THE BET (A MENAGE ROMANCE)

A MENAGE IN MANHATTAN NOVEL

TARA CRESCENT

My editor Jim takes the comma-filled words that emerge from my keyboard and shapes it into a story worth reading. As always, my undying gratitude.

Cover Design by Eris Adderly, http://erisadderly.com/

FREE STORY OFFER

Get a free story when you subscribe to <u>my mailing list</u>!

Boyfriend by the Hour

This steamy, romantic story contains a dominant hero who's pretending to be an escort, and a sassy heroine who's given up on real relationships.

Sadie:

I can't believe I have the hots for an escort.

Cole Mitchell is ripped, bearded, sexy and dominant. When he moves next door to me, I find it impossible to resist sampling the wares.

But Cole's not a one-woman kind of guy, and I won't share.

Cole:

She thinks I'm an escort. I'm not.

I thought I'd do anything to sleep with Sadie. Then I realized I want more. I want Sadie. Forever.

I'm not the escort she thinks I am.

Now, I just have to make sure she never finds out.

THE BET

A rash bet leads to a steamy ménage, but will my unconventional love affair be the biggest mistake of my life?

Sexy-as-sin billionaire CEO Daniel and tattooed bad-boy chef Sebastian bet fifty thousand dollars that I'd win a game of pool, and they offered to coach me...

I wasn't supposed to want them.

I shouldn't have become romantically involved with both of them.

But I couldn't resist.

Then all hell broke loose.

Now the three of us face the loss of everything we've worked for our entire lives, and we're left to ask – *can our love survive?*

NOTE: The Bet is a **standalone ménage romance (mfm) with a HEA ending and no cliffhangers!** It is full of steamy scenes featuring a billionaire businessman, a bad-boy chef and a curvy redhead. Spare panties are recommended.

The Bet was previously titled Betting on Bailey.

In Armenia, on the Day of St. Sargis, single women fast all day and eat a slice of very salty bread before they go to sleep. The man that brings them water in their dreams is the man they are meant to marry.

— FROM BAILEY'S JOURNAL OF INTERESTING FACTS
FROM AROUND THE WORLD

Bailey:

"Professor Moore," Maria Rivera knocks at my office door and sticks her head in. "Do you have a moment? Sameer's reviewing my grant application, and he suggested you look it over as well."

I glance at the clock at the bottom of my computer screen. It's a quarter to seven. I'm supposed to meet my boyfriend Trevor at seven thirty to watch him play pool, and he gets extremely irritated when I'm late. There's no point telling him that my job is demanding and leaving on time isn't always an option. According to Trevor, if my job was important, I'd make a lot of money. I don't, therefore my career is not to be taken seriously.

"I have," I tell Maria, rising to my feet and gathering the small pile of rings and bracelets that I've taken off to type, "exactly fifteen minutes, then I have to leave."

"Thanks so much," she says gratefully as I follow her into Sameer Shah's office, slipping my turquoise ring on my finger and fastening the coral bracelet around my wrist. I like the gemstones. I dress, in typical New York style, in black almost all the time. The jewelry adds some color. "It's the section on gender roles in the Taiga that we thought you should review," she elaborates.

Ah. That makes sense. I'm the resident expert on the Siberian Taiga, having spent a year there as part of the research for my doctoral dissertation.

"Hey Bailey," Sameer greets me as I walk into his office, his eyes glued to the computer screen. "Pull up a chair, will you? Can you tell me what you think of this bit?"

I read over his shoulder. Maria's done a reasonable job describing why the people who live in the remoteness of Siberia are important and why they deserve study. She's mentioned all the important points — the arrival of the Internet is eroding cohesion in the community, language is being lost and we are, in essence, in a race against time to study and preserve this slice of the world that has so far remained untouched by modern influences.

"Who's funding this grant?" I ask her. "The National Science Foundation?"

She shakes her head. "No, the NSF's budget has been halved. This grant is from a private company. Hartman. Have you heard of them?"

"Nope." I'm not really listening to Maria's words; I'm digesting the impact of her first sentence. Damn it. I knew the National Science Foundation wasn't going to budget very much money this year for liberal arts. Everything's about science and technology these days. It's a great time to be in the STEM fields, and a terrible time to be in the humanities.

Thank heavens they've already approved my grant to go to Argentina in the fall.

Of course, thinking of Argentina reminds me of Trevor's reaction last week when he heard I needed to be away for five months doing research on the myth and the reality of the *gauchos* in Patagonia. Let's just say he wasn't supportive.

Since I seem to be becoming an expert on ignoring the many reasons Trevor is wrong for me, I push those thoughts to the background and focus on Maria's problems instead. "Okay," I pull up a chair and reach for a pad of paper, pushing the bangles back from my right wrist so I'll be able to write. "This is a great start, but you also need to add..."

I have multiple mechanisms in place to prevent me from being late. Alarms going off on my phone in fifteen minute intervals. Flashing screens on my laptop warning me to stop working. My computer is even programmed to shut down automatically at seven thirty.

But I've left my cell phone in my office, and engrossed as we are in strengthening Maria's grant application, none of us hear the alarm when it goes off at seven. There's another alarm that's supposed to chime at seven fifteen, but if I can't tell you if it went off — I don't hear it either. When I finally look up at Sameer's screen to check the time, I'm horrified to note that it's seven thirty five. "Fuck," I swear. "Fuck. And fuck again. Sorry, Maria. Pretend you didn't hear me." I don't bother apologizing to Sameer. He has the office next to me. He's heard me curse before.

She laughs. "Sure thing, Professor Moore," she says easily. "Thank you so much for your help. This is fantastic."

"Sorry to keep you here late on a Friday night," Sameer adds apologetically. "You doing something fun?"

"Not really. I'm going to watch my boyfriend Trevor play pool. You guys met him at the faculty mixer two months ago, right?"

"Ah." Sameer's voice is flat, and he exchanges glances with Maria. "Yes, Trevor. You should go."

I furrow my brow. Trevor had too much to drink at the mixer, and he'd insulted a bunch of my co-workers by going on an extended rant about the pointlessness of liberal arts. Finally, mortified by his rudeness, I'd had to drag him away. It had not been a good evening, and judging from Sameer's reaction, Trevor has left an impression.

I ignore the big honking signs the universe is giving me about my relationship. Making my excuses, I head back to my own office and dig around the stacks of papers till I find my phone. Crossing my fingers, I dial Trevor's number. As luck would have it, I get his voicemail. "Hey, I'm running late," I tell the machine. "Sorry! I'm leaving right now, and I'll see you soon." The bar Trevor's team is playing at is in SoHo, a ten minute walk away. With any luck, I'll only be fifteen minutes late, and he won't be too pissy.

THREE HOURS LATER, I'm wondering why I even bothered to come out tonight. Trevor's been in a snit all evening long. I've been reduced to sitting in the corner with a beer, trying to pretend that he isn't looking down the shirt of the size-two blonde as she bends over the pool table to make her shot.

The brunette standing next to me has been openly flirting with Trevor, though she knows we are together. I'm not the jealous kind, but even so, I'm getting a little irritated. *Come on,* I think. *Have some class.*

Of course, Trevor isn't exactly discouraging her flirting. That's the kind of special guy that he is.

"What do you think this is?" Even her voice is whiny. There's a few of Trevor's teammates within hearing distance, but she's looking straight at me. *Shit, she's talking to me. I have to make conversation?*

She's holding her finger out to me. For a second, I think she's making a rude gesture, then I realize she's saying something about a wound. "Something bit me when I went camping a month ago," she pouts. "Look, it's still swollen."

It's *barely* swollen. Apart from everything else, she's a hypochondriac. Absolutely *fucking* lovely.

I know I'm being cranky and anti-social, yet I can't stop myself. A devil-may-care attitude grips me. *Flirt with my boyfriend right in front of me? Honey, you don't know what's going to hit you.*

"Oh my god," I yelp, bending over her finger and pasting a serious expression on my face. "Did you go to the hospital?"

"No," she shakes her head. "My sister," she gestures to the blonde whose rack Trevor's still ogling, "told me it was nothing."

I make a tut-tut sound, allowing urgency to infuse my voice. "I'm a professor of anthropology. When I trekked in the jungles of Indonesia, a spider bit our guide. His wound looked exactly like this."

I *am* a professor of anthropology, and I *have* trekked in the jungles of Indonesia multiple times. But I assure you that I know absolutely nothing about infectious diseases.

Brunette Barbie, who clearly doesn't know what anthropologists do, has no idea that I'm making up the story of the guide's finger.

"He had the same kind of swelling," I continue, my voice hushed. "Same red color. Nothing happened for a few weeks..." I swallow a sob. "Then..."

"What happened?" Her voice is shrill, her eyes are wide with fear. *I've got her.*

"The eggs were incubating. One day, they all hatched." I clench my eyes shut, and my voice is very low. "That poor man. He had three children."

Her face pales, and she lets out an ear-splitting shriek, which causes her sister to miss her shot at the table.

Ladies and gentlemen, my work here is done.

ONCE THE BLONDE misses her shot, I watch my boyfriend strut up to the table. The cocky swagger is earned - Trevor is an exceptional pool player. The American PoolPlayer League ranks all their players by skill, and Trevor is a seven, which is the highest level.

They don't rank douchebaginess, but if they did, Trevor would be a seven there too.

I wince at that churlish thought. I'm being unusually crabby tonight. But everything is irritating me - the way Trevor's opponent is flirting with him, the way he's responding, the way the bartender has served all the thin, pretty girls, while ignoring the fact that I've been standing at the bar for the last five minutes, waiting for a beer.

The sad truth is - I don't really care how many women my boyfriend checks out. I don't even mind if he's sleeping around - that'll give me the push I need to break up with him. Our relationship has been on life-support for a long time now, but I'm too embarrassed to pull the plug.

'Why are you with him?' my friend Gabby asked me once. She's made no effort to conceal that she doesn't like him.

I don't know, I wanted to reply. Maybe because I'm the chubby girl and I get friend-zoned by guys. When Trevor, a good-looking and successful guy showed interest in me, I was flattered and swept off my feet. At the six month mark of our relationship, I even hoped I was in love with him. When he suggested moving in together, I'd been so thrilled that I'd held my tongue when he picked an apartment that I could not afford. I wanted the fairy tale.

Five months later, I've come to the unpleasant realization that fairy tales are for children. As uncomfortable as the truth can sometimes be, hiding from it won't solve anything. Trevor doesn't love me. The reason he's dating me is because I can open some doors for him in Manhattan's cultural scene. Trevor's a social climber, and it's prestigious to date a professor at NYU.

And I'm dating him because I'm too passive to end it, which is *pitiful*.

Something my dad told me when I was ten comes to mind. We'd been on a hike that had felt never-ending, and I had been tired and cold and miserable. "Can we go home yet?" I'd whined.

My father had crouched down so he was level with my face, and he'd looked into my eyes. "Look Bailey," he'd gestured to the path, which curved round a corner. "Don't you want to know what lies ahead? If you stay right here, how will you find out?"

And though the ten-year old me hadn't thought very much of my dad's reasoning, the adult version can appreciate those words. Life might not be a fairy tale, and true love might not exist. But I'll never know if I stay with Trevor. I'll never find out what lies ahead.

ONCE TREVOR FINISHES HIS GAME, his teammates beckon me over. They've won handily tonight, and consequently, everyone's in a good mood. "Bailey," one of them, a guy called Peter says, his expression jovial, "why don't you play a game with Trevor?"

Oh, dear god no.

I've tried to play a few times, but I'm dreadful. I have terrible hand-eye coordination. Trevor always looms over me, making me nervous. My overly-generous boobs graze the table, and I'm very self-conscious about them. One time, my breasts had knocked a ball out of the way. You would have thought I had tortured a puppy from the way Trevor reacted to that.

Trevor looks just as unhappy as I feel. "Bailey can't really play," he says. "I've tried teaching her, but she's hopeless."

At that, my temper, normally held well in check, flares, and I straighten my back. I know he'll beat me. But I'd be damned if he's going to talk me out of playing.

"Come on, man," another one of his teammates says. He's looking at me with pity in his eyes. "Don't be a jerk."

Trevor flushes. He's generally pretty careful to treat me well in public. "Of course, honey," he says, gritting his teeth.

I select a pool stick from the rack on the wall, knowing without even asking that Trevor isn't going to offer me one of the cues in his case. "Do you want to break?" I ask him.

"No," he says. There's an unpleasant curl to his lips. "Why don't you show us what you can do?"

I hate breaking. I can never hit the cue ball fast enough

and with enough accuracy. The hallmark of a successful break is a satisfactory scattering of the balls all over the table. Me, I consider it a win if my cue ball even makes contact with the racked balls.

It feels like the entire bar is watching me. I don't want to bend over the table - the black t-shirt I'm wearing will show too much cleavage if I do so. Trevor called my breasts cow-like once in the heat of an argument, and I've never forgotten those hurtful words.

I try to hold myself so I'm standing straight and I take the shot, but even before I make contact, I know I've failed. My cue stick careens out of control and barely grazes the white ball, which rolls a foot down the table and stops, humiliatingly, before it even hits the balls in the center.

My face is fiery. Trevor mutters a curse before he stalks forward. "You are supposed to bend over," he says. He lines up his shot. "Like this."

Thwack. He hits the rack of balls dead on. Three balls roll into pockets and Trevor walks around to make his next shot.

"I've taught you how to break." He doesn't look at me, and he's careful to pitch his voice low so I'm the only one who can hear the corrosive words. The solid green ball rolls into the side pocket. "But this isn't book learning, is it? You can't study your way to success." The four slides into a pocket, followed by the three. He lifts his head up and chalks his cue tip. "Face it, Bailey. You huddle in academia because you can't cut it in the real world."

Everyone's looking at us. Why wouldn't they? My boyfriend's running the table. *All I wanted to do was come out and have a nice evening.* Instead, this has turned into another 'Let's humiliate Bailey' exercise.

The warning bells swell to a choir. I've had enough.

Before he can preen and take the shot at the eight ball, I set my beer down on the table. "It looks like you have things under control," I say quietly. "I'm going home."

Not supportive of my career? *Check*. Being a jerk to my friends? *Double-check*. Looking down the boobs of every available chick? *Triple-check*. Humiliating me in front of his friends? *The final straw*.

It's time to pack my bags.

IT TAKES Trevor two hours to come back home, by which time I've packed one suitcase with my essentials. I don't own much stuff - at heart, I'm a traveler, and it shows in my rather meager possessions. As tempting and movie-like as it would be to march out of Trevor's apartment clutching my Kitchen-Aid stand mixer in one hand and pulling a suitcase with the other, I can come back for the rest of my stuff on a different day.

The ending of our relationship shouldn't have come as a surprise to Trevor, but he looks shocked when he sees me dressed to leave. "You're joking," he says flatly.

I frown. He doesn't love me. If anything, he acts irritated with me most of the time, as if I'm a troublesome child that needs to be managed, not a grown woman. He's probably just upset because I'm breaking up with him, not the other way round.

I'm a little sad that it's over, but mostly, I'm relieved. "It's time, Trevor," I say softly. "Neither of us have been happy in this relationship, and we both deserve more." I pause. "I'm going to Piper's place tonight, and I'll come back for the rest of my stuff in a week." I take a deep breath. "I hope we can still be friends."

"Friends?" His voice is icy, sending shivers down the back of my neck. "You'll be begging me to take you back in no time. You stupid bitch. Have you seen yourself in the mirror?" He shakes his head. "Pathetic and fat."

There's an ugly glass vase that sits on a side table in the tiny foyer of our apartment. It belonged to Trevor's grandmother, and is something of a family heirloom. I've always hated where it's located - I'm terrified that I'll knock it off and it'll break.

Right now, it's everything I can do to keep myself from throwing it at his head.

"Goodbye, Trevor." *Forget about being friends, you jerk. I never want to see you again.*

THERE'S a scene in Kill Bill that has always stuck with me. It's almost at the end of the second movie. Beatrice has finally found Bill in a remote Mexican village and is in the process of confronting him. Bill's attempting to interrogate her and in the process, he talks about superheroes. Specifically, the myth of Superman.

I'm enough of a geek that I can quote the exact phrase, though the precise wording isn't important. The gist of it is that there are superheroes and their alter egos. Bruce Wayne puts on a costume to become Batman. Peter Parker becomes Spider Man. Superman however, is the exception to the rule, because Clark Kent doesn't become Superman. No, Superman is *always* a superhero. Clark Kent is his disguise. His way of mingling with us mortals.

I first saw Kill Bill back in my graduate school days, when I still felt like Superman. Then, I was publishing papers and making an impact in my field. I was set to finish my PhD in record time, and I was being recruited by universities from around the world. I'd come off a difficult field assignment, living in Siberia for a year. I had felt invincible.

The girl who had been Superman would have never put up with Trevor's insults and cruelty, but for the last year, I've been stuck in Clark Kent mode. I've forgotten how to be amazing.

It's time for that to end.

2

Tell me what you eat and I will tell you what you are.

— JEAN ANTHELME BRILLAT-SAVARIN

Sebastian:

Neither of my two New York restaurants are open for lunch during the week, so it's not often that I see my staff during the day. This sunny Friday morning in May is the exception.

We are gathered in the bar area of *Seb New York*, tense and waiting. All eyes are on my cell phone, which rests on top of the polished mahogany bar. Bottles of champagne dot the counter, but no one pops the cork yet. We aren't a superstitious bunch, but to open the bottle before we receive the call? We won't tempt fate that way.

The Michelin staff calls at noon on Friday. Five minutes to go.

Seb New York has one Michelin star, an honor shared by only twenty-three other restaurants in New York. In a few minutes, we'll find out if we've earned the coveted second star. If we have? Then, I can write my own ticket. Not bad for a kid from Mississippi who didn't even finish high school.

I look around the room. Helen, my sous-chef at *Seb New York*, is pacing back and forth. Ben, the sous-chef of my second restaurant, *Seb II* is watching her, absently chewing on a nail. The expression on his face is a mixture of anticipation and envy. *Seb New York* gets all the accolades, and *Seb II* is the new kid on the block. Ben's an ambitious chef, and I'm sure he'd love to be in Helen's place right now.

Next to me, Juliette's playing with her phone. She's the outsider in this gathering. The rest of us cook together, night after night. There's a rhythm that comes with that, and a shared sense of camaraderie that can be exclusionary.

Juliette, on the other hand, doesn't belong in the kitchen. She's cheerfully confessed that she can't even make toast without burning it. She doesn't need to. She's my business manager, smart, ambitious and driven. I hired her six months ago, and already, she's got me my own show on the Food Network and arranged a book deal with a top New York publisher.

There's only one person missing. Daniel Hartman, my partner in both restaurants, and my best friend. He's in Kansas City today on an unavoidable business trip. It feels odd to face this moment without him. Daniel has been my biggest supporter throughout my career. If it wasn't for him, I'd probably still be cooking in the diner I worked in when I first moved to New York.

The phone rings and silence falls over the room. I take a deep breath and answer. "Sebastian Ardalan?" the disembodied voice on the other end of the line asks.

"Yes." Helen crosses her fingers, and my restaurant manager Katya is chewing on her nails.

"Congratulations, Chef Ardalan," the voice continues. "I'm happy to inform you that we've decided to award *Seb New York* a second Michelin star."

Yes! I give the room a thumbs-up and everyone erupts in cheers. Without waiting for me to hang up, Helen pops the cork open on one of the champagne bottles. The staff are cheering, laughing and congratulating each other. Juliette jumps up and down in excitement, dancing a duet with one of the line cooks. I utter some words of thanks and hang up, grinning at the scenes of celebration in the room. Everyone in this room has toiled for this moment, and they deserve every bit of attention they'll get when the word gets out about the second star.

My phone beeps. It's a text message from Daniel. *'Congratulations.'*

I laugh out aloud. I have no idea how Daniel already knows. I likely never will. If I ask, he'll merely look mysterious and tell me it's his job to know. I'll never be able to tell if it is a lucky guess, or if he does have a source at Michelin.

That's okay. The second star is mine. All the work has been worth it. The long hours, the personal sacrifices... it's all paid off in this moment. *If only my parents could see...*

I smother that thought. My parents never cared. I was too much of a dreamer for them. Too interested in women's work, as my father put it once. My teachers thought I'd end up broke and washed up, worse than useless. All my life, failure has been expected of me, and I had lived up to that potential, until the day I ran away from home, hoping for a fresh start.

Juliette ropes me into her dance, and I shake my head to wipe away thoughts of the past. Helen hands me a flute of champagne. "We thought about emptying a bottle over your head, Chef," she grins. "But Colin wouldn't let us."

Colin, the wine sommelier, sniffs disapprovingly. "It's Krug Grande Cuvée," he says with a grimace. "It's bloody expensive."

I laugh. Juliette's distracted by her phone again. I drink my champagne and circulate the room, shaking hands and exchanging high-fives. I'm chatting with Katya about the spike in reservations that's going to result when the news becomes public knowledge when Juliette finds me again. "Sebastian," she says, pulling me aside. "I'm already getting texts and emails. Now is the time to talk to investors who are pushing for a nationwide franchise. Think about it. A Sebastian Ardalan restaurant in every city in the country."

We've talked before about this idea, but it's remained the stuff of dreams. But with a second star? The world's my oyster.

It's tempting to want what Juliette's offering. My restaurant makes a respectable amount of money, but the income from a nationwide franchise would dwarf what I make now. More than that, I want all the people who expected me to fail to see me succeed beyond their wildest dreams. The high school counselors who thought I'd amount to nothing. The teachers that called me stupid. Everyone in my small town, who sneered at me - I want them to see the restaurants and know, they were wrong.

My emotions run too close to the surface. My parents, the people whose approval I wanted the most, are dead. Yet I still crave fame, and I'm too swayed by past hurts and injustices.

I should be cautious. Yet when I open my mouth to answer Juliette, the words that emerge aren't the ones I should utter. "Call them," I tell her. "Let's see what the offers are."

I turn away from her and raise my glass to the room.

Tomorrow, the phones will start ringing, with all of New York clamoring to eat at Michelin's newest two-star restaurant. We will be sold out every single night. In a halo effect, *Seb II* will be busy as well, and Ben's going to have to raise his game significantly in the face of that attention. Helen's ready for the challenge, I know. Is Ben? I'm not sure.

So much work to be done, and this franchise idea could be a fatal distraction. I wonder what Daniel would think of it. I should really consult with him before I make too many commitments.

Yet when I turn back to Juliette to tell her to tread lightly, she's not there anymore. She's all the way in the far corner of the room, her attention on the glowing screen in front of her, her fingers typing out a message.

Already, things are in motion. I shelve the unease I feel, and I throw the champagne down my throat and demand a refill. No regrets. Today *will* be a day of celebration.

3

He will win who knows when to fight and when not to fight.

— Sun Tzu, The Art of War

Daniel:

There are many places I want to be on a Friday afternoon, but this windowless Kansas City boardroom, with its taupe walls and its faded grey chairs, is at the bottom of the list.

"Mr. Hartman," the blonde assistant slides in, looking apologetic. "Mr. Ryan's been delayed in another meeting. He'll be with you momentarily, as will the rest of the board."

Fuck this shit. Keeping us waiting is Wayne Ryan's version of a power play, but he's missing one important point. As much as Hartman & Company would like to acquire Ryan Communications, we can afford to walk away from this deal and they cannot. Their stock price has dropped thirty percent in the last quarter and the only thing that has kept it from free-falling even more is the rumor that we are interested in buying them.

"Ms. Parker." I eye Ryan's assistant pointedly, and my voice is icy. "My flight leaves in three hours. I intend to be on it whether I've met Mr. Ryan or not. Perhaps you can pass that message on to him."

Her face pales and she hurries out, no doubt to tell Ryan that I'm getting restive. Next to me, my Uncle Cyrus makes a disapproving sound. "You shouldn't have done that."

Things between Cyrus and me have always been tense. My best friend Sebastian, who never minces his words, has called our relationship the most fucked up thing he's seen. Cyrus has worked at Hartman & Company all his life. I can't deny that he's given me some helpful advice since I became the CEO, though his condescending and lecturing tone always grates at me. "Why not?"

"This isn't New York, Daniel," Cyrus replies, frustration in his tone. "We are in Kansas. Here, deals are done over a game of golf or at a neighborhood barbecue. You have to learn to play the game. Act like you are one of them."

This is the one area that Cyrus and I cannot agree on. My uncle is old-school. He hires his friends and he does business with his golf-club buddies. Me? I'm more direct. I have absolutely no patience with small-minded, judgmental assholes like Wayne Ryan and the rest of his board. Last year, Wayne Ryan divorced his wife after thirty years of marriage, and married the twenty-one year old woman who babysat his kids. At the same time, Ryan Communications fired three employees for *'behavior unbecoming to the company,'* which was a codeword for being gay.

"I'm not here to be Wayne Ryan's buddy," I respond. "I'm here to buy his company. We've made them a fair offer. They'll be fools to turn us down."

Cyrus shakes his head. "There's so much about the world that you don't understand. Not everyone is motivated by logic. To make a deal here, you'll have to learn to belong. Fit in. Live their values."

I've run Hartman for seven years, Cyrus, I want to retort. *I've doubled our profitability in that time. I don't need you to tell me how to run my business.*

Before I can open my mouth to snap at him, Wayne Ryan hurries in. "Sorry, sorry," he blusters. "Another meeting ran over. You know how it is."

I'm not in a good mood. I hate being kept waiting and Cyrus' attitude has pissed me off. My voice reflects my ill-humor. "Let's get going, shall we?" I say curtly. "Like I told your assistant, I have a plane to catch. Was the rest of your board planning to join us today?"

THE MEETING PROCEEDS very much as I anticipate. There's some posturing about the financial terms, but Ryan's not a complete fool and he knows the amount we've offered is more than fair. There's some hinting around what our plans are for the management - Ryan's way of asking if he'll still have a job once Hartman buys his company. *Not if I have anything to do with it,* I think to myself, and I avoid answering the question.

As we talk, I get the sense that Ryan Communications' board has reservations about this deal, and I'm somewhat at a loss to understand why. Without us, Ryan Communications will declare bankruptcy this year. The board isn't composed of idiots. They have to know they are out of options.

On the way to the airport, I lean back in the seat and

close my eyes. "What did you think?" I ask Cyrus. As much as he irritates me, he *is* the Chief Operating Officer of Hartman, and he's been the primary driver of this deal.

"This is by no means a done deal," he replies. "There was a lot of hesitation in that room."

"Why? I don't get it. Without us, they are going to go under."

"It's not that simple, Daniel," he says. "These guys do business with people they are comfortable with. Wayne Ryan has known the members on his board his entire life. They worship at the same church. They went to the same private school. They were in the same fraternity. Brant Hollister was even Wayne's best man."

I snort. "For which marriage? The first one, or the one where he married the woman who is thirty years younger than him?"

Cyrus waves aside my snark. "That's not the point. You, Daniel, are about as different from them as it gets. You," he continues with a disapproving glare, "live your life in the spotlight. You date models and socialites. Your photo is in the tabloids more often than not. They can't relate to your lifestyle, and if they can't understand you, these guys will not listen to a word you have to say."

There might some merit in what Cyrus is saying. "What do you suggest we do?"

"Let me continue to negotiate with them," he says. "And while we are doing this deal, you stay out of the spotlight."

I'm tempted to walk away from this deal. Cyrus is making it sound like I'm manwhoring my way around New York, which couldn't be further from the truth. Yeah sure, I date. But my work comes first, and my personal life is a distant second. Everyone I go out with knows the score.

Yet I bite my tongue, because it's become a habit for me

to place Hartman & Company ahead of my own happiness. The acquisition will be good for us. It'll give us access to markets in Kansas, Oklahoma, Arkansas, Mississippi and Alabama. It should increase our revenue by twenty percent over the next five years. The money is nothing to sneeze at.

"Fine," I say finally. "Let's do it your way."

"Remember," Cyrus warns. "No scandals. I can't convince them that Hartman is exactly what they need if the CEO keeps appearing in the tabloid press with women draped all over him."

Cyrus should stop talking when he's ahead. "I said okay," I snap. "Stop pushing it, Cyrus. I'll toe the line."

Let your plans be dark and impenetrable as night, and when you move, fall like a thunderbolt.

— Sun Tzu, The Art of War

Bailey:

Trevor thinks that I'm going to be begging him to take me back? He couldn't be more wrong. I'm not alone. I have my best friends to lean on, the five women that make up the Thursday Night Drinking Pack.

There's calm and stable Katie, who is married with twin two-year old daughters. She lives in Chappaqua with her husband Adam. Miki moved away to Houston two years ago, but we Skype her in every time we get together and valiantly pretend it's the same as hanging out in person.

There's Gabby, who is going through a justifiable man-hating phase. Wendy, despite being a barracuda divorce lawyer, still believes in love. And last but not least, is my former roommate Piper, who, five months ago, inherited a restaurant in Hell's Kitchen.

It's Piper I call right after I leave our apartment. *Not our apartment anymore,* I correct myself. *Trevor's apartment.*

She picks up on the first ring. "Bailey? Is everything okay?" she asks into the phone, before even waiting for my hello. The concern in her voice is obvious, and hearing it, I choke up for the first time this evening.

"I left Trevor." It sounds so stark when I hear it. "I was wondering if I could crash at your place tonight?"

"Of course Bails," she says instantly. "Always."

"WHAT HAPPENED?"

I'm holding a cup of hot chocolate and sitting on Piper's couch. Her cat is curled up in my lap. Though I haven't lived in this apartment for five months, it still feels like home in a way that my place with Trevor never did. "Jasper's missed having you around," she adds.

"I missed him too," I admit, stroking the ginger cat's head. "However, I think that as far as Jasper is concerned, human laps are interchangeable."

"There is that." She hesitates before broaching the topic that's on both of our minds. "I don't have to know what happened with you and Trevor, if you don't want to talk about it."

"No, it's okay." I fill her in on my evening.

"You have to be kidding," she interrupts loudly, when I get to the part where he was being a dick at the pool table. "He said what?"

"I'm hopeless." I repeat those hurtful words. "Still, he's

right, isn't he? I am hopeless. I've never had any hand-eye coordination, and I wilt under pressure."

"You," she glares at me, "are the furthest thing from hopeless." She holds up her hand. "One," she counts, "you spent six months in Indonesia, studying remote tribes, and you spent how long in Siberia?"

"A year."

"Exactly. Wilting under pressure, my ass. Trevor's dick wilts under pressure."

There's enough truth in that statement that I bite my tongue to keep from laughing aloud. I'd never mentioned Trevor's problems to my girls, because he was my boyfriend and that would have seemed disloyal. After the breakup, I feel perfectly justified giggling a little.

"Second, you were the youngest hire ever in your department in NYU, weren't you?"

I nod. I should miniaturize Piper and carry her around in my pocket everywhere to be my own personal cheerleader. She's fantastic for my ego.

"Third," she says. "I've seen Trevor trying to teach you how to play. He's mean and he yells at you. He's a horrible teacher."

"He is that," I agree. "I had a teacher like that in high school for French."

"And do you speak French?" she asks pointedly.

I shake my head. "She put me off the language forever," I confess.

"Exactly." I've made Piper's point for her. "So, can we agree that Trevor's a terrible human being, and you would be excellent at pool if you were taught by someone even the slightest bit encouraging?"

"The former point, I concede." I laugh. "The jury's out

on the latter. Incidentally, you sound like a trial lawyer. Taking lessons from Wendy?"

She grimaces. "I've inherited the kitchen staff from hell, so I need to channel my favorite shark in order to get people to fear me." She sips at her cocoa and we are both silent for a while, submerged in our own problems. "Listen Bailey," she says finally. "Would you like to be my roommate again? I could use a hand with the rent, and you need a place to stay."

"Are you sure?" Piper had just inherited her restaurant when Trevor had asked me to move in, and it seemed like we were both getting what we wanted. I was living my fairy tale, and Piper was getting some space. Five months later, it seems that we are both back to square one. "I don't want you to feel obligated to offer. I can find something else..."

"The money will help," she admits, refusing to meet my eyes. "Business isn't good."

Piper's situation is very strange. Her eccentric aunt left her a restaurant in her will, but she only inherits it free and clear if she can make the place survive for three years. But the place is run down, and the staff is surly and unprofessional. In New York's hyper-competitive restaurant market, it's a recipe for disaster.

I don't know what to say, so I keep it simple. Piper doesn't like to get mushy anyway. "That sucks ass."

She smiles wanly. "Look at us," she mocks. "The Tragic Two." She shakes her head. "You know what we need? A drink, something stronger than hot chocolate. We need to celebrate that you finally left Trevor, and I need to remember that life could be so much worse. I have friends and I have my health."

Things must be worse than I think at the restaurant if

Piper needs cheering up. "Let's do it. I'd get up and help you, but..."

"We don't want to annoy Jasper." She gazes fondly at her cat, before she goes into her kitchen and comes out with a bottle of red wine. I take the glass she hands me without displacing the purring bundle of fur on my lap.

"You know he had the nerve to imply I'd come crawling back?"

"He did what?" Piper's voice rises in anger. "I don't know why you put up with him for as long as you did. You deserve to be with someone who is kind to you, Bailey. Who thinks the sun rises because of you, and who sees stars when they look in your eyes."

Piper has a poetic, romantic streak in her that even New York can't kill. I sip at my wine and think about her words. Why did I stay with Trevor once he revealed his true colors? "I guess part of me," I answer slowly, "was hoping that he was just going through a rough patch. I thought it was because we'd just moved in together, and that can be stressful."

"You made too many allowances for him."

"Yeah, maybe." Jasper purrs in satisfaction as I pet him, and his warm body is very therapeutic. Some company will make a fortune one day by packaging up kittens and wine as part of a gift basket for women that have just broken up with their boyfriends. "I think part of me was preparing for the break up. I mean, I applied to go work in Argentina for six months. Surely that was a sign."

She shrugs. "Normal healthy relationships can survive a six month absence."

I'm still thinking about why I stayed with Trevor. "Dating is hard in New York," I muse. "It seems like there are two women to every guy. And I'm not skinny. Guys prefer women who look like models."

Piper rolls her eyes. "Two failed relationships does not qualify you to talk about what guys prefer. If all guys wanted skinny blonde women, I wouldn't be sitting here on Friday night with my cat and my best friend for company."

We sit in the living room for a long time, listening to the street noise outside. People walk about, partying and celebrating, and I feel removed from it all. Finally, Piper yawns. "Bed?" she asks. "My mom always used to tell me that everything looks better after a good night's sleep."

"Bed," I agree. Nothing has gone according to plan today but I'm too tired and too numb to figure out what to do. I dislodge Jasper from my lap, enduring his indignant yowl as punishment. I brush my teeth, using the dentist-issued toothbrush that resides in my travel bag, since my electric one is still at Trevor's place. I'm asleep the instant my head hits the pillow, and though I don't expect it, I sleep deeply and without dreams.

THOUGH WE CALL ourselves the Thursday Night Drinking Pack, we've recently taken to hanging out on Monday nights, because Piper is too busy running a restaurant to drink on a Thursday with her girlfriends.

When I get back to Piper's apartment after work Monday night, Katie, Gabby and Wendy are crammed together in the small living room, and Jasper's purring happily on Katie's lap. *Traitor.* "The time for an intervention has passed," I quip. "I left him."

A bottle of rum, several cans of Coke, and a tray heaped

with sandwiches jostle for room on the coffee table. Gabby must have brought the food. She's told me that her mother's response to every crisis is a plate filled with egg salad sandwiches. It's a habit that's stuck.

"This isn't an intervention," Gabby retorts, handing me a rum and coke. "This is a celebration. Since you've ended things with him and I don't have to bite my tongue anymore, can I tell you how much I hated Trevor?"

"Fuck yes," Piper agrees from her spot on the floor. Her words are slightly slurred. "Patronizing asshole." She holds up a FedEx envelope to me. "This came for you, by the way."

I frown at it. I'm not expecting anything. "Was he really that bad?" I ask as I rip the package open.

"Yes," they all answer in unison, but I'm not looking at them. I'm reading the letter that was in the envelope, and I'm starting to see red. Blood red.

"Bailey?" Katie asks me. "Is everything alright?"

"No." I take a big gulp of the drink in my hand. "You guys, listen to this." I wave the sheet of paper at them. "This is from Trevor's lawyer. The fucker's demanding that I pay ninety days of rent, since I didn't give him adequate notice before moving out."

"What the…" Gabby exclaims.

"He can't do that, can he?" Piper cuts in. "That's not fair."

We all turn toward Wendy. She's a divorce lawyer, and while rents and tenancy aren't really her area of expertise, she'll know more than any of us.

Wendy makes a face. "He probably can," she says. "I'm sorry, Bailey, but you both signed a lease, didn't you?"

I nod. "One year." I empty the glass, and Gabby helpfully refills it for me. That's my girl. Rum is exactly what I need right now.

"And you've lived together for five months? So technically, you owe seven months' rent. A court will see the ninety days that Trevor's suggesting as a reasonable offer." She grimaces. "I'm sorry, Bailey. But you are probably best off paying him and moving on. I'll loan you the money, if you need."

"Hang on," Gabby says slowly. "He earned almost a half a million dollars every year, and you made a teacher's salary, and he still wants you to pay rent?" She glares at Wendy. "And you are agreeing with this?"

"I'm not agreeing," Wendy protests. "I'm just telling you that if Bailey goes to court, she'll probably lose. She's best off cutting her losses."

"Motherfucker," Piper grits out. "I want to put Trevor's balls in my pasta machine and roll them out, bit by painful bit."

I toss back my second rum and coke, but the sour taste in my mouth isn't from the drink. I'm furious. In that moment, fueled by Gabby's rum and fortified by her egg-salad sandwiches, I want to get even. I want Trevor to feel as stupid as I felt right now. "Fine," I look at Wendy. "I'll pay. But I want revenge."

"Whatever you are planning to do, if it's illegal, don't tell me," she says hastily. "I can't hear about it."

I roll my eyes. "It's not illegal, I'm not stupid." A plan is forming in my befuddled brain. There's one place that I can hit Trevor where it would really hurt. "Guys," I hear myself ask. "Does anyone know how I can get really good at pool quickly?"

"Tell us more..." Piper says. Her tone suggests she thinks I've lost my mind, but she's wrong. For the first time in a really long time, the way forward is clear. I want Trevor to hurt.

The words tumble from my mouth in a rush. "I want to beat him. Every year, his pool league plays in a tournament. There's a stupid trophy that they compete for, and the winners get to fly to Las Vegas and play in yet another tournament. Trevor lives to compete in Vegas." I take a deep breath. "I want to play on the opposing team, and I want to take that away from him. I want to beat him."

"A pool league?" Gabby's voice is thoughtful. "I might know someone." She shoots me a look. "It would be a lot easier to just throw a lot of dishes against the wall in anger. If you want to get good at pool, it'll take time and effort."

"I want this." There's no doubt in my voice.

Gabby already has her phone out and is scrolling through her contacts. "A coworker of mine plays in a league. Let me see if his team needs another player." She stands up and takes her drink on to Piper's rickety balcony. "Hey Clark, it's Gabriella," I hear her say before she shuts the door. "Listen, a friend of mine wants to play pool. Didn't you say you needed more players?"

I sip my third drink and ponder what I've set in motion. I'm crazy busy at work. I have two papers to publish and one of my graduate students is planning on defending his PhD soon. In addition, I'm in the tenure window at NYU, which means my teaching load is heavy. I'm teaching four undergraduate classes this semester. Spending an evening every week playing pool feels like a luxury I cannot afford.

But the Department of Anthropology isn't well-funded, and my chances for tenure are quite slim. Besides, the need for revenge burns hot in my blood.

Gabby opens the door and comes back in. "You are in," she announces. "The team meets Wednesday nights at the Maxwell Club. Get there at seven and ask for Clark. He's expecting you." She reaches for a sandwich and munches it before speaking her next words. "Clark can be annoying," she says. "But he tells me their team is very, very good."

"They know I'm not, right?" I want this to be clear. If they are expecting some kind of pool shark, they are going to be sorely disappointed. I've never been sporty. I was the kid that always had her nose buried in a book. When I bend over the table, my breasts knock the balls out of place.

Maybe Trevor was right. Maybe I am hopeless. Maybe wanting to beat him is just some kind of pipe dream. Then the advice from my dad sounds once again in my head. *Don't you want to know what lies ahead? If you stay right here, how will you find out?*

He's right, and Piper's right as well. I probably am never going to be any good at pool, but I owe it to myself to find out.

Gabby nods. "He said they need some players that aren't experts. It has to do with some kind of handicapping system."

I know what she's talking about. Having lived with Trevor for five months, I've learned much more about the mechanics of pool leagues than I ever wanted to know. If there's a finite amount of memory in my head, knowing about the equalizer system that the American Poolplayers Association uses has probably replaced something more important in my brain. If you find me walking around gibbering like an idiot, blame Trevor.

Gabby's grinning to herself, a secret little smile that means that something's afoot. "What?" I ask her, pointing my finger at her. "I know that look. What aren't you telling me?"

Her reply is airy. "I was at the Maxwell Club one night when Clark's team was playing," she says. "Let's just say that your teammates are very easy on the eye. I predict a rebound fling."

I normally keep the details of my sex life private, but I'm also on my third drink, and the rum has loosened my tongue. "A rebound fling sounds really good," I sigh. "Trevor was... underwhelming."

Everyone leans forward for more dirt. The last time we giggled and spilled the beans about our sex lives was two months ago, when Gabby regaled us with the story of her ménage à trois with two guys she met in a bar. *Ménage à trois.* It even sounds exotic. "What do you mean, underwhelming?" Wendy asks.

"Missionary with the lights turned out, precisely twice a week." I make a face as I remember my lamentable sex life. "Once in a while, if he was being adventurous, I was allowed to get on top and do all the work."

Shrieks of horror greet my answer. "Seriously?" Katie sounds astonished. "Not even doggie?"

I snort inelegantly. "Doggie? Trevor preferred to pretend I didn't have a butt. He called it the *'out hole.'*"

Gabby almost chokes on her rum and coke, she's laughing so hard. "I'm assuming anal was out of the question, then?" she quips. "So tell me again, why were you with him?"

"I thought there should be more to a relationship than sex." I gulp back the rest of my drink. "Stupid me. Instead, I got a shitty relationship and a lackluster sex life. That'll teach me. A rebound fling is exactly what I need. Wild crazy sex? I'm in."

They all giggle and the talk turns to Wendy's last blind date from the internet. I laugh and make conversation, but underneath all of it, my resolve hardens. Trevor was a mistake - a bad one. I was ready to move on until he sent me that stupid bill. Now, I want to kick his ass in front of all his friends. A rebound fling does sound nice, but if that doesn't happen, I'm not going to get too worried. I am going to Argentina in September, and I have my career to worry about. Guys are a distraction, and anything more serious than casual sex isn't what I need right now. I'm too busy for love.

5

Victorious warriors win first and then go to war, while defeated warriors go to war first and then seek to win.

— SUN TZU, THE ART OF WAR

Daniel:

I t seems ridiculous to come to a private, members-only club in Manhattan to play pool, but there we are. That's the kind of insanity that's to be expected in my life. Still, at the Maxwell Club, absolutely no-one calls me Mr. Hartman in the deferential tone of voice that drives me crazy. People even disagree with me from time to time. It's very refreshing.

"Good of you to show up."

I grimace. Clark Ellis' tone drips with passive-aggressiveness. If he's going to chew me out for missing the opening three weeks of this season, then I wish he'd just man up and yell at me. Instead, I'm going to have to endure not-so-subtle digs about the importance of showing up all night long. Sebastian, my best friend and instigator of this pool league idea, owes me big-time.

"Do you want me to quit the team, Clark?" I look straight into his eyes, and there's steel in my voice. "If you've found a replacement, I'm happy to withdraw."

I'm being a dick. Right now, there's only four of us and the league's rules require five players in each team. Clark's getting desperate. He's managed to annoy most of last season's players and three of them have flat out refused to come back. If he can't get a fifth person to show up tonight, we'll forfeit a game all season long.

I don't care a shit about the pool league. I'm here strictly for relaxation purposes. My father died from heart disease and hypertension when he was only fifty-five, brought on by many years of stressful work heading up the family firm. The family firm is now listed on the Dow Jones, and I'm the CEO. The pressure is constant and unrelenting and to mitigate its effects, my doctor has mandated recreational activity. So I make it a point to hang out with Sebastian at least once a week, and we shoot some pool and drink some beer.

But I'd be damned if I'm going to listen to Clark's bitching and moaning all night long, especially after listening to Uncle Cyrus all *day* long. Life is far too short for that.

"I found a fifth player," he says smugly, ignoring my threat. "There's this hot piece of ass that works with me, and she said one of her friends wants to play. One of her *girlfriends*." He smirks. "I can't wait."

Seriously, who talks like this? This guy sounds like a dickwad that reads *The Game* and boasts about his imaginary conquests. Before I give in to my urge to punch him,

Sebastian walks over. "I was going to the bar to grab a beer, Daniel," he says with an amused grin. "Then I remembered you're buying today."

I laugh. "Of course," I agree. "We cannot expect Manhattan's newest star chef to pay for his own drink, can we?"

We walk away from Clark. "Thanks for the rescue," I tell him. "Was it that obvious I wanted to hit him?"

"Not to everyone. What was Clark being a dick about tonight?"

"Some woman who's joining our team." I grimace in distaste. "He's hoping she is, and I'm using his words, *a hot piece of ass.*"

Sebastian shakes his head. "Classy guy, Clark. Still, punching him isn't going to do either of us any favors."

"Sad but true." I turn around to look at Ellis, who is shaking the hand of some young guy, his chest thrown out. No doubt he's now introducing himself as the team captain. Good for him.

The bartender brings us a couple of bottles of beer without being prompted. We take a seat at the bar as Juliette steps forward to play the first match. "I'm glad you came out tonight," Sebastian says. "For the last three weeks, I've just had Clark and Juliette for company. It's been rough."

I laugh. Sebastian has a very conflicted relationship with his business adviser. She's relentless about making sure he's in the public eye, and at heart, Sebastian's a low-key guy. "Juliette's not that bad."

"She's really gung-ho about this franchise idea," he says. "What about you? How's the takeover going?"

I frown. "If they weren't strategically important to us, I'd be tempted to just walk away. They've been consuming all my time in the last month. Each conference call produces some bullshit objection. Now, it looks like their board is going to fight." I pour half the bottle of beer down my throat. "And do you know why? Because they don't want to be exposed to New York values. Those were their actual words."

"What *are* New York values? Paying too much money for real estate? Ordering takeout more than five times a week?" Sebastian asks dryly. "Is Cyrus riding your ass, then? Telling you to stay out of the tabloids?"

Sebastian knows my family dynamics well. I'm about to confirm his guess when I'm distracted by the sight of a woman walking toward Clark.

She's not Clark's type, that's for sure. Her figure's more generous than Clark typically prefers, and her black dress wouldn't be out of place at a nunnery. She's wearing sensible flats and her red hair is pulled back into a ponytail.

Though she's sending out absolutely no signals, there's something about her. I can't tear my eyes away. The primness of her dress can't hide her body's curves. Her breasts are round and lush, and I can't wait to see her ass as she bends over a table.

At that image, my cock stirs. Pavlov would have been proud of me. Bend a woman over a table, and I either want to spank her or fuck her, or both.

"That's the woman Clark was talking about?" Sebastian's eyes are glued on her as well. "She *is* a hot piece of ass. Let's go over and say hello."

When we reach them, Sebastian sticks out his hand. "Hi," he says smoothly. "I'm Sebastian."

"This is our newest teammate," Clark interjects. "Bailey Moore, meet Sebastian and Daniel."

"Welcome to the team." I smile at her. "Can I get you a drink?"

"Thank you, but it's probably not a good idea before I play." Her voice is soft. *Pretty.* She makes a face. "I'm already terrible at pool." She looks at Clark. "Gabby warned you, right? But I'd really like to learn."

The sincere, fervent need in her voice startles me. She wants this. Though she's doing a good job hiding it, she's nervous. I can feel the tension emanate in waves from her, and I wonder why. It's just a stupid pool game.

Clark nods ungraciously. "Juliette's almost done," he says. "Why don't you go up next so I can see what you can do?"

"Okay." She bites her lip, and desire clenches through my groin as I see her straight white teeth indent her tender pink flesh. A sideways look at Sebastian reveals that she's having the same effect on him. Clark's the only one who is immune. *Fool.*

SHE's as dreadful as she said she'd be.

Clark's set her up to play a game opposite a woman on the other team. Pool players are ranked based on skill level. Bailey's been marked as a three - the default skill level assigned to a new woman player until the league figures out how to rank her. Her opponent is a two. Technically, less skilled. It's still slaughter.

Clark shakes his head next to me as he watches. "Great." He sounds pissed. "She's a dog, and she can't play. Fucking perfect."

"Come on, man," I say, a little shocked. Seriously, that crosses a line. I guess no one ever told him that women exist for more reasons than to look pretty for him. "Don't be a prick. Besides, we need newbies on our team. Aren't we skating close to twenty-three right now?"

The league mandates that the total skill level of the entire team is less than or equal to twenty-three. I'm a seven. Sebastian's a six. Juliette's a solid three, and Clark is a wobbly four. This week, Bailey's playing as a three, though she'll drop a level for next week after today's scores have been tabulated.

Long story short, Clark shouldn't be bitching. We need Bailey to be terrible.

"What's going on?" Sebastian's at my side again. He's got a great nose for trouble, and my clenched expression must have given me away. I'm not going to hit Clark. That'll make the headlines of every tabloid in the city. But it doesn't mean I'm not tempted.

"What do you think?" Clark points to Bailey. "Hot or not?"

Sebastian shakes his head. "She's not a piece of meat, jackass," he says in disgust. "She's a person."

"Hot or not?" Clark repeats. There's a note of rancor in his voice. I'm really hoping he's had too much to drink tonight, not that alcohol is any justification for acting like a douchebag. "You guys. You want to act like you are above it all, don't you? Daniel with his billions, Sebastian and the bad boy chef routine. You can't stand admitting that you look at women and think, *I'd tap that.*"

Sebastian stiffens next to me. I might not be willing to get into a fight, but I know Sebastian, and if Clark doesn't stop talking, he's going to get hit. I'm about to say something to try and diffuse the tension, when Bailey bends over to make a shot, and her breasts graze the table.

Fuck yes, I'd tap that in a heartbeat.

"Oh, she's hot, alright," Sebastian says next to me. His

voice sounds hoarse. It's not just me that's feeling the effect of her curves. "She just doesn't know it."

Clark grits his teeth when Bailey misses an easy shot. She has absolutely no confidence in herself, her hands shake when they grip the cue stick, and she takes each shot in some kind of weird hunch over the table, but *she doesn't give up, and she doesn't leave.*

When her opponent wins her final game, Clark goes up to Bailey. "Well," he says, his voice patronizing, "you have plenty of room for improvement."

Her face whitens, and she whirls on her heel, looking for the closest exit. When she spots it, she makes a beeline for it. I want to follow her, and I will, in a moment. But Clark needs to be dealt with. I walk up to him, murder in my eyes. "Did you just make her cry?"

"Fuck off, Hartman," he snaps. "You saw her. She's terrible and she's inconsistent. I want a two who can win a game or two, not just act as a sacrifice."

Clark's obsessed with winning the tournament and going to Vegas, and he's forgotten to be kind. "She'll win more than a game or two," I tell him. "I guarantee it."

"She's dreadful and she's ugly," he says viciously.

Next to me, Sebastian's temper is one thread away from snapping. "Listen to me, asshole," he growls, his voice thick with menace. "I will get her good enough that she'll win at the end of the season."

"Bullshit," Clark says. "She'll be a two next week, and in July, I'll sacrifice her to draw out a seven. She doesn't have a chance. In fact, I might not even play her. It'll be easier to take a forfeit."

"You'll play her," I say. "Let's bet on it. You play her in July and she'll win her match."

"How much?"

"Fifty."

"Fifty dollars?" he sneers. "Fuck off, Hartman."

"Fifty grand."

From the look on Clark's face, I know we've got him.

6

We know what we are, but not what we may be.

— WILLIAM SHAKESPEARE, HAMLET

Bailey:

You have plenty of room for improvement. The words themselves weren't cruel, but the tone was scathing. Clark, who looks exactly like the comic book Clark Kent, right down to the square black nerd glasses, didn't bother to gentle his voice and listening to him, I had a bad flashback to Trevor's cutting words.

As I stand in the alleyway behind the bar, I twist my turquoise ring round my little finger, trying hard to calm myself. Right now, I wish I were more like my friends. Gabby, whose temper erupts hot and fiery when she's enraged, would have never let Clark speak to her the way he had just done to me. Wendy, who can turn icy when provoked, would have come up with a cutting response. Piper would have given him a contemptuous look and walked away. Me? I ran away and I'm fighting back tears behind the club. *Great job, Bailey,* I tell myself. I wish I'd grabbed my bag before fleeing. I don't want to go back in there and feel the eyes of the entire team on me. A team that includes two of the hottest men I've ever met. Daniel and Sebastian.

The door opens, and as if thinking about them can actually conjure them from thin air, the two of them come out into the alleyway. And when I see them so close to me that I can reach out and touch them, all thought flees my brain, and I forget to breathe.

"WHAT DID CLARK SAY TO YOU?" the big dark-haired man who had introduced himself as Sebastian growls. There's a hint of stubble on his face and his ocean-blue eyes are clouded with concern. His fists are clenched, his arms are thickly muscled, and his biceps are tattooed, though his t-shirt sleeves obscure the images. For some strange reason, he looks vaguely familiar.

"Just that I need improvement," I mutter. "No biggie."

"He upset you," Daniel, the leaner of the two says.

I shrug uncomfortably. These guys are perfect strangers - I'm not sure what I'm expected to say to them. Am I supposed to pour my heart out and tell them my insecurities? "It's okay," I say quietly. "He didn't say anything that wasn't true. I'm not sure I'm going to come back anyway."

"Why not?" Sebastian comes closer, so close that I can see each hair on his chin glimmer under the outdoor light in the alley. A sudden yearning to reach out and touch his face fills me, and I back away until my shoulders hit the wall. "You played two games," he says. "The woman on the other team kicked your butt, but you didn't quit. I liked that." His eyes hold mine captive. "Why quit now?"

Daniel is watching our interaction. His nostrils flare, and his breathing is ever so slightly quicker. Under his intent gaze, I feel very exposed, but I like it. I feel like I am tap-dancing at the knife edge of danger.

I drag my wandering mind back to our conversation. Back to the humiliating scene at the pool table. "Did you see me in there?" My voice rises with frustration. To my horror, I can hear the tears just under. One word will crack the fragile barrier and release them.

"Everyone starts somewhere." Daniel's voice is deliberately reassuring, as if he's soothing a cornered animal. "Everyone's a beginner once."

"I've been trying to learn to play for eleven months." Ever since I met Trevor. Almost a year, and what I have to show for it is less than nothing.

"Your teachers are not very good at their task," he says. Sebastian's the one watching me now, and he's so close I can almost feel him. There's a weird energy that's humming between the three of us, some kind of undercurrent of attraction that zings under the surface of our conversation, peppering each word with a heated spice. "We'll be better."

"You?"

"Sebastian and I can teach you." There's a pause in the conversation. "If you want."

They are way, way above my league, but I'm attracted to these men. I want them. I want to be sandwiched between them. I want to feel suffocated by their hard weight pressing against me. "You'll teach me how to play pool?" I stammer, in an effort to calm my raging hormones.

They both look amused. "Yes Bailey," Sebastian confirms. "We'll teach you how to play."

"Next Wednesday," Daniel says. "Get here an hour early." He fishes a business card from his wallet and hands it to me. "My address and personal phone number is on the back. Call me if something changes."

My brain cannot seem to string together enough words to form a sentence. I'm so caught up in their spell. An observer of this scene must think that it must be laughably easy to earn a PhD.

A full-blown grin covers Sebastian's face. "We're going to enjoy coaching you, Bailey. Don't be late."

Unless I'm imagining things, there's a gleam in Sebastian's eyes, a subtle emphasis on the word *coaching*. They aren't coming on to me, are they?

7

To receive guests is to take charge of their happiness during the entire time they are under your roof.

— Jean Anthelme Brillat-Savarin

Sebastian:

For every good, there is a bad. I learned this the painful way. The day after I got my first Michelin star, my dog Buddy died. He'd been ailing for many months, and his death was only a matter of time, but I still can't think back to that day without sorrow. Such is life.

So I'm not entirely unprepared when I'm sent an absolutely brutal Yelp review of *Seb II* Thursday morning.

This place sucks big hairy eyeballs.

Sebastian Ardalan might have two fucking Michelin stars, but if the food we ate last night was any indication, the people that hand out these stars have no taste buds.

First, my girlfriend ordered steak, well done. The snotty

waiter looked down his nose at us for that. Apparently, when you are paying over a hundred dollars for meat, the only option is rare. Eating raw meat is not an option for her — she's pregnant. And hey, douchebag waiter, if you are reading this? I'd prefer to tell our family that we are having a baby first, before letting you know.

Then the meat comes out, and of course it's still bloody. We send it back to be cooked. Comes back thirty minutes (!) later, cold and bloody. I point out how long we've been waiting for our food, and the waiter shrugs.

Absolutely terrible experience. We ended up eating at Taco Bell, where some cheerful minimum wage workers made us a delicious steak burrito, and yes, they made sure the steak was well-done without the attitude.

And those two Michelin stars? The chef can stuff it up his ass.

Damn it. If this were a one-time thing, I could ignore it. Sometimes, customers get disgruntled, but this is starting to feel like a pattern. I've seen many reviews in the last three months talk about slow service, snotty waiters and more. I need to head down to *Seb II* right away, and I'm long overdue a conversation with the staff there. I don't like to go Gordon Ramsey on their asses, but after this review, it seems necessary.

"WHAT THE ABSOLUTE FUCK?" I wave my phone, with the offending Yelp review visible on the screen, in the small office space in Seb II. Crammed in there are the sous-chef Ben and the restaurant manager Mina, who is in charge of the front.

Mina looks uncomfortable, but she doesn't say anything. Ben starts to roll his eyes, then catches a sight of my face and thinks better of it. "Look, Sebastian," he says. "I wouldn't get too bent out of shape. They were just tourists."

"They were just tourists." My voice is dangerous and my blood pressure is rising. "That's your response to this? *They were just tourists?* Do you know how much money tourists bring to *Seb II*? Do you think our business is all investment bankers and Wall Street analysts? Are you fucking kidding me with this shit?"

Ben quails, but I'm not done yelling. "Is this review fair?"

Mina finally speaks up. "Yes Chef," she mumbles. "It's true. They did send back their steak, and they did wait more than thirty minutes for a refire." She shoots Ben an irritated look. "I was told the kitchen didn't feel that tending to the steak was a priority."

"Bitch, don't you put this on me," Ben snarls. "There was a large party of regulars in the room and we were dealing with their orders."

I've been too lax with these guys. Ben's casually uttered slur against Mina is a sign that the front and the back of the restaurant have become dangerously fractured. I'm not going to tolerate this kind of disrespect. There's only one person in this room that's allowed to curse, and that's me.

"Ben." My voice is quiet. "If that's how you want to speak to my staff, you can leave."

He realizes how close he is to the line. Fuck, I'm not sure he hasn't *crossed* the line. He gulps audibly before he speaks. "Sorry, Mina," he mutters. "Sorry, Chef."

Mina nods curtly. She doesn't seem surprised by either the swearing or the half-assed apology. "Mina, I'd like to speak to you alone," I tell her. "Ben, can you excuse us? I'll send for you."

Ben looks unhappy, but leaves without protest. He's smart enough to know that when you are knee-deep in shit, you need to stop digging. "Okay," I tell Mina, when we are alone. "Tell me your side."

"What makes you think I have something to say?"

"Because you are from Nebraska, and are the last person in the city to treat tourists badly. So, what gives?"

She looks at her nails. "Permission to speak frankly, Chef?" she asks finally.

"Go ahead." I'm not sure why she feels the need to ask, and I don't like it. *Seb II* has always been a bit of a problem child, but I sense that things are spiraling out of control.

"The waiter who was rude to the couple is a friend of Ben's," she says. "He's snotty and arrogant."

"Why is he still employed? We have no place for that here."

She doesn't meet my gaze. "I didn't want to piss off the kitchen," she replies. "We work on tips. Those guys don't."

Okay, this is bullshit. "Did Ben suggest that he'd slow down food service if you fired his friend?"

"No, Chef."

"So you jumped to conclusions and did nothing about a problem employee?" I cannot believe Mina. I thought she was better than this.

She doesn't say anything in her defense. But I can read it in her stance. She genuinely believes Ben would have retaliated, and more than anything, that gives me pause. Mina's been a rock steady manager. She was my fifth hire. I'd prefer not to lose her to Ben's dismissive misogyny.

"Okay, here's what we are going to do," I tell her. "Helen's going to come in here for the next month and get the kitchen in shape." I give her a steady look. "In the meanwhile, I want you to clean house. And Mina, I'm not thrilled that it needed to get to this. I expect you to raise a red flag if you are running into issues, not just wait for shit to blow up in our faces."

She bites her lip. "Sorry, Chef."

"Let's get Ben in here and break the news to him."

Ben is, as expected, thrilled that he's moving to *Seb New York*, even if it's just for a month. Coming right after a second Michelin star, it feels like a promotion to him. I don't like it. I'm sure Ben's responsible for as much of the bad behavior as Mina, maybe more.

When Mina's gone and the two of us are alone, I turn to him. "You aren't being rewarded," I say through clenched teeth. "Helen's going to get your crew ready, and I'm going to be riding your ass at *Seb New York*. I don't like a sloppy team, Ben. If you aren't prepared to put in the work, you don't belong here."

"I belong, Chef," he insists. "You aren't going to regret this."

He's wrong - I *already* regret this. I don't have the time to babysit Ben, especially not if this franchise deal that Juliette's pushing falls into place. I don't want to give up my Wednesday evenings playing pool to make sure things at *Seb New York* are working smoothly. If my intuition about this stupid mess is correct, this is going to be a clusterfuck.

8

In the Kreung tribe in Cambodia, fathers build a love hut for their daughter when the girl reaches marriageable age. Different boys spend the night in the hut until she finds the one she wants to marry.

— FROM BAILEY'S JOURNAL OF INTERESTING FACTS
FROM AROUND THE WORLD

Bailey:

We are going to enjoy coaching you.

When Sebastian had spoken those words to me, I had gaped at him, unable to think of a witty repartee. I still cannot.

But I wonder about his words all weekend. What did he mean by *we*? It wasn't an expression of interest, was it? And if it was, did he really mean both of them wanted me?

Trevor was my third lover. My first was nothing to write

home about - a fumbling encounter in Kevin McNamara's bedroom before his parents got back from work. After that first brief moment of pain, I remember lying back and wondering why people made such a fuss about sex. It was okay, but hardly life-changing.

So I stayed away from boys, much to the delight of my parents, and I focused on my studies. I graduated college with straight A's, and started my Masters degree immediately after. In my early twenties, all my energy and focus had been on my research.

Things had been better with Ivan in the Taiga. It had been a relationship that had been based on sexual attraction rather than any real underlying compatibility. It hadn't mattered - we never had a future. Ivan was interested in hunting, fishing and in surviving the harshness of Siberia. I was on the cusp of getting my PhD, and I couldn't see myself staying in Russia past my research year. When it was time for me to leave, we ended things amicably and without sadness.

The pendulum had swung the other way with Trevor. On paper, he had seemed like the right guy, but our sex life had been pretty dismal.

Which brings me to Daniel and Sebastian. They are two of the hottest guys I've seen in a long time, guys whose sex appeal exudes off them in powerful waves. Guys who make my body tighten with longing.

You must have misunderstood them, Bailey, I tell myself. *Guys like that aren't interested in you.* In many parts of the world, men are attracted to curvy women, but North America isn't one of them. Here, men who look more like gods don't date chubby girls. They date supermodels.

But they'd been nice. When Daniel had smiled at me, the warmth and sincerity were hard to disguise. When

Sebastian had grinned conspiratorially at me, I'd felt included. I'd wanted to belong in their little charmed circle.

Gabby's the only one of us who's been with more than one person at the same time. In March, she met two men at a bar, and she'd gone to their hotel room. *Best sex I've ever had,* she said dreamily, when she told us. Even now, two months after the fact, I know she can't forget that one-night stand.

I wonder what it would be like to be with both Sebastian and Daniel. Two men, one with chocolate-brown eyes, the other with eyes that remind me of the ocean. Two strong bodies. For an instant, I close my eyes and allow myself to imagine what it would feel like to be sandwiched between them, engulfed in their heat. Four hands would caress every inch of my body. Two mouths would pleasure me. Two sets of eyes would look at me, heavy with lust.

Yeah. That's going to happen. Get your head out of your ass, Bailey Moore.

"LEVEL WITH ME, Bailey. You're attracted to them, aren't you?"

I'm having lunch with Gabby Monday afternoon at a small Italian bistro overlooking Washington Square park. The Thursday Night Drinking Pack couldn't meet this evening. Katie's husband Adam is out of town and she can't find a sitter for the twins. Piper's bowed out as well, and Wendy's texted us that she's going to be working late. Since that just left Gabby and me, we decided to take advantage of the lovely spring day and meet for lunch instead.

There's a mountain of corrections at my desk that I'm playing hooky from. My colleagues in the science world can test their undergraduates with multiple-choice questions. I have no such luck. In Cultural Anthropology 101 at NYU, the students write essays. Five 25-page essays per student per semester, essays that need to be read and corrected - *by me.*

"I didn't say that."

"No, you didn't," she agrees with a grin. "However, you have spent the last five minutes talking about how kind they were. How nice. And when I asked what they looked like, you went bright red." She winks at me. "Also, your nipples are hard."

"They are not." I look down automatically, and her chuckle turns into a full-throated laugh. "Damn it, Gabby. Maybe I'm just attracted to you."

She's not fazed. "Sorry, dollface, you aren't my type."

"Dollface?"

She shrugs. "Someone I know speaks like that," she says vaguely. "Stop changing the subject. Talk to me about Daniel and Sebastian. Which one do you want?"

If she thought I was blushing earlier, I wonder what she thinks of my coloring now. "It doesn't matter," I mutter. "It's not all about what I want. They have to want me, and that's not going to happen."

"Hang on." She leans forward, her pasta primavera forgotten. "You didn't say Daniel had to want you. Or Sebastian had to want you. You said *they.*"

I can't keep the defensiveness out of my voice. "It doesn't matter," I repeat. "My fantasies don't count."

"So you have been fantasizing about them?"

"A little bit," I confess, lying only a little. I've been fantasizing *a lot.* "Does that make me weird? I mean, shouldn't I be fantasizing about the perfect white dress, a house in the 'burbs and two-point-five children instead?"

Gabby shakes her head. "You are an adventurer, Bails.

Why on earth would your fantasies be conventional? You love to explore. You need someone that can keep up with that." She giggles. "Or two someones." She sips her iced tea. After a pause, she adds, "I could never understand why you dated Trevor. He was stodgy. And more than that, he wasn't nice."

She's right, but Trevor's not what I want to focus on right now. "Daniel and Sebastian *were* nice," I say aloud. "I mean, they offered to teach me how to play pool, and they didn't have to do that. But come on, Gabby. I barely know them."

She rolls her eyes. "As if knowing someone is a prerequisite to good sex," she quips dryly.

Gabby might like to pretend that she's the queen of casual hookups, but I know better. Her desire to keep things superficial with the men she dates isn't because she doesn't want something more lasting. Rather, it's because a succession of absolutely vile men have broken her heart, and she's formed a shell to protect herself.

"It is for me," I reply. "I don't have to fall in love with them, you know? I don't walk around with stars in my eyes. But I think I have to like them before I sleep with them."

Is that a lie? Had I ever actually *liked* Trevor? He'd taken me to fancy restaurants and he'd bought me flowers and I'd become smitten because I wasn't used to being wooed. The luster had, however, faded fast.

"So Google them," she suggests. "Talk to them, get to know them."

She makes it sound so easy. "Would you do it again?" I ask her. "Your threesome, I mean." I don't know why I'm talking about this. Perhaps I need to say the word *threesome* out loud, as if hearing the words spoken would snap me out of my crazy thoughts.

"I don't do relationships, Bailey," she responds quietly.

"Not anymore. But," she continues, "if I did, I would. Absolutely." A wistful look crosses her face. "They were so good. For the space of one evening, I was the most treasured person in the world. They were very... attentive."

It's my turn to laugh at her. "Who's getting all hot and bothered now?" I tease. "Sorry, dollface. You're not my type."

She shakes her head with a smile, but not before I catch a fleeting glimpse of the look of regret in her eyes. "Here's my advice, Bailey, whether you want it or not. Everyone's a consenting adult. If they are interested, then what's the harm in something casual?"

"It's only a fantasy, Gabby. Just because I have naughty thoughts about Daniel and Sebastian, it doesn't mean they'll come true. I'm not married to Brad Pitt, am I?"

She laughs. "Brad Pitt isn't playing pool with you every week. Daniel and Sebastian are. It seems to me that you have an opportunity to make things happen."

"I'm leaving for Argentina in the fall," I respond.

"So what? I'm not suggesting a relationship, just some good sex to make up for the drought. The pool league isn't a long-term commitment, is it?"

She's right. Once this season is over, I won't see my teammates again. A casual fling with Sebastian and Daniel will have a built-in shelf life, the same way my relationship with Ivan did. I was able to survive my breakup with Ivan unscathed, and I'm sure things would be similar with Daniel and Sebastian.

I'm sure of it.

Really sure.

Okay, I might be trying to convince myself. I can close my eyes right now and picture both of them in crystal-clear detail. I remember every word of our brief conversation. Thinking about the look of intent in their eyes, my skin erupts in goosebumps. I never had such a reaction to Ivan.

When it comes to my personal life, I'm extremely good at ignoring the obvious. "You are right," I tell Gabby. "I'm done with the pool league in July, and I leave for Patagonia at the end of August. This might be a really good idea."

9

To thine own self be true.

— William Shakespeare, Hamlet

Sebastian:

It's Wednesday. I've been working all week at *Seb New York* with Ben, and it's been exhausting. The guy doesn't pay attention, he can't see problems starting to form, and he can't get production out of the line chefs. The kitchen, normally a smoothly functioning machine, is struggling to cope with his waffling and his indecisiveness.

God, I miss Helen. I call to tell her that on Saturday night, after a grueling shift in the kitchen, and she snickers. "I should ask for a raise, Chef," she jokes.

"It's yours," I tell her sincerely. "I didn't realize how good I had it with you. How are you making out with your clowns?"

"They aren't that bad," she replies. "Just needed a little whipping into shape. Some of them thought a woman couldn't lead a kitchen." She snorts. "I corrected that impression."

Helen stands five feet tall, and weighs ninety pounds soaking wet. Still, I feel sorry for the idiots who dared to even hint that she didn't belong. Helen can kick ass with the best of them. "The fools." The phone chimes in my ear. Another call's coming through. "Hey, Helen, I have to go. I'll call you back over the weekend."

Juliette's on the other line. I pick up the call. "Hey, what's going on?"

"Sebastian," she says, her voice urgent and slightly irritated. "Where have you been? I've left you a couple of messages today. Don't you check your texts?"

"I work in a kitchen, Juliette," I point out. "I'm hardly going to be fiddling with my phone when food's about to burn on the stove. What's going on?"

"A couple of the franchise deal investors are in town tonight, and they want to meet you at *Seb New York*," she says. "Can you skip pool so they can meet you?"

I think of Bailey. I've been looking forward to this evening all week long. In the shower, I've closed my eyes and imagined her slick, wet body next to mine. Her eyes had widened when I'd hinted we were interested, and her breathing had caught. She'd definitely picked up on the signal.

I can't wait to see where this evening might go. It's been years since I've felt this kind of anticipation for a woman. Juliette's franchise opportunity pales in comparison. "Sorry," I tell her. "I can't. I'm busy tonight."

"Sebastian, this is really important. We just need thirty minutes. What if I can get them there in an hour?"

I'm leaving in twenty minutes to head to the Maxwell Club, where Daniel and I are teaching Bailey how to play pool. Then again, the franchise deal is important, isn't it? For so many years, I've dreamed about showing everyone in Mississippi that I defied their expectations and made something of myself. What's a pool lesson in comparison?

My phone buzzes. It's a text message from Daniel. *Leaving work now,* it says. *See you in thirty minutes?*

I make my decision. "No can do, Juliette," I tell her, my voice steady. "I'm far too busy running my restaurants for last-minute meetings. Next time, give me a little more heads-up."

There's a long pause, then she clears her throat meaningfully. "Running your restaurants?" Her voice has a hint of suspicion in it. "Is that the real reason you can't meet us today?"

"What are you saying, Juliette?"

Her voice is curt. "The window of opportunity is small, Sebastian. We may never get another chance like this. Our entire focus should be on this deal."

"*Seb New York* and *Seb II* are always going to come first. You have to know that."

"Make time for this, Sebastian," she says. "Else this might slip through your fingers." She sighs. "I'll look through your calendar and arrange another time. Oh, tell Clark I'm going to be really late. I need to take these guys out for drinks first."

"Stay away from *Seb New York*," I warn her. "Ben's not ready for prime time yet."

As I get ready to leave, I dwell on my warped sense of priorities. I should have blown off Daniel and Bailey, and met with the investors, but I don't want to. The only place I want to be this evening is at Maxwell Club, helping a curvy redhead improve her pool game.

10

Who wishes to fight must first count the cost.

— Sun Tzu, The Art of War

Daniel:

I'm back in that alley behind the Maxwell Club, and I can't tear my eyes away from Bailey. She's wearing lingerie. Lines of leather and lace crisscross her breasts. The thong she wears shows the lush curves of her ass. Bailey's dressed for sex, and I'm ready to oblige and next to me, so is Sebastian.

Our shared desire hangs heavy in the air.

Sebastian moves closer and pins Bailey in place against a wall. "Spread your legs for me," he growls and she obeys instantly.

"Is she wet?" I ask from my position opposite her. I don't come closer, not yet, but my voice is thick with lust. "Check her, Sebastian."

He kneels between her feet, his hands gripping the sides of her panties. He yanks them down harshly. The fabric rips, but she

*doesn't care. She thrusts her hips into Sebastian's face. "Please..."
she begs.*

My cock jumps in reaction to her pleas, her open need.

*Sebastian pushes three fingers into her wet, waiting pussy.
"She's soaked, Daniel." His voice is rich with satisfaction. "Take
off the bra, Bailey."*

*"Here? Anyone can see," she protests weakly, but her hands
are already reaching behind to unclasp the offending garment.*

*"Are you questioning us, Bailey?" I ask her, my voice taut. I
come closer now and my hand grips at her jaw before I press a
hard kiss on her waiting lips. My tongue runs at the seam of her
lips till she permits me entry.*

*Blood pounds in my head. She whimpers as Sebastian's
fingers thrust in and out of her pussy, his tongue dancing over her
clitoris. "Please," she begs again. Looking at her, I can tell that her
climax is close. Another few seconds...*

*Sebastian and I exchange glances, then he thrusts his fingers
in and out of her, faster and harder. At the same time, I pinch
Bailey's erect nipples between my fingers. She erupts between us
in waves and waves of pleasure.*

When I wake up and my head clears from its sexual fog,
I shake my head in chagrin. I can't remember the last time I
had a sex dream about a woman.

Bailey Moore is trouble.

BAILEY ISN'T THERE when I get to the Maxwell Club, but
Sebastian is, idly shooting some pool. I grab a beer at the
bar, and walk over to him. "Want to play a game or two
while we wait?"

"Sounds good," he agrees. He racks the balls efficiently,
and we toss a coin to see who breaks. Sebastian wins, and he

bends over the table. "Be honest with me. What do you think of Juliette's franchise proposal?"

We haven't had a chance to talk about this. I've been spending a lot of time in Kansas City, and he's been busy sorting out the mess with Ben. This is the first opportunity we've had to talk about Juliette's ambitious plans. "I'm always honest with you," I respond. "It's a terrible idea."

He breaks. Three balls hurtle into pockets. "I thought you might say that."

"Don't you think so? You have to know that setting up a chain of franchise restaurants will take too much time away from your operations in New York. Already, you're writing a cookbook and you're filming a Food Network show. Where are you going to fit it in?" I shake my head. "You are spreading yourself dangerously thin."

Sebastian doesn't deny the truth of my words. "You're right," he says. "I know I'm crazy to think about this. *Seb New York* is my home. I'd rather shove bamboo skewers underneath my fingernails than to see it languish because of my inattention." The nine slides into the top right pocket. "Still," he says slowly. "The vision of a restaurant in Hattiesburg shimmers and beckons."

"Why are you still trying to prove yourself to them, Sebastian?" I ask him, though I know the answer. Sebastian's upbringing was hell, and I do understand his desire to rub his success in the face of his hometown. "There are people here in New York who believe in you, who want you. Can't you just let Mississippi go?"

He misses his shot and I move to the table. "You did that deliberately," he accuses with a faint grin. "Let's change the topic. What do you think about Bailey? I'm looking forward to tonight."

"As am I." My smile dims as I shake my head. "I checked

up on her," I tell him. "She just moved out of a man's apartment. I'm assuming he's the ex. His name is Trevor Decker. The guy owns about a dozen sandwich shops in the city. And he plays in the league. *What?*"

Sebastian's trying hard not to smirk. "It's my job to know things," I tell him, sounding defensive. "Besides, most of this was just Google."

"Someone's very interested," he chuckles. "It's good to see you focus on something that isn't work."

I grimace. We both have our flaws. Sebastian can't let his past go. I have an all-consuming focus on the family firm, leaving me no time for women or relationships or anything else.

"What are you going to do about our bet if Bailey doesn't show up this week? Clark was a douchebag to her. Maybe she doesn't want to play anymore."

"My bet," I correct him. "I believe it was me that put forward the number." I shrug. "It's fifty grand. I'm not going to get bent out of shape about it."

Sebastian gives me a shit-eating grin. "If she shows, I'm totally going to enjoy coaching her. I think I caught a vibe from her."

I roll my eyes and refuse to rise to the bait. "Please. You think you are going to score all the fucking time." I lift my head and I see that Bailey's walked in while I was taking my shot. She's at the bar, laughing and saying something to the bartender as he hands her a shot of vodka. She's wearing black again today - black pants and a black shirt, but unlike last week, her hair isn't pulled back into a ponytail. It cascades in lush waves over her shoulders and down her back. She looks softer this way. *Prettier.*

She downs the drink before she turns and heads our

way. "She's here now, hot-shot," I tell Sebastian. "Let's see what you can do."

SHE LOOKS wary as she approaches us. "Hey," she says, and there's a definite note of unease in her voice. "You guys are here."

"Is something wrong?" I ask her.

"I didn't realize who you were when you offered to teach me how to play pool," she says, making a face. "Daniel Hartman - billionaire CEO of a Fortune 500 company. Sebastian Ardalan, the youngest chef to earn two Michelin stars. Shouldn't you be too busy to tutor me?"

Sebastian chuckles. "You googled us," he teases. "I'm flattered."

She flushes, and I interject before her embarrassment worsens. "We googled you too," I reassure her. "You're a cultural anthropologist at NYU, right? What brings you to our team?"

She grimaces ruefully. "My ex-boyfriend thinks I'm hopeless at pool. I want to prove him wrong. You didn't answer my question, by the way. Why *are* you helping me?"

I bite back my smile, and Sebastian laughs aloud. I should have guessed she would be smart enough to notice the half-answer. I've been reading the blog she kept when she was in Russia in my spare time, and her entries reveal a bright, curious, enthusiastic woman. Already, I'm fascinated by her. There's not a single woman in my social circle who would voluntarily spend a month in the wilderness of Siberia, let alone a year.

"Daniel bet Clark fifty grand you'd win in July." Sebastian tells her with a grin, ignoring the withering look I send him.

I expect her to yell or rant, but she surprises me by bursting out laughing. "That is such a cliché," she says, her eyes sparkling with mirth. "Bored billionaires betting on the lives of mere mortals like myself."

"Daniel's the only billionaire," Sebastian corrects her. "I'm just a cook."

She rolls her eyes. "Of course, Chef Ardalan. So let me see if I get this straight. The two of you are going to teach me how to play pool so Daniel won't lose fifty *thousand* dollars." She's still amused. "Will you even miss the money?" she asks me.

I'm more intrigued by her with each passing second. "That's not the point," I reply. "I don't like to lose. So what do you say, Bailey? Are you in? Do you want us to coach you?"

She gives me a challenging look. "Will I get good enough to beat Trevor?"

"If you follow directions." There's definitely innuendo in my phrasing.

"Directions." She tests that phrase out on her tongue with an arch of her eyebrow.

"Mmm-hmm."

She looks from me to Sebastian, then back to me. Finally, she shakes her head with a laugh. "So, about that pool lesson. What do I need to do?"

11

It takes courage to grow up and become who you really are.

— E.E. Cummings

Bailey:

Unfair though it is, I blame Gabby for my confused state of mind. If she hadn't told us about her threesome, such a forbidden fantasy wouldn't have even been in the realms of possibility.

Now, as Daniel bends over me, helping me aim my pool cue, I can't stop imagining him doing other things to me in the same position. As Sebastian gives me instructions, I wonder if he's just as dominant in bed. I have butterflies in my stomach and sex on the brain.

When Sebastian mentioned the bet, my heart had sunk to my toes. They hadn't made the offer to coach me because they were being nice, or because they wanted to help me. It was about winning the bet and nothing else.

Then I stopped to think, and realized that it didn't

matter. I'm not looking for anything from them. Some people flirt as easily as breathing, and Sebastian seems to be one of them. Daniel's more of an enigma, but I can't spend time analyzing them. I need to get dramatically better at pool to beat Trevor in July, and Daniel and Sebastian want to win their bet against Clark. For the moment, our goals are aligned. That's all.

~

"TELL ME ABOUT CULTURAL ANTHROPOLOGY," Daniel says to me as we play. "I thought you joined the team to use us as research subjects. And don't jerk your head up as soon as you make your shot. Keep your movements slow and steady."

Heat pools in my lower belly at his words. Slow and steady. I can imagine him saying that to me under *very* different circumstances, circumstances that would involve a lot less clothing, but I push the lust back and respond to his question. "'Gender *relations and interpersonal dynamics in a modern sporting environment*' would make for an interesting paper," I agree. "But no, I'm just here because my ex-boyfriend is a jerk."

"What did he do?"

I tell Daniel about the letter from Trevor's lawyer, and he laughs. I glare at him, but he's unconcerned. "Come on, Bailey, think about it. You must have hurt his feelings quite a lot for him to retaliate with such a dick move."

"I doubt it," I say dryly. "The Met Gala's coming up, and Liberal Arts faculty at NYU get an invitation. Trevor's pouting because he can't go rub shoulders with celebrities."

Sebastian's listening to our conversation, but he doesn't interrupt. "Is that all you think it is?" Daniel asks gently.

"You are a beautiful woman, Bailey. Your ex-boyfriend is an idiot if he missed that." He drinks the last of his beer. "Can I get you a drink while I'm at the bar? You were drinking vodka, right?"

Trevor's never called me beautiful before. My heart feels like it's beating faster as I raise my gaze to Daniel's chocolate brown eyes. "You were watching me when I walked in?" I ask faintly. *Damn it, why is my body so aware of these men? I barely know them. I'm not supposed to react this way.*

"I would be a fool not to." His eyes are warmly appreciative as he looks at me with a grin. "As horrible an outfit as this is, it can't hide all your charms."

"Vodka neat," I tell him, barely registering his assessment of my attire. "The bartender knows my preference."

He nods and walks away, and I tear my eyes away from his butt with difficulty. "Ready to play?" Sebastian mutters in my ear, making me jump once again. "Steady, Bailey," he soothes, his hands on my arms. "I didn't mean to startle you."

He is touching me, and I don't know what to do. Things like this don't happen to me. I'm a chubby girl. I tend to be invisible to guys. Men rarely look at me with open heat in their eyes, the way Sebastian is right now, and it both arouses me and terrifies me.

"Is it my turn to break?" I mumble. I need to distract myself from the desire that swirls in my body, pulling me like a helpless marionette toward these men.

An amused smile creases his lips. Sebastian Ardalan is not unaware of the effect he's having on me. "Go ahead," he replies. "Break."

Pull yourself together, I scold myself, resolving to focus on the true reason I'm here. I have to beat Trevor and wipe that smug expression off his face. I slide my bracelets off my wrists and put them on a nearby table. "Can you keep an eye on them?" I ask. "They aren't valuable, but I don't want to lose them." He looks curious, so I elaborate. "They're souvenirs from trips."

"I get refrigerator magnets when I travel, and Daniel buys coffee mugs," he confides as I chalk my cue.

"Really?" I look up, surprised by Sebastian's revelation. I didn't expect to have something in common with a billionaire or a celebrity chef, but it's nice to know that even they shop at kitschy souvenir shops.

He nods. "Really. Daniel drinks about eight cups of coffee a day, so he collects coffee mugs as a memento of his vacations. I used to take photos, but I never looked at them after I got back home. The magnets, I can look at each time I open the refrigerator."

Sebastian gives me some tips about breaking. He shows me how to move the tip of the cue closer to my hand so I have more control when I make the shot. When Daniel comes back with three shots, the three of us lift our glasses in a toast and gulp down the vodka, then Daniel shows me where to aim so I don't scratch. They make me practice scattering the balls, over and over again, and each time I make contact, they speak encouraging, supportive words.

Their coaching works. After fifteen minutes, I stop dreading walking up to the table to try and dispel the tightly racked triangle of balls. I start hitting the cue ball cleanly, and when I follow Daniel's advice - *slow and steady* - I even have my first legal break. Three balls hit the rails.

"I did it!" I exclaim. "I can't believe it. I actually did it."

"Yes you did," Sebastian agrees cheerfully, handing me my stack of jewelry. "Congratulations, Bailey. We'll make a pool player out of you yet."

For the first time ever, I believe him. Less than an hour

of instruction and I've learned how to break? Daniel and Sebastian are miracle workers.

CLARK'S in some kind of snit when he shows up and reads the paperwork that the bartender hands him. Sebastian sneaks a look and comes away grinning.

"What?" I ask. After hanging out with Daniel and Sebastian for a little over an hour, chatting about work and vacations and my pool game, I feel a sense of camaraderie with them.

Sebastian laughs out aloud. "Clark's rank dropped. He's now a three. Idiot."

"That's not very nice." Though Clark was a dick to me last week, given my general ineptness at the pool table, I feel sympathetic for anyone that's struggling at the sport. Even douchebag Clark.

"Trust me, it's perfectly justified," Daniel replies. "You know why his rank dropped? He can't play opposite a woman."

"Huh?"

"He's way more aggressive when he's playing a woman," Daniel explains. "His shot selection is reckless. He hits the balls too hard. Sound and fury, but no substance. He's trying to prove something." He shakes his head. "Clark's been playing in the league for a while. Other teams have figured this out, so they always put up a woman when he's playing. Of course, he loses far more often than he wins. Watch."

Just as Daniel predicts, when Clark puts himself up to play, still muttering about the incompetent American Poolplayers League, the other team confers briefly, and a petite Asian woman comes forward. Both Daniel and Sebastian are struggling not to laugh, and to tell the truth, I too am fighting my urge to giggle at the thunderous expression on Clark's face.

Bailey, I think to myself, *you might be in trouble.* I'm extremely attracted to Daniel and Sebastian, but as I told Gabby over lunch, attraction is not enough for me. Liking them is a pretty necessary part of the equation. The problem is, after this evening, I like them a lot.

"Where's Juliette?" I ask them, to try to distract myself from that train of thought. We'd been introduced last week, and we'd even had time for a brief conversation, where I'd learned that she had known Daniel and Sebastian for more than a year. She'd been polite enough, if a little aloof.

"She's meeting with some potential partners of mine," Sebastian says.

Daniel raises an eyebrow. "She didn't want you there?" he asks curiously.

"She did," Sebastian replies shortly. "I declined."

Daniel looks amused. "Of course." He looks as if he's going to say more, but he stops himself short.

I look back and forth at them, intrigued by this conversation. "Partners of yours?" I ask. "Other chefs?"

"No, these guys are investors," Sebastian replies. "Juliette's my business adviser."

"Oh." I feel a strange sense of relief that I'm unprepared to examine. Instead, I turn toward the pool tables, where Clark is, as predicted, losing to his opponent. He's just scratched while trying to pocket the eight-ball - an automatic loss. For anyone other than me, it wasn't really even a difficult shot. Had Clark not tried to be flashy, he would have made it without any problem. "Wow, he really can't play against a woman, can he?"

"Nope," the guys confirm. We watch in silence as he

racks up the balls for the next game with bad grace, but the second game goes no better. His opponent has her foot on the throttle, and she doesn't let up.

"If he doesn't win the next game," Daniel mutters next to me, "he's going to lose the match."

"Aren't you bothered?" I ask him.

He shrugs. "It's just a game," he says. "I like to play, and I'm competitive enough to want to win. But if I start getting irritated every time Clark fucks up, I'm going to be angry all the time. It's not worth it."

"How very zen of you," I quip, and he laughs. "Are you going to be this laid-back if I lose your bet too?"

"Is that any way to talk?" Sebastian chides from his spot on the other side of Daniel. "Have some confidence in yourself, Bailey. You can absolutely win. Oh, for fuck's sake."

That last exclamation was directed at Clark, who scratched on the eight-ball again. Yikes. Three-zero. Clark's face is red with anger. He shakes hands with his opponent stiffly, and comes over to us. "Juliette not here yet?" he snaps. "Fine. Bailey, you're up."

Daniel gives me an encouraging nod. "Remember what we taught you," he says quietly, as Sebastian racks the balls for me. "Steady. Long strokes, nothing jerky."

I wink at him, hidden devilry appearing from nowhere. "I've heard that before," I joke. "Not quite in the same context though."

He laughs aloud. "Do me proud, Bailey."

CLARK'S not the only one who has dropped a rank. Not unexpectedly, my rank has fallen as well. Last week, I was a three, but after my abysmally poor performance, the league has downgraded me. I'm now a two - the lowest skill level of anyone in the league. *You have nowhere to go but up, Bailey*, I tell myself encouragingly, trying to ward off my nerves ahead of my match. Daniel and Sebastian are watching me, and I do want to do well for them. In one evening, they've taught me far more than Trevor's taught me in months, and I'm really grateful.

My opponent is another two. He's a geeky looking guy, and he's a dead-ringer for Sheldon Cooper, on the Big Bang Theory. As I shake his hand, I ask him if people ever tell him that. "Who?" He looks blankly at me. "I don't own a TV."

It takes difficulty to keep from rolling my eyes. I don't understand the hate some people have for TV. I like to escape reality by watching home decorating shows. Sue me.

I'm actually so busy getting annoyed by his attitude that I don't tense up as I break, and because I'm not paying attention, I have the break of a lifetime. *Well, my lifetime.* This isn't just a legal break. No, this time, when the balls scatter, one of them actually rolls into the pocket.

Little orange ball, I want to take you home and put you on a display shelf.

Even more shockingly, I follow up that opening shot, that miraculous exciting break, by sinking another ball, the solid green. I miss the next one, because sadly, no fairy godmother has been by sprinkling fairy dust on my pool cue. But still - two balls in a row? *This is unheard of.*

Nerd guy - whose name is Michael - tries to aim for a striped yellow ball at the far end of the table and misses, and it's me again. Luckily, he's left me with an incredibly easy shot - the ball I'm aiming for is only inches away from the pocket. It rolls in.

Three balls. I've managed to sink three balls. This is beyond awesome. This is stupendous.

My streak continues. Nothing dramatic - I still miss far more balls than I make, but I realize something. When I was playing with Trevor, if I missed a shot, he'd take advantage by clearing the table. Today, since I'm playing with an opponent that's as bad as I am, the game is much more evenly balanced, and the coaching that Sebastian and Daniel have provided me is helping. It's really, *really* helping. I'm keeping all the instructions I've heard from them in mind. Eyes on the tip of my cue. Keeping my head down while I take the shot. Steady and slow, with no sudden movements...

And then, it's time for a shot at the eight ball. I close my eyes and mutter a small prayer to the universe. *Please,* I ask. *I really want this.*

I miss.

Crap, I mutter under my breath. *Crap, crap, fucking crap.* I move to the side to let Michael take his shot. Sebastian's talking to Juliette, who must have come in at some point while I was playing. She's gesturing at him angrily, and they look like they are having some kind of argument. Daniel comes over to talk to me. "You are doing really well," he says. "You know that, don't you?"

"I missed the shot at the eight." My voice is disconsolate.

"So what? The game's not over yet. Your opponent still has two balls left, and he hasn't made two shots in a row all night long. There's an excellent chance you are going to get another try at this."

He's absolutely right. I just need to keep this in perspective. Sure enough, as Daniel has predicted, the guy misses and I get another go. It's not going to be easy - the eight ball is all the way on the far end of the table. Since I have almost no chance at it, I just go through the motions. I mark my pocket and I chalk my cue, and I aim, and *wham.*

There must be a fairy godmother.

Because that ball?

That sweet, precious eight-ball?

Rolls into the pocket.

I have won my first pool game.

I squeal like Alicia Silverstone in Clueless, jumping up and down with gleeful excitement. "I won," I shriek in Daniel and Sebastian's direction, but they aren't looking at my face. Their eyes are glued to my chest. "Oh come on," I flush, getting closer to them so they are the only people that can hear my next set of words. "My face is up here, you know."

"I know," Sebastian says, unabashed. "I wasn't looking at your face." He puts an arm around my waist and draws me in. "Now I am," he mutters, his lips so close to mine that I stop breathing in reaction to his nearness. "Congratulations, Bailey," he says. Then he dips his head toward my lips, and kisses me.

He smells like musk and sandalwood and man. His kiss is soft but insistent, and I yield, parting my lips and deepening contact as if I can't get enough of him. Forgotten is the pool hall and my opponent. I ignore Clark's slack-jawed stare and Juliette's narrowed eyes, and I kiss Sebastian Ardalan, bad boy celebrity chef, strong, tattooed Sebastian Ardalan, and it is so good. My hands come up to hold onto his waist, and the blood pounds in my ears, and I am helpless and aching for more.

We pull away slowly from each other as he breaks the kiss. In his eyes, I see the same hazy lust as I'm feeling. Then he leans in for one more brief kiss. "The match isn't over," he says hoarsely. "First one to win two games, remember?" He shakes his head, a wry smile on his lips. "A pool game has never been more inconvenient."

My head's still spinning as I walk back to the table. My

focus isn't on the game. It's on the very public kiss that Sebastian just gave me. As much as I'm trying not to think about it, I can't help it. *What does that kiss mean? What's going to happen next? And most importantly, what does Daniel think about it?*

Distracted as I am, I promptly lose the next two games. Clark glares at me as Michael pockets the eight-ball to win. "Sebastian, you're up next," he says curtly. "And try to win your match, damn it."

Sebastian winks at me and goes up to play, and I shake my head again, confused. I need to go to the washroom and splash my face with cold water, and wonder what the heck is going on.

12

Courage is not the absence of fear, but rather the judgment that something else is more important than fear.

— AMBROSE REDMOON

Bailey:

Juliette's waiting for me when I get out of the stall, her expression thunderous. *Shit. Is this about Sebastian's kiss? They aren't dating, are they?* "Is something wrong?"

"Is something wrong?" she repeats. Her voice rises with frustration. "Yes, Bailey, I'd say something's *fucking* wrong. Do you know that Sebastian blew off a really important business meeting tonight to come hang out with you?" Her fists are clenched at her side.

"Sort of," I reply. "He mentioned something."

"Well, good for him," she drawls the words out, sarcasm oozing out of every syllable. "Isn't that nice that Sebastian mentioned blowing off a meeting I've been working on for months to put together?"

I'm not sure why I'm the target of her ire. Sebastian's a big boy, and I'm not responsible for his behavior. "Why are you getting pissy with me?" I ask directly, refusing to pussy-foot around the fact that she's being a bitch right now. "I don't control Sebastian."

"Listen to me, Bailey." She steps close to me, and I fight the urge to take a step back. "There's a narrow window of opportunity here. Sebastian knows it, even if he's ignoring it at the moment. *Seb New York* was just awarded a second Michelin star, and we have to strike when the iron's hot." She glares at me. "If there's ever a time for Sebastian not to lose focus, it is now. The last thing he needs is a *distraction*."

Me. I'm the distraction.

Here's the deal. All my life, I've had to fight the redhead stereotype. Everyone always assumes that redheads are prone to anger and rage, but I've never been that person. I'm pretty even-tempered. I avoid conflict. I don't call people out on their bullshit.

Until now. "No," I tell her. "*You* listen to me. Sebastian is an adult who can make his own decisions. If you have a problem with him, you can talk to him. But you don't get to hurl accusations." I meet her eyes evenly, though I'm quaking inside, wondering how she's going to react to my speech. "Are we clear?"

The Thursday Drinking Pack will be so proud of me.

Juliette doesn't reply. She just glares at me for a few long seconds, then she spins on her heel and walks away without saying another word.

∾

I WASH MY HANDS, somewhat shaken by the whole confrontation. As I calm myself, a surge of sympathy for Sebastian flows through me. He's a two-star Michelin chef, and he's in his early thirties. He must have worked incredibly hard to achieve everything he has. I can't believe that his own business adviser is acting like he's slacking off for playing pool with his friends. Poor Sebastian.

All of those thoughts flee my brain when I push the door open and walk out, because standing in the dim passageway, waiting for me, is Daniel.

My heart jumps in my throat at the gleam in his eyes. Amused, heated, dark. The instant I absorb that look, I swallow, unable to conceal my own desire. These guys are like some kind of Bailey catnip.

"Unlike Sebastian, I didn't get a chance to congratulate you on your win," he says, his voice smooth as velvet. I watch his head dip toward mine, his body nearing, then his lips are on mine, and I stop thinking and just feel.

His kiss is slowly sensual. Sebastian's kiss could have been passed off as a gesture of celebration, but the message in Daniel's kiss is clear. *This is a prelude to sex.* I whimper as his tongue slides into my mouth, hot and insistent. His fingers slide through my hair, wrapping around the strands and tugging my head back so my neck is exposed. His lips press butterfly-soft kisses against my throat, my jaw. His teeth graze my skin and I shift, restless with longing.

Then he pulls away and I blink pressing my fingers to my swollen lips. Some of my lipstick is on his mouth. I move to wipe it away, but his mouth captures my fingers and he sucks, and my knees almost buckle as liquid, molten heat runs through my entire body. "Daniel," I whisper. "What are you doing?"

"Congratulating you."

"I didn't win my match." Why am I standing here arguing with Daniel about whether I won or not, when there's the two kisses to think of?

"You won a game, didn't you?" His gaze never leaves my face. "Do you want to take this further?"

"With you?"

"With Sebastian and me."

I swallow nervously. There's no dancing around the topic now, no way to pretend that I'm not interested in both of them. There's no hiding from my desire and my forbidden longings.

"Both of you?"

He just nods.

Shit. I just ended a relationship. What am I doing, playing with fire the way I am? I shake my head back and forth, frantically. These guys have crawled in and staked claim over my libido. I need to dislodge them. A threesome is a ridiculous idea.

"When?"

This time, he smiles, a surprisingly sweet smile that softens his face. "Friday night, my place?" he asks. "Sebastian is usually done working at ten."

Ten at night. There's no way to pretend that this isn't a booty call. Every sensible voice in my head is screaming at me to turn him down.

"Ten," I whisper, quieting those thoughts with ruthless efficiency. "Okay. I'll see you there."

13

If your opponent is temperamental, seek to irritate him. Pretend to be weak, that he may grow arrogant.

— SUN TZU, THE ART OF WAR

Daniel:

I wake up Friday morning with a smile on my face. I can't wait for tonight.

Bailey had been so beautiful on Wednesday. Her face had been flushed with triumph, her smile victorious as she watched the eight ball roll into the pocket. My dick had hardened when I saw Sebastian kissing her, and I had to kiss her myself and taste her sweetness. And just as I'd anticipated, it had taken real effort to pull away from her after that kiss. I had to struggle to keep from sweeping her out of the club, into a cab, and to my house.

My smile fades as I scroll through my email. One from my Uncle Cyrus jumps out at me. *'Call me ASAP'* is the ominous subject line, and the body of the message is empty. *Damn it.*

Wandering into the kitchen, I pour myself a cup of coffee before I dial his number. When he answers, he sounds apoplectic with rage. "I thought I told you to stay out of the news," he snaps.

"Hello to you too, Cyrus," I say coolly. "I have no idea what you are talking about, so perhaps you can fill me in."

"I told you to keep a low profile," he rants. "I warned you that we are at a crucial state in the negotiations." I can feel his glare sear at me through the phone. "Your photo is in the New York Times."

"Hang on." My laptop is in my bedroom, so I head back there and turn it on. We don't talk as I navigate to Google and search for *'Daniel Hartman New York Times.'* Before I manage to find it, a beep in my inbox announces an email from Sally in Corporate Affairs, who manages my public presence. She has a link to the article in her message, but there's nothing in her email that expresses concern.

Okay. If Sally's not worried, Cyrus is overreacting. I sip at my coffee and scan the article. Sure enough, it's a completely harmless piece on the history of the Maxwell Club, and I'm only mentioned in passing. I remember the journalist who has written it, a young guy called Oliver. Marty, the club president had introduced him around about a month ago, and Oliver had several fascinating things to say about the club history that I didn't know about.

"Cyrus," I sigh into the phone. "This article isn't even about me." I glance at the alarm clock. Ten after six. "Did you wake up at the crack of dawn to yell at me about this?"

"Your photo is in the paper," he repeats. "I thought I told you to stay out of the tabloids."

I lose my patience. "The New York Times is not a

tabloid. All I'm doing in the photo is playing pool with a group of people. Even in Kansas, I'm sure that's an approved activity." I need to calm down. In my head, I count to ten before continuing. "I told you I won't do anything scandalous. I never promised to quarantine myself until Ryan Communications' board made up their mind about our offer."

"Fine," he exhales. "I'm going to be in Kansas City tomorrow playing golf with Wayne Ryan. I'll smooth this over."

There's nothing to smooth over, Cyrus.

"Which reminds me," he continues, not noticing my frigid silence. "Sophie said you were unavailable, but I have some numbers about this deal to go over with you. I'm booked solid in meetings until eight in the evening. Let's meet after that?"

"Nope, that's not going to work. I'm busy tonight."

"You are?" His voice sharpens with surprise.

"Yes, Cyrus," I say with forced calm. "It is Friday night. Some people use the onset of the weekend as a way to wind down."

"What can be more important than this deal? Is it a woman?"

"That's none of your business," I snap. "Send me an email if you absolutely need me to look at something, but I'm not available to meet tonight. And in the future, when Sophie says I'm busy, you should listen to her."

I hang up on him, then I stare into space, my pulse still pounding from my phone conversation. I'm thirty four, and my uncle wants to ground me for the good of the company. And the last minute meeting about some mysterious numbers? I know Cyrus well enough to know that this is just another attempt to control me.

And in the past, you've allowed him, my conscience reminds me. *Cyrus is acting this way because you've set a precedent. What's different about tonight?*

The answer is stark in its simplicity. Bailey. Bailey is what's different. I'm fascinated by her. Fantasies of her in my bed, writhing between Sebastian and me, moaning, whimpering as she succumbs to pleasure fill my head. I wonder what tonight's going to be like. Will she show up interested in exploring the obvious sexual energy that flows between the three of us?

Or will she be coy? I can't see her in that role. She's completely unaware of her appeal, but at the same time, she's not shy, and her joke about steady long strokes suggests she's not a blushing, virginal type. Thank heavens, because the things I'm thinking of doing with her over a pool table are far from innocent. I can't even enter my rec room anymore without sporting a semi.

As I EAT BREAKFAST, I'm not thinking of Bailey and sex, though I wish I were. Instead, I'm thinking morose thoughts about Cyrus and the sacrifices I'm expected to make for Hartman & Company.

I became the CEO of the company seven years ago when my father died of a heart attack. Since then, everything's come second to running the firm. I haven't dated anyone seriously - I don't have the time. The crazy adventures I used to have with Sebastian have all been shelved for more profitable pursuits. Friends have fallen away, to be replaced by lackeys and sycophants.

I hate it.

I'm definitely feeling rebellious, though this is not the

time for rebellion. The deal with Ryan Communications will help our top line growth over the next decade. It's an important deal for Hartman.

It is, in short, the absolute worst time to be contemplating a threesome. If my sex life somehow becomes public knowledge, there's a real risk that the deal will fall through. Sebastian, I trust with my life. He'll be discreet.

From everything I've found out about Bailey, she's motivated, dedicated and amazing at her work. She's in the tenure window at NYU. She's unlikely to sell me out to the tabloids. My gut tells me to trust her.

Yet I don't know her at all, and I wonder if I'm being a fool to want her.

14

In Wales, it's common for a man to gift his lover with a carved wooden spoon, as a symbol that he will never allow her to go hungry.

— FROM BAILEY'S JOURNAL OF INTERESTING FACTS
FROM AROUND THE WORLD

Bailey:

I've masturbated more times than I can count to relieve the pressure. Each time I close my eyes, I see their faces, and I hear their voices. I want *more*.

Yet my desire isn't the only thing that matters. I'm still unconvinced that they really want me. Sure, they say they do. But when they see me naked? There are rolls of fat. Things are squishy where they should be firm. I look nothing like a model.

Two kisses, and a whispered invitation, and I'm going over to Daniel's place to have sex. Shouldn't I be more interested in finding a more conventional relationship with guys that are more in my league?

"What should I do?" I ask Gabriella, who has become my unofficial threesome coach. "What should I wear?" It's Friday night, and she's at Piper's apartment, watching me fret with an amused expression on her face.

"You like adventures, don't you Bailey?" she asks. "Go have one." Then she grins wickedly. "And it doesn't really matter what you wear - it doesn't sound like it's going to stay on for long."

I throw a pillow at her. "You are not helping." I smooth my palms against my jeans. "I'm really nervous about this."

"Why?"

"What if I don't know what to do? What if it just sucks? What if they just laugh at me and tell me they were joking about wanting to sleep with me?"

She rolls her eyes at me. No doubt she thinks I'm ridiculous, fluttering around like an anxious sparrow, picking up everything in my room and setting it down, not knowing what to do with the restless energy that's running through my blood.

"I'm not even going to dignify that last question with a reply," she retorts. "As for the rest, if it sucks, don't do it again. And what to do?" She forms a ring with the fingers of her left hand, and mimes her right thumb pumping in and out. "Surely you *know* what to do?"

"Stop laughing at me," I say crossly. "I know all about..." I mirror her gesture. "I just don't know what to do when you add another hand to the mix. Or another dick."

"Have you ever had anal sex?"

"Whoa," I feel my face turn fiery. "Way to be direct, Gabby." She's identified the heart of the problem. I don't think I have enough sexual experience for something as adventurous as a threesome. Trevor was a missionary man, with an occasional bit of oral when he was feeling extra-frisky. Ivan would sometimes spank me, but that was in the early stages, and it was never more than a swat or two.

"Well?" she persists. "Have you?"

I shake my head. "Nope. Never."

"Are you opposed to it on principle?" she asks curiously.

I snort. "Gabby, I'm contemplating a threesome here. No, I'm not opposed to anal sex on principle. I just haven't…"

She shrugs, unconcerned once more. "In that case, just be honest with them, Bailey, and everything will be fine. Being an anal virgin isn't a sin, you know." She laughs. "In fact, I'm sure the opposite is true in some parts of the country. Isn't having anal sex illegal in parts of the country?"

"Sodomy is still against the law in fourteen states," I quip, then I become serious. "Should I go, Gabby?"

"I can't make that decision for you, Bails," she says. "But ask yourself this. Are you hesitating because you don't want them or because you are scared?" She curls up on the couch and bends forward to lift Jasper into her lap. "You want to know what I think?"

"Do I?" I ask wryly, more than a little afraid of what she might say. "Okay. Hit me."

"Remember I love you," she warns. She gestures at me. "But seriously, look at what you are wearing."

I look at my outfit. Black t-shirt, dark wash jeans. That's the uniform on days I don't have to teach. When I have students to deal with, I upgrade to a black pantsuit. "Let me guess, you don't like black?"

"I like black just fine," she responds. "You, on the other hand, dress in boring clothes and date boring men. You're smart and you're bright and you are really pretty, but you like to hide all of that, because it's easier to do that than to risk failure by putting yourself out there."

I stop and look at her, stung by her words. "That's not true. It isn't my fault that Trevor was a jerk."

"No, but it's your fault that you moved in with him anyway." She waves away my protest. "Look, forget Trevor. Tell me, do you think these guys are attracted to you?"

I think about the feel of their lips on mine. "For the moment."

She glares at me. "Stop putting yourself down. You are beautiful and you are interesting. And if you want to have a threesome, just do so. Own that shit."

I exhale. "Okay," I agree. "I'm going over." I glare at her. "Now, come help me decide what to wear before I lose my mind."

GABBY HELPS me pick out a swishy, green printed skirt with a hem that hits just above my knees and a white v-neck t-shirt that reveals more cleavage than normal. "Remind me to take you shopping," she says, sifting through my closet. "Where are your slinky dresses?"

"College professors and slinky dresses don't go hand in hand. Just be glad it's not black." I look in the mirror, my brow furrowed. Clothing can serve as both armor and a message, and I hope my outfit says I'm casual but flirty, open to the possibility of something happening, but if it doesn't, no biggie.

It's best that I don't dwell on what I'm doing. Two weeks ago, I left my boyfriend of eleven months. My stuff is still at his place - I haven't been able to make myself call him and arrange a time to pick it up. I'm still living out of the suitcase I packed that night.

Yet, I appear to be on my way to participate in a three-some. Sometimes, I can overthink things, but at the moment, I'm just operating on instinct. It's been a long time since I've allowed my thirst for adventure to guide my choices.

I've left myself plenty of time on the subway, and I arrive ten minutes early to Daniel's tree-lined neighborhood. Rather than knock at the three-story brownstone, I just pace on the street outside. It's late enough that no-one is around. There's a slight chill in the air, and I pull my coat tight around me and wince at the wind that sneaks up around my ankles and makes me shiver. Warm light spills out from the windows. It appears to be a surprisingly normal neighbor-hood, until I remember that we are in Manhattan, and each of these townhouses is probably worth more than ten million dollars. I'm in Billionaire World. This is strictly one-percent territory.

Finally at ten, I lift my hand and bang the carved lion knocker. The door is opened instantly, and Daniel smiles at me. He's casually dressed in a faded linen shirt and grey slacks, but it doesn't muffle the hotness, not even a little bit. It just makes him look more approachable. *Dangerous.* "Bailey," he greets me with a pleasant smile. "Come on in. We're in the kitchen."

I follow him through the foyer that's almost as large as Piper's entire apartment. In the massive kitchen, Sebastian is by the stove, chopping some peppers with easy competence. "Have you eaten?" he asks as I enter. He's casually dressed as well, a black t-shirt, worn jeans, and bare feet. If you'd told me before this moment that I'd be turned on by a man's naked feet, I would have laughed.

I'm definitely turned on. Cue the laugh track.

"No." I was too nervous to eat earlier. Now the aroma wafting from the wok causes my stomach to growl.

"Good, us neither," he smiles. "This should only be another five minutes or so."

"Pull up a seat, Bailey," Daniel says at the same time, gesturing to the table in the center of the room. "Make yourself at home. Can I take your coat?"

I shrug off my practical black jacket and hand it to him. This whole situation is so surreal. A two-star Michelin chef is cooking a meal for me and a billionaire is hanging up my jacket, which cost less than a hundred bucks at Target. A giggle wells up in my throat, and I just can't hold it back. I snort out aloud, a distinctly unladylike sound.

"What's funny?" Sebastian asks.

"I'm just wondering how many people in New York would give up their first born child for this experience. Sebastian Ardalan cooking a meal for them."

Sebastian makes a face. "They should hold on to their children, this is just a simple stir-fry. It bears no resemblance to anything on my restaurant's menu."

Daniel joins me at the kitchen table. In the apartment I shared with Trevor, we had a narrow table in the kitchen, with two barstools that were designed to fit underneath the tabletop. It had enough room for two plates and two glasses of water, and absolutely nothing more. But in New York's real estate market, even that felt like luxury.

Not here. Daniel's table is large enough to seat six people. The rich, I'm rapidly discovering, live very differently from the rest of us.

"Can I get you a drink, Bailey?" he asks me. "Vodka, wine, beer, something else?"

As much as I'd like to do a shot of vodka to ease my nerves, I think I should stay relatively sober. "Beer, please."

He opens a bottle and pours the beverage into a glass for me, grabbing one for himself at the same time. At the stove, Sebastian takes a drink from his own beer while adding a bunch of spinach to the wok, moving the leaves around to wilt them. His movements are sure and unhurried, and watching him, my insides clench with need. Is this the way he'd touch me? Calmly, surely, as if he has all the time in the world to explore my body?

I'm on edge, but I force myself to relax and make conversation. "How long have you two played in the league?" I ask them curiously.

"I've just been playing for three months," Daniel replies. "Sebastian talked me into it."

"I needed sane company," Sebastian explains. "I played for Clark's team last year. We lost in the finals of the tournament, and Clark does not know how to lose with grace. He was so much of a dick that half the team swore they'd never come back. So I recruited Juliette and Daniel to keep me company."

"And to keep you from strangling Clark," Daniel jokes.

"There is that," Sebastian agrees with a grin.

"You guys must have lost to Trevor's team," I realize. "Trevor won last year. He couldn't stop talking about it."

"Probably." Sebastian shrugs. "It's just a game. People take this shit far too seriously." He puts two plates in front of us, heaped with brown rice and a colorful mixture of chicken and vegetables. Steam rises in spirals from the dish, and it smells wonderful. "Dig in," he says, and I attack my food like I've never eaten before.

The stir-fry is a revelation. A perfect medley of sweet and spicy and salty flavors dance on my tongue, and each vegetable is cooked exactly right. "God, this is good," I moan. "Why isn't this on your menu?"

Sebastian laughs. "It's too simple," he says. "I can't make any money on it."

For a few moments, the only sound in the kitchen is the noise of our forks scraping at our plates. Then something strikes me. "Hang on, you said you bet Clark that I'd win in July. Isn't that when the tournament is played? What happens if we don't qualify?"

"I presume that the bet becomes a non-issue in that case," Daniel says. "But," he adds confidently, "if you allow us to coach you, that won't happen. We'll qualify."

Coach me. Again, he's said it with just a little bit more emphasis than required. There's heat in his eyes and a trace of roughness in his voice.

Sebastian doesn't say anything, but he's sitting in front of me, and I can see his eyes linger on my body. There's appreciation in his gaze, one that makes me very glad I'd worn my prettiest, laciest pink underwear beneath my clothes.

I can hear the desire in Daniel's tone and I can see the heat in Sebastian's eyes. Suddenly, all the doubts that have plagued me vanish. It was the same way when I went to Russia. The entire flight, I thought I was mad for going so far away, but the moment the wheels of the airplane touched down in Vladivostok, I'd been ready.

I'm ready now, ready to be adventurous. I can't wait to finish my meal and see what happens next.

15

In 19th century Finland, a girl of marriageable age would wear an empty sheath in a belt around her waist. Interested men would put a sword in her sheath. If she returned the blade, she wasn't interested in the would-be suitor, but keeping the blade meant she agreed to marry him.

— FROM BAILEY'S JOURNAL OF INTERESTING FACTS
FROM AROUND THE WORLD

Bailey:

"You look nervous." Sebastian's blue eyes pierce into me.

Dinner's done and cleared away. There's no food to hide behind, and my nerves have made an encore appearance.

I remember Gabby's advice to be honest with them about my sexual inexperience. After all, based on the fact that I'm here, Daniel and Sebastian might think that I've done a lot more exploration in bed than I actually have. Yet it's hard to broach the conversation, and I find myself tongue-tied and anxious.

At work, I know exactly what I want, and I will do everything in my power to get it. But when it comes to guys, relationships and sex? I'm not good at asking for what I want. Gabby was right. I do find it easier to hide behind drab clothes and pretend that men like Sebastian and Daniel could never be attracted to me.

"Bailey," Daniel's voice is steady. "Are you alright?" His eyes are warm and concerned.

"Yes." I force the words out past my too-dry throat, and I take a fortifying gulp of my beer. "I have a confession to make. I've never done this before."

"Define *this*." Sebastian gives me an encouraging look.

"This..." I gesture to the two of them with my beer. "With more than one guy at once." I screw my eyes shut as a wave of heat washes over my face. "Sorry."

"Bailey, open your eyes."

Hang on, is Daniel laughing at me? My eyes fly open and I glare at him. "This isn't funny."

He doesn't smile back. "One question," he asks, and the strained intensity of his voice catches me by surprise. "Do you want to do this?"

"Yes." Heaven help me, yes. I haven't been able to think of anything else. Desire and burning curiosity prickles at my skin, threatening to erupt from me like a molten, heated volcano. "I really want to."

Sebastian lets out a huge breath. "That's all that matters." They move closer to me. "We won't do anything you don't want to."

Daniel looks at me with a slight frown. I guess I must

still look wary. "Tell you, what," he says after a minute, his expression clearing. "Why don't we head to the game room and play a game of pool? No pressure."

"You have a game room." I shake my head in disbelief. *Sheesh. Billionaires.* The guy has a rec room in Manhattan, on the Upper East Side. "Must be nice. Lead the way."

Daniel is entirely unperturbed by my eye-rolling, as is Sebastian. The sound of their chuckles fill the air, warming me from the inside out.

THEY MAKE ME BREAK, because they are jerks and because Daniel reminds me that he has serious money riding on my performance. Now that I've seen his place, I know that fifty thousand dollars is a drop in the bucket for Daniel Hartman. A rounding error.

Despite their tips the other night, breaking remains a mortifying experience. "Come on, Bailey," Sebastian chides as I chalk my cue tip elaborately in an effort to stall the proceedings. "Stop delaying. I know what you are doing."

Daniel moves behind me, his expression gleaming with anticipation. His hands come up to stroke the outside of my arms. "We can teach you how to play," he mutters into my ear, his breath warm against my skin, "or..."

"Or?" My voice comes out breathy and fluttery, a perfect match to the feeling in my belly.

"Or we can do *more.*"

"And what does *more* involve?" All I want to do is lean back against Daniel's hard chest.

Sebastian moves in front of me, effectively trapping me between the two of them. They don't close in yet, but their intent is clear. "What do you want it to involve?"

I've been thinking about what my limits are. I don't want to be a prude, but I also know that these guys are significantly more sexually adventurous than I am. "No unprotected sex," I say firmly. My safety isn't up for negotiation. "Beyond that, I don't have a lot of experience. I'm game to try almost anything once."

Sebastian's eyes fill with startled surprise, then he starts laughing. Behind me, Daniel wraps his arm around my waist, pulling me toward him. "Ah Bailey," he says into my ear, before nibbling at my earlobe, sending a spike of pure desire through me. "This is going to be so good."

Sebastian places a finger on my chin and inclines my jaw up toward his face. I watch as he dips his head down to kiss me. I can see each bit of stubble, and I want to rub myself against it, like a cat seeking a scratching post. I reach to pull his head toward me, impatient for his kiss, but Daniel makes a noise of disapproval and seizes my hands in his.

Ah. This is how it's going to play out.

I moan in my throat, my anticipation making me fidget between them. I incline my face up as his lips descend on mine, then I stop thinking and kiss Sebastian back. My breasts press into his chest, and his hands come up to caress my sides. Behind me, I can feel Daniel's erection against my ass as his hands roam all over my body, his legs urging mine apart.

"Here's how it's going to work, Bailey," Daniel rasps. "You can always say no, and we will stop. But until then, you'll do as you are told. Okay?"

Fuck, fuck. Too much, too intense. I feel like I'm about to burn up from his dominant tone. Every bone in my body has melted into lava, and I'm only being held up by their bodies.

Sebastian's eyes search my face. "If you want us to stop," he says reassuringly, "we will. We want you to be turned on."

In an odd way, their dominance soothes me. I feel very inexperienced, but they are telling me I don't need to worry about anything. All I need to do is obey.

"What turns *you* on?"

"You do." Daniel's voice whispers, nibbling my ear till I'm grinding against him like I'm in heat. Which, to be fair, is exactly right. "You turn me on."

"What should we do with her?" Sebastian asks, his voice amused but with a distinctly ragged undertone.

"Take her top off," Daniel suggests.

Sebastian promptly moves in front of me. "Lift your hands up, princess," he says. I obey, and his fingers find the hem of my shirt, tugging it over my head. This is so much like my fantasy. "And the bra too, I think."

They pause for an instant, no doubt to give me an opportunity to protest. But the time for protestations is past, and besides, despite my inexperience, I'm hardly going to act like a blushing virgin. I came to Daniel's place fully aware of what was on offer. I knew there were two of them, and if I'd stopped to think about it, I could have even guessed that they would be all dominant and alpha in the bedroom. I knocked on Daniel's door knowing all of that. I nod. "Yes," I whisper. "The bra too."

"Good girl." Daniel's voice is encouraging. He inhales sharply as Sebastian moves behind me to unclasp my bra, letting it slide to the floor. "Fuck," he groans. "Those are fantastic tits. Touch them, Sebastian."

Sebastian doesn't need any prompting. His hands circle my body and pin me in place, my back touching his chest. His fingers tease my nipples, pinching and pulling, rolling them between his thumb and forefinger. "What pretty breasts," he growls. "I could stay here and play with them for hours... Would you like that, Bailey? Would you like to be taken right up against the edge? Again and again?"

No. I want to orgasm now. Though my clitoris hasn't been touched, and I never come without direct stimulation, I'm at the edge now, and my entire body trembles. "Yes," I moan. I'll agree to anything. Anything as long as either of them parts my legs and touches my cunt.

Daniel's hands hoist me onto the pool table. His fingers curl around the hem of my skirt, lifting it up so it bunches around my waist. Sebastian claws at my panties, pushing them down to my knees, then still lower, until I kick them off frantically, unwilling to let a scrap of fabric come between me and my reward.

I have no idea what's come over me, but I'm burning up. My lust crackles like a sparkler on a dark night, all sharp edges and fierce sounds. I'm moaning, panting as one of them slides a finger into me. "So ready," Daniel marvels. Is that Daniel's finger? If so, where's Sebastian?

My legs are being parted. A tongue runs at my slit, nibbles at my labia. "I'm going to drip on the surface," I worry.

A sharp smack on my inner thigh makes me bite my lip. That felt unexpectedly good. If that's what a spanking feels like, I want one.

Then the tongue touches my clitoris, and thinking becomes impossible. Mouth and lips feasting on me. Fingers pistoning in and out of my cunt. Hands gripping my knees, forcing them open. The faint scratch of the wool of the tabletop against my naked ass.

A finger circles my asshole and I flinch. "Never done that," I pant out. "Be gentle."

Daniel smiles at me. "Don't worry," he soothes. His

finger smears some of the wetness that's dripping off my cunt into that tight hole, and I concentrate on not tensing up. "Relax," he says again.

Another smack on my thighs brings back my focus to Sebastian's mouth on my clitoris, where he's demonstrating some seriously formidable oral skills. I've never been eaten out as skillfully. My pleasure is cresting, threatening to overflow. My thighs stiffen on either side of Sebastian's head, and his hands move quickly to hold me still.

My focus jumps from one of them to the other. From Sebastian's mouth on my pussy, licking my slit, teasing my clitoris, to Daniel's finger, slowly exploring my asshole. When he slips one finger up to the first knuckle, I groan. The sensation is so strange, yet so oddly arousing.

"Yes," I clench out, pushing my pussy into Sebastian's face. "Please…"

Sebastian groans, and the sound vibrates through my sensitive flesh. "Fuck me, you are amazing," he growls. "If this is what all college professors are like, I'm going to give higher education a serious rethink."

"Mouth," I beg. "Back on my pussy. Don't stop."

He obligingly gets back to work. This time, he increases the suction and grazes my pulsing flesh ever so slightly with his teeth, a move that has my hips bucking and grinding into his face. Daniel adds another finger to the one already in my asshole, and the burning stretch makes me stiffen in pain for an instant. But then it dissolves into pleasure, and I'm lost again in my haze of need.

"Fuck, fuck, fuck," I moan. "Please…" That last word is a warble, because though the arousal has been building steadily, it's suddenly too much. I shudder and scream, and hands lock me in place against that tongue, against those fingers battering my pussy with pleasure.

Wave after wave washes over me, till I am left, limp and sated, drenched with sweat. If this is the carrot they are going to dangle in front of me, I'm aiming to be their star student.

16

Hearts will never be practical until they can be made unbreakable.

> — L. Frank Baum, The Wonderful Wizard of
>
> Oz

Daniel:

Holy fucking shit, she's incredible. All I want to do is sweep her into my arms, take her to my bedroom, and taste her sweetness, hear her moans as she comes again, this time, because of my mouth, my touch.

I'm about to suggest that we do exactly that when my phone pings, alerting me to an incoming message. I glance down at it by habit. Cyrus never did send in the numbers he said he wanted me to look at, and I've been waiting for them all evening. But the email is not from him. It's just one of many messages that routinely come in late in the night, ready for me to deal with when I get into work tomorrow morning.

Cyrus. His image pops uninvited into my mind, looking grim and disapproving. *What are you doing?* he would ask. *Do you not care about Hartman and Company? The firm has prospered for hundreds of years - are you going to be the person who runs it into the ground? For what? Sex? Can't you keep it in your pants, boy?*

Damn it. Cyrus' admonishments rip me out of the moment and my lust disappears. I still want Bailey, yet the caution I felt earlier this morning comes to the fore. *You don't know her at all,* I remind myself, in a voice that sounds very much like my uncle. *You have an image to maintain, and obligations to your company. Make sure Bailey can be trusted before taking this any further.*

Bailey stands up unsteadily, and she has a sated, satisfied expression on her face. She looks like a sleepy kitten. "I might not know much about threesomes," she smirks, her eyes resting pointedly at our crotches, "but I think it's your turn now."

I clear my throat. I'm about to do one of the stupidest things of my life. "Can we take a raincheck?" I ask her. "I have an early morning meeting."

Sebastian's head snaps toward me, and he surveys me with a puzzled expression. Bailey's face falls. "Is everything okay?" she asks hesitantly. She gnaws at her lower lip, and seeing the tip of her pink tongue sweep over her soft lips, I grow even harder than before.

"Everything's fine," I lie. "See you Wednesday at the Maxwell Club? I'll call you." Even before I say the words, I feel like a louse. "And Bailey, I'm sure it goes without saying that you'll keep the details of our encounter out of the press?"

Out of the corner of my eye, I see Sebastian tense, but I'm not looking at him. I'm looking at Bailey, who has gone sheet-white with shock.

Fuck. I've screwed up. I should have never opened my mouth.

~

SEBASTIAN:

I see the hurt on Bailey's face as Daniel utters his ill-thought out words. Daniel does too, and his shoulders hunch and his expression turns bleak. He opens his mouth to say something, then closes it, his arms dropping helplessly to his sides.

Bailey quickly pulls her clothes back on, and glances at the door. "I should go," she says, not meeting our eyes, her fingers fiddling with the strap on her embroidered bag. I can hear her discomfort in her voice. She clears her throat and looks in Daniel's direction. "Don't worry," she says. "I understand your need for privacy." She laughs, a false little trill that doesn't sound like her at all. "I'm sure that NYU wouldn't approve of what we did either…" Her voice trails off, and she stands up. "See you Wednesday, I guess?"

If you don't know Daniel, his face is an unfeeling mask. But I've known Daniel for a long time, and I see the regret and the shame etched in his features. He knows he's screwed up. Bailey is not like the women he's dated half-heartedly in the last seven years. She's not going to date him for publicity, and she's not going to spill details of our tryst on social media. I can't believe Daniel can't see that.

I want to ask Bailey to stay, but her distress is obvious and I don't want to cause more pain. "Come on," I tell her, standing up. "I'll take you home."

"No, there's no need. I'm fine," she demurs.

As much as I want to respect her desire to be alone, I'm not going to let her take the subway or a cab alone in the dark. I had a deeply conflicted relationship with my parents, but they did raise me to be chivalrous. "I need to go home too," I point out with a friendly smile. "Let's share a cab."

"Okay," she says reluctantly.

I see her desire to flee in the set of her shoulders, in the hands clenched into fists at her side. So does Daniel. He finally speaks. "Bailey," he says, his voice barely audible. "I'm sorry. I was out of line."

She doesn't meet his gaze. "I told you, Daniel," she says in a deliberately neutral tone, "there's nothing to be sorry for." She turns to me. "I'm leaving now."

I give Daniel a warning look. He's done enough for the moment. Bailey had drawn into herself, and she's too bruised to listen to anything he has to say. There will be another time to make amends. "Let's go." I grab Bailey's jacket from Daniel's coat closet and hand it to her.

Behind us, Daniel takes a deep breath and closes his eyes. He's tense again. Earlier this evening, as we'd eaten dinner and played pool and pleasured Bailey on the pool table, he'd become a person he hadn't been in a very long time. Easy-going, amused, his eyes filled with ready laughter.

Now, that person has retreated once again into the shadows, and in his place I see Daniel Hartman, CEO of a Fortune 500 Company, ruthless businessman. And he's miserable.

"YOU CAN YELL, YOU KNOW," I tell her in the cab. The taxi

driver has a cell phone pressed against his ear, in total violation of New York City laws, and is engaged in a heated argument with someone on the other end of the line. He's not paying any attention to our conversation. "You'd be justified."

"It's not a problem," she says tonelessly. "Like I told Daniel, I understand."

The hair on the back of my neck stands up. She's sitting on the far side of the cab, pressed against the door, and the gap between us right now seems huge and insurmountable. She's not okay, not even close. "Bullshit. It was a dick thing to say, okay?"

She doesn't move any closer to me, but she does raise an eyebrow. "I thought you were good friends."

"We are," I agree. "It doesn't mean I blindly agree with everything Daniel does. And it doesn't mean I can't admit he was wrong."

She stares out of the window. Her hands are tightly clenched in her lap, a sure sign of stress, but she doesn't respond to me. *Fuck.* I don't want to lose her. Not like this. Not when there's so much potential, so much promise. You ever go out on a date and you find you can't stop yourself from smiling for hours after? That's kind of how I feel around Bailey.

I want to kick Daniel in the nuts right now.

"Daniel shouldn't have said what he did," I say quietly. "But he does have his reasons. Will you listen?"

"I'm in a moving cab," she replies. "I can't stop you from talking."

"He didn't always used to be so circumspect," I explain. I can't help grinning as I remember some of the crazy shit we used to do when we were younger. "When his father died, the board almost voted to break up the company. Daniel's mom had to swoop in and appoint him CEO. Three members of the board resigned in protest. The stock price dropped twenty percent. It was a disaster."

"We all have jobs that we care about, Sebastian," she snaps. "Don't tell me that Daniel's job is more important than mine because he's a billionaire, or that he should receive some kind of special pass for being a dick because he's loaded. That's the kind of crap Trevor used to pull, and I'm absolutely not going to take it anymore."

Red's got a temper, though in this case, I don't blame her. "I already told you that he was wrong," I reply. "Daniel's company is in the middle of some sensitive negotiations, and he needs to keep a low profile till this deal is done. And women he's been out with have sold him out to the tabloids before. He's cautious for a reason."

She looks briefly sympathetic, before her expression turns blank. "You are in the public eye as well, probably more than Daniel," she points out. "I didn't see you tell me to *keep things quiet.*"

She practically snarls the last three words, and I have to fight to keep a grin from breaking out on my face. She's not giving any quarter. "I'm a chef," I reply. "If it's revealed that I'm in a threesome, my company stock isn't at risk of a free-fall. Board members aren't going to ask me if I'm fit to run the company."

"You know what the worst thing is?" She continues on her tirade, not listening to me. She sounds furious. "I'm an assistant professor at NYU, and I don't have tenure. If the school decides tomorrow that they don't approve of what I do in my personal life, I'm out of a job. I have far more at stake than Daniel. Unlike him, I don't have a billion-dollar cushion to land on."

"You know, you really are yelling at the wrong guy," I say

mildly. "I'm not concerned about the press - I'm completely in favor of fucking you. Heck, let's do it right now."

She giggles at that. At first, the laughter is reluctant, but soon, we are both laughing openly. When she sobers up, I lace my fingers in hers. "Give him time, Bailey. When his father died, everyone was dead-set against him running the company. He responded by putting his head down and out-working everyone. He's finally learning to live again. He just needs to process this at his own pace."

She doesn't reply. I spend the rest of the cab ride wondering if she's going to walk away, and hoping against all hope that she'll give us another chance.

The last time Daniel and me were in a threesome, it had been an uncomplicated thing. All three of us had been interested in sex and nothing else, and the affair had remained casual. There had been no feelings or emotions on the line.

This time, everything isn't going to be quite that simple.

17

Hell is empty, and all the devils are here!

— William Shakespeare, The Tempest

Daniel:

I have a sleepless night, tossing and turning, unable to get the hurt expression on Bailey's face out of my mind. When my phone rings on Saturday morning, I reach for it, fully prepared to hear Sebastian read me the riot act about last night.

But it isn't Sebastian, and it isn't Cyrus either. Instead, it's someone I actually like to hear from. My mother, Alexa Hartman.

"Hey mom," I mumble blearily into the receiver. "What time is it?"

She tsks impatiently. No doubt she's already been awake for three hours. She's probably meditated and done her yoga, and eaten her scrambled egg whites or a kale smoothie. She has more energy than someone half her age. "It's nine thirty," she says. "Why are you still in bed?"

"I had a rough night." I wince as I hear how whiny I sound.

"Why?" Her voice is dry. "Did some numbers on a spreadsheet not add up?"

My mother is very free-spirited. She was protesting something in Central Park when she bumped into my conservative, businessman father. *It was love at first sight,* she says fondly, when asked about it. They were married for thirty years, and they made each other incredibly happy every single day. Growing up, my grandparents and Uncle Cyrus would lecture me about the family legacy, but my parents would just laugh and tell me to do what made me happy. "I did," my father would say, squeezing my mother's hand. "Best decision I ever made."

"I met a girl," I answer her question. "Then I said something stupid and chased her away."

"What'd you say, Danny?" she asks.

Even though my mother is unlikely to judge me, I'm not going to tell her that I'm sharing women with Sebastian. It takes me a minute to formulate my thoughts. I fumble my way out of bed and into the kitchen on autopilot, seeking coffee.

"We are trying to buy a company and Cyrus thought I should keep a low profile." I grimace at the memory of what a dick I'd been last night. "So I told her to keep our encounter out of the tabloids. Not surprisingly, she walked out on me." My head feels like there are a bunch of dwarfs with very tiny hammers inside my brain, digging for gold. Aspirin. There has to be aspirin somewhere in my apartment.

She hisses in anger. "Daniel Stuart Hartman," she snaps

at me. "I thought your father and I raised you better than this. Is this how you talk to a woman?"

"No mother." I feel about ten, waiting to hear that I was grounded. "I'm sorry."

She sniffs. "Yes, well, there's not much point apologizing to me, Danny. What is wrong with you? Should you be listening to Cyrus for dating advice? Cyrus, who has not had a single meaningful relationship in his life?"

Okay, she has a valid point. I tell her that, and she snorts. "Of course I do," she says. "So Cyrus told you that the family firm had been around for hundreds of years, and your only role was to pass it down safely to the next generation, and you listened to him and scared away some poor woman?"

"More or less," I concede.

"Yes, well, what next generation?" she asks sharply.

Oh, there's not enough aspirin in the world for this particular conversation. "Go bother Susan if you are going to start badgering me for grandchildren," I tell her. Thanks to the coffee, my wits are slowly returning to me. "I'm not interested in kids."

"Yes, honey," she says. "I know that. This isn't the grand-kids lecture, this is a different lecture. Cyrus is miserable and alone, and the company is his entire life only because there's nothing else to fill it. If you start listening to him, you'll end up in the same place."

"Trust me," I rub my throbbing forehead, "I already feel like shit. The yelling isn't necessary. Did you call for some specific reason, by the way, or do you have some kind of maternal voodoo instinct that tells you when I screw up so you can lecture me?"

She chuckles. "I called to remind you that we are having drinks this afternoon with the President of NYU to discuss the endowment the Hartman Foundation has been planning to make to the school."

"Shit, I forgot." I'm dropping balls all over the place. "What time was that?" As I speak, a glimmering of an idea occurs to me. I need Bailey to forgive me, and in order for that to happen, I need something good. Something big and bold.

"Four. Don't be late."

"I won't," I promise her. I hang up and gulp back the coffee. I have some groveling to do, and I'm prepared for it. Better still, I have a plan.

18

First we eat, then we do everything else.

— M. F. K. FISHER

Sebastian:

As soon as I wake up Saturday morning, I text Daniel. *'Lunch at one?'* I ask, sending him the address of a Hell's Kitchen eatery that Helen's told me about. I'm going to tackle two birds with one stone. Taste the cooking of a talented chef that Helen thinks we should hire, and chew Daniel out at the same time. Perfect.

His reply comes instantaneously. *'See you there.'*

So he's up. Knowing Daniel, I'm assuming he slept like shit, and he's already formulating a plan to make amends. That's good.

Last night, in the cab, I realized something. I like Bailey, and I find her intriguing. Some of the things she's done - living in Siberia for a year, doing field research in the jungles of Indonesia, trekking through North Africa in search of stories of the Silk Road - absolutely amaze me. She's in her late twenties or in her early thirties, but she's already crammed in so much travel, so much living and adventure into her life.

If my cock could talk, I'd be hearing an earful about the case of blue balls I was left with after Daniel decided to be an idiot. Even now, thinking about the taste of her, the way her soft creamy thighs had fallen open as I'd pleasured her with my mouth...

Damn it. We better fix this. Because I definitely want to see Bailey Moore again.

∽

"THIS IS an out of the way spot," Daniel looks up as I walk in.

"My kitchen staff cannot stop talking about this place," I tell him as I pull up a chair. "They tend to be a jaded bunch. If they are excited, I want to know why."

The place is small and tired-looking. The wooden tables are weathered and worn, and each one has a dented metal lamp on it. Faded beaded curtains hang on the wall, completing the Arabian Nights theme. My lips twitch. The restaurant is called Aladdin's Lamp, and the decorator has not been subtle. *It's very kitschy.*

"You fucked up last night." My words are direct. Daniel's my best friend, and I don't need to tread tentatively with him.

"I'm quite aware," he grimaces. "My mother's already yelled at me."

I grin at that. "Has she?" Daniel's mom is quite the firecracker.

"Oh yes." He shakes his head. "She told me I was brought up better."

"Yeah." I'm going to say more, but the pretty waitress behind the bar comes over to us at that point, her notepad at the ready. "Hello, my name is Piper," she says. "Can I get you something to drink?"

We order beers, and she walks away. When she's out of earshot, I look at him. "She's right," I tell him. "I'm concerned for you."

"Why?" His voice is tight with tension. With anyone else, I might take that as a warning sign to tread lightly, but my concern for Daniel outweighs my caution.

"Because..." I think through my words, trying to find the best way of expressing my worries. "The version of you that I met in that greasy diner thirteen years ago would have never even thought that Bailey might go to the press. What the fuck is wrong with you, Daniel? She's an assistant professor at NYU. She's as ambitious in her career as you are in yours and as I am in mine. You think she doesn't know how to be careful on keeping her sex life private?"

He hunches his shoulders. "I am a dick."

"A little bit, yes."

"A lot." He lifts his head up. "The moment I said those words last night, I was horrified. Not just because Bailey was hurt, and not just because you were shocked. I did something that I swore I'd never do." He sighs. "When my father wanted to marry my mother, my grandfather threatened to cut him off and never speak to him again. My mother was not from the right social set." He makes a face. "My grandfather told my dad that the future of the family company rested on him, and his focus should be on that."

"Ah." It all begins to make sense.

"Yeah." Daniel's not done. "When I was sixteen, I liked a

girl who was definitely from the wrong side of the tracks."
He grins in memory. "She had a nose ring, and a pierced
tongue, and most interesting to a teenage boy, nipple rings. I
was nervous about bringing her home. I was afraid my
parents would sneer at her."

I can't imagine Daniel's parents reacting that way. They
certainly hadn't sneered at me when Daniel had invited me
to lunch. They'd welcomed me warmly and we'd talked
about food, and one week later, I had a job as an assistant to
one of New York's most creative chefs.

"That was when my dad told me the story of bringing
my mother to meet his parents for the first time. My grandparents more or less told him to fuck her out of his system
and move on to a more appropriate woman."

I wince. "I'm assuming that your dad didn't listen?"

Daniel shakes his head. "Nope. Both my parents are far
too stubborn." Then his smile fades. "Last night, I didn't
follow my father's example." There's regret mingled with
sadness in his voice. "I followed my grandfather's. I focused
on business and nothing else. No wonder my mother is
ashamed of me."

"Stop." There's a hopelessness in his eyes that I'm
unused to seeing. Daniel always has a solution, he always
has a plan. The waitress is approaching us to take our order,
but I wave her away, signaling to her to give us another
minute. "You fucked up. So fix it."

He raises his eyes toward my face, and my worry eases
when I see the steel in his eyes. He's not giving up. "Oh, I
am," he responds. "I have a plan in motion. Now, onto other
topics. How's Ben working out at *Seb New York*?"

I groan as I think about the unpredictable mess that is
my sous-chef. Ben is a walking personification of every
angry chef stereotype. He yells at the line cooks. He curses

and pouts and stomps around, and the worst thing is that most of the time, he's responsible for the kitchen crisis he's on a rant about. "I think he might have a drinking problem."

Daniel frowns. "That's not good."

I shake my head. "Tell me about it. Last night, I had to intervene before every single one of our staff walked out en masse. He messed up the tickets, he screamed at the wait staff, and he almost caused a fucking riot. I had to send him home and take over. I was almost going to bail on you."

"I thought you looked exhausted when you walked in. Fire him."

"Come on, Daniel."

"Nope, listen to me." His voice is firm. "I run into shit like this all the time. Some people are a cancer. They ruin everything around them. You want to help Ben - do it outside your restaurant. Don't poison everyone else by exposing them to his antics."

"I'll think about it," I concede reluctantly. I hear the wisdom of his words, but I don't like what he's suggesting. Ben's from the South too, and I feel a sense of kinship with him. The memories of my early struggles in New York intrude when I'm tempted to give up on Ben. Daniel had given me a helping hand when I needed it - shouldn't I do the same?

The waitress is back to take our orders and I try to decide if I should order the halibut or the lamb. The menu is a disjointed mess. The owner of this place might have lucked out with an exceptional chef, but they are missing the mark in so many other ways. I wonder how long the place will last.

Daniel rolls his eyes at my hesitation, but doesn't push it. He turns to the waitress and orders the lamb, and I promptly get the halibut. I want to see what these guys can do.

We chat about other things as we eat our lunch. As my crew has promised, the food is really exceptional. "Is this place going to make it?" Daniel asks me.

I shake my head. "I don't think so. The decor and the menu need an overhaul. The pricing is all wrong as well. I give it six months. A year, if they get lucky."

"Pity," he lifts his fork up to his mouth. "The food's amazing."

"Why do you think I'm here?" I grin. "I'm going to hire the chef when this place goes under, Daniel. Whoever he is, he's too good to leave in a place like this." I thank the waitress, who has just topped up our water. She's looking upset, for some reason. I wonder why.

19

In the midst of chaos, there is also opportunity.

— Sun Tzu, The Art of War

Bailey:

Lying in bed after Sebastian dropped me off, I contemplated quitting the pool team. Then I'd grown angry at myself for thinking about running away. Why should I? I'm not the one who is in the wrong here. That's definitely Daniel.

Sebastian isn't much better. Seriously, I want to roll my eyes when I think about Juliette confronting me in the bathroom on Wednesday and telling me to stay away from him. *So much drama.* It's like I'm in high school all over again, and she's warning me to stay away from the cute boy that she likes.

The whole thing is ridiculous. I have work to do. I've had to spend all of Saturday at school, catching up on grading and my own research. I don't have time for a moody billion-aire and a brilliant chef.

SUNDAY MORNING, I wake up early. I've been putting off getting the rest of my stuff from Trevor's place, and I'm determined to get it done today. It's not like Trevor can say anything to ruin my mood — Daniel already did that pretty thoroughly Friday night.

I've texted Trevor to let him know I'll be by to grab my things, but because I'm in a spiteful mood, I make it a point to use my key to let myself into his apartment. This won't be a long visit - I just have my Kitchen Aid mixer, a few clothes and some jewelry to pack.

When I walk in, Trevor's in the living room eating a bowl of cereal in his boxers and nothing else. He almost drops his spoon in surprise when he sees me. "You can't just waltz in here, Bailey," he says angrily. "You should have knocked."

"Is that what you think?" I'm spoiling for a fight; I've been spoiling for one since Friday night. "I'm pretty sure that charging me for rent for the next ninety days means that I still live here." I smile pleasantly at him. "That's how my lawyer interpreted it for me. Perhaps you need to have a chat with your own attorney?"

I'd called Wendy on my way over to confirm the legality of what I was doing. She'd sighed over the phone and she'd tried to dissuade me from being petty, but in the end, she'd given up and told me that yes, I could indeed just walk in. I can see Wendy's point - I should just let this go. However, I'm still furious that Trevor charged me rent. The slimy dirt bag. It would be one thing if he needed the money, but Trevor is rich enough to easily cover the cost of the apartment. He wants to mess with me? Bring it on. The new Bailey, the one who won a game of pool on Wednesday night, isn't going to roll over and play dead.

Trevor splutters angrily. I ignore him and go to the spare bedroom, where I store all my clothes. They are still there, untouched. Good. I pull out my two battered suitcases from their spot at the bottom of the closet. I took these suitcases on my one year trip to Siberia. I know that everything I own will fit in them.

Trevor stands in the doorway, watching me pack. "Do you want some coffee?" he asks finally.

"Sure." I follow him, since I need to go to the kitchen anyway for my stand mixer. My anger is dying down. As much as I like this newfound righteous indignation of mine, it's tiring to be annoyed all the time. I'm not tempestuous enough. Gabby's better at being fiery.

In the kitchen, he leans against the counter and surveys me with a sly smirk on his face while I unplug the mixer from the power strip. "How've you been?" he asks. I'm a little puzzled about his grin, until it dawns on me that he expects me to be attracted to his almost nakedness.

Oh. *Oh.*

Poor Trevor. He doesn't know that Daniel and Sebastian fill my thoughts and haunt my dreams. I only have to close my eyes, and I can feel the scratch of the pool table fabric against my buttocks. The rasp of Sebastian's stubble against my inner thighs. The feeling of Daniel's fingers in my most forbidden hole.

Damn it. I'm some kind of sex-crazed fiend. Worse than that, though I don't really like either of them very much right at the moment, if they told me to spread my legs, I would be seriously tempted. I'd probably obey.

"I've been fine," I answer shortly. "I joined a pool league."

He snorts in derision. "Oh Bailey, that's just pathetic. If you want to get back together, just say so."

"I don't want to get back together," I say evenly, holding onto my temper with an effort. Guys. They always think it's about them. "But you were a shitty, *shitty* teacher, and you made me think I was hopeless." I meet his gaze squarely. "And I'm not."

He just shakes his head. "Whatever, Bailey," he says condescendingly. "This is what you new age chicks called empowerment, right?" He makes air-quotes as he says *empowerment,* and I want to punch him.

As furious with Daniel as I am, neither he nor Sebastian ever dismissed me this way. Instead, they were interested in me. They'd never once made me feel that I wasn't important.

I consider it a win that I don't smash Trevor's stupid ugly vase on my way out. I'm tempted, trust me. I'm *seriously* tempted.

MONDAY MORNING, I'm at work, snowed under by a pile of essays, when there's a knock at the open office door. I look up, expecting some undergrad who has come to argue about his grade, but instead, it's Steve Ashworth, the head of the Department of Anthropology. Uncharacteristically, he has a beaming smile on his face.

"Bailey," he booms. "Good job, great job. I can't even begin to tell you how delighted I am. How delighted we *all* are."

I blink at him, confused. "What's going on?"

He frowns at me, entering my office. "You don't know?"

I clear some paperwork off a chair for him to sit down. "I promise you, I have absolutely no idea what you are talking about."

"The endowment, of course," he exclaims. Then he looks at my expression. "Hang on, you don't know what I'm talking about."

"Yes, I *have* been saying that," I agree blandly. "What exactly are we celebrating?"

Sameer, alerted by the noise, appears in the doorway. *It's a party at Bailey's, everyone. Bring your own coffee.* "What's going on, Steve?" he asks.

Steve's grin stretches from ear to ear. "Our Bailey here has friends in high places. You've heard of the Hartman Foundation?"

"Yeah," Sameer says. "They're sponsoring Maria Rivera's trip to Siberia."

"Oh, did that get approved? Good for Maria," I say automatically, then I register Steve's words. Hartman Foundation. *Daniel Hartman.* How did I not connect the dots? And what has Daniel done that has Steve so pleased?

"Right. Well, they were going to fund an endowment to the university," Steve says. "Of course, I didn't think twice about it. Most of these grants go to the business school or the engineering school."

I want to tell Steve to hurry up and get to the point. "And instead?" Sameer prompts, suppressing a smile at my impatience. Steve's legendary within the department for telling the longest, most rambling stories.

"Instead they gave it to Liberal Arts," Steve announces, sounding thrilled. He's almost dancing a jig in his excitement. "One hundred and fifty million dollars over the next five years. The official press conference is tomorrow, but I wanted to thank you personally, Bailey. George told me that Alexa Hartman mentioned in passing that you were a friend of her son." George is the president of the NYU.

Steve winks at me and leans in, continuing his sentence in a lowered voice. "Good job, Bailey. I won't forget this when it's time to evaluate your tenure application."

When he departs, Sameer looks at me curiously. "What did Steve say to you at the end?"

I swallow back the sour feeling from my mouth. "That he'd make sure to keep in mind at tenure time that a billionaire name-dropped me. You know, because the work I do doesn't matter at all."

Sameer shrugs. "Bailey," he advises calmly, "these are tough times to be an anthropologist. Stop sweating it and use every advantage you have. NYU won't give you tenure if your work isn't good enough."

The feeling of bitterness doesn't go away. As I think about the situation, I start getting angry. If Daniel wanted to apologize, a bunch of flowers would have done admirably. He didn't need to spend a hundred and fifty million dollars.

I've already dated one guy who thinks that his money makes him better than me. I don't need another one.

THINGS DON'T IMPROVE when I get home. Monday night drinking is at our apartment, and Piper's emptying a packet of chips listlessly into a bowl. Gabby, Katie and Wendy are due any minute now, and Miki's going to Skype in.

I've barely seen Piper all week. When I'm home in the evenings, she's working at her restaurant, and in the mornings, she's still asleep when I leave for work. "Are you okay?" I ask. "Is something the matter?"

She turns to me. Her eyes are red, as if she's been crying. "Can I talk to you for a second, Bailey?"

"Of course, sweetie. What's wrong?"

"Sebastian Ardalan ate at my restaurant on Saturday," she says. Her voice is oddly flat. I would have thought that she'd be squealing and dancing a little jig. A two-star Michelin chef eating at Piper's restaurant? That's huge, and her lack of excitement is conspicuous.

"Why aren't you more excited?"

"I was waiting on his table because Kimmie didn't show," she says. "And I overheard a little bit of his conversation." She doesn't meet my gaze. "Sebastian Ardalan said that Aladdin's Lamp wouldn't last six months. A year tops, he said."

"Oh honey," I put down my laptop bag and envelop her into a hug. "He doesn't know that. Don't listen to him."

"No," Piper's voice is muffled into my shoulder. "He's right. His words hurt because he's absolutely correct. And I don't know what to do to prevent it."

I love Piper. She's like a sister to me, but she's at her best in the kitchen, comfortable with her herbs and spices, combining ingredients and enjoying the creative process. Unfortunately, it takes more than creative genius to run a successful restaurant. You have to formulate a menu that's familiar, yet exciting. You have to find and hire attentive wait staff in a city where it's hard to find good talent. You have to know how to get reviewers to review your restaurant, and how to create buzz. There's so much more to it than just cooking and the New York restaurant scene is a cauldron. It will burn you.

I wish there was something I could tell her, something I could do to make this better. She was there for me, readily and without question, when I needed her after I left Trevor.

She's always been there for me. It kills me to see her hurting like this.

"What can I do?" I don't know what else to say. I wish I could wave a magic wand and make this better.

She sighs and pulls away. "I don't know, Bailey," she confesses. "Sebastian Ardalan loved my food. Once upon a time, that would have been the highlight of my month. Now, all I can do is stress about what he said." Her expression turns wistful. "It used to be so much simpler."

"You are doing a great job," I say loyally. "You had the place dumped on you. You are doing fantastic."

She shakes her head. "No," she corrects me. "He was right. I'm going to fail."

A sudden flash of anger runs through me at the power of careless words. Trevor's corrosive words convinced me I couldn't play pool. Daniel's warning about the press on Friday night had sent me into a tailspin. And now stupid, gorgeous Sebastian Ardalan has hurt my friend with his throwaway words. *Guys should not be allowed to talk, ever. Their only use is to look pretty and open jars with too-tight lids.* "Listen to me. You cannot let some stupid arrogant celebrity who probably hasn't been inside a kitchen in months knock you off your game. You are a fucking excellent chef, and everything's going to be okay."

She nods, unconvinced at the start, but as I stare into her eyes, willing her to believe me, she nods with more faith. "Okay," she giggles, "If I agree with you, will you stop staring at me? It's getting creepy. Oh, by the way, there was a FedEx slip on the door. They tried to deliver a parcel for you."

I let her go, barely registering her words. I'm angry with Sebastian and this time, I'm not going to run away. *I'm going to do something about it.* "I'm not expecting anything," I tell her, going into my bedroom to grab my coat.

"Where are you off to?" Piper asks me. "Everyone's going to be here in a few minutes."

"I am going," I say grimly, "to find Sebastian and Daniel, and give them a piece of my mind."

"What did Daniel do?"

"He told me to keep our threesome out of the tabloids, then gave our department millions of dollars to make up for being a dick."

Piper looks confused at my brief explanation. "I know it doesn't make any sense," I say over my shoulder, walking toward the front door. "I promise I'll explain everything tomorrow. I'll swing by the restaurant."

"Hang on," she grins, "are you dropping out of Monday Night Drinking so you can get laid?"

"Are you even listening to me?" I ask in exasperation. "I'm really pissed off with them. I'm going to kick their asses."

"Sure, Bails, whatever," she says. Her eyes twinkle. "Somebody's going to get laid. I can't decide if I should sing *'bow-chika wow, wow,'* or tell you to *'go forth and fornicate.'*"

"There's going to be no fornication," I insist weakly. "You have the situation all wrong."

But the words feel like a lie as they leave my mouth, and judging from the amused grin on Piper's face, I'm not doing a very good job convincing her.

20

Wealth is the ability to fully experience life.

— Henry David Thoreau

Daniel:

At seven, not too long after I walk into my home, there's a knock at my front door. I go downstairs to find Sebastian standing there, a frown on his face. "I need to punch something or someone," he says. "I thought I'd come here instead."

"I have beer." I stand aside and he walks in. "What happened?"

"You know Mina, the restaurant manager at *Seb II?* She fired a waiter who is a buddy of Ben, and Ben was a surly bitch the whole day yesterday." Sebastian clutches at his hair. "Don't tell me to fire Ben."

"Fire Ben."

"Yeah, yeah, I know. Lead me to the liquor, Hartman." He enters the kitchen and grabs a beer out of the refrigerator, handing me one at the same time. "Any word from Bailey?"

"No." I'm nervous. I thought I might hear from her today about the package I sent her, but there's been no word. And if news of the Hartman Foundation grant has reached her? I shudder to think of the conclusion she will draw.

Sebastian reads the expression on my face. "What did you do, Daniel?"

I tell him about the grant and he laughs out aloud. "Daniel," he shakes his head at me, "did you really spend a hundred and fifty million dollars to apologize?"

"Of course not." I even sound defensive, damn it. "I sent her a gift with an apology. The NYU grant has been in the works for a long time. I merely suggested to my mother that she shouldn't give it to the business school. They would have just built a fancy building and named it the Hartman School of Business. An endowment to Liberal Arts is much more useful. They'll hire professors and fund scholarships for graduate students." I roll my eyes. "You know, the actual purpose of higher education."

"Dude, I wouldn't know about any of that," Sebastian says. "I didn't finish high school, remember? Despite my lack of education," his voice is laced with sarcasm, "I'm going to hazard a guess that Bailey isn't going to be thrilled when she finds out that the billionaire who owes her an apology gave her department a hundred and fifty million dollars."

"Come on," I protest, "she can't possibly hold the grant against me." I down the beer as I think through his words, a sinking feeling going through me. Then I get a short, terse text message from Bailey, asking if I'm at home and announcing that she's coming over. She says she wants to talk to both Sebastian and me. I quickly reply in the affirmative. "She's coming over," I tell Sebastian, showing him my phone. "She sounds irritated, don't you think?"

Sebastian looks puzzled as he reads her message. "Why does she want to know if I'm here? You fucked up, not me."

"Thank you for the support, asshole," I reply, but there's no energy in my words. Sebastian is right. I've fucked up, not once, but twice.

"I can explain," I say as I open the door.

She sweeps in without saying a word. She's dressed in her usual black. The only jewelry she's wearing are silver hoop earrings and a chunky bracelet. Her hair's loose and soft over her shoulders. She smells like flowers and for an instant, all I can see is her beautiful, naked body lying on my pool table, sweet and open. The only sounds I can hear are her breathy moans.

Then I see the ire in her violet eyes, and I grimace. Yeah, as Sebastian predicted, she's furious.

She stalks in, her back held ramrod straight. I lead her toward the kitchen, where Sebastian waits. It might be cowardly of me, but I need support here and I'm counting on my best friend for help. Though, in fairness, he's had to do some heavy lifting in the last two days.

"I really want to get published in the Smithsonian Institute Press, Daniel," she snaps. "Can you buy me a spot?"

Sebastian snickers and she shoots him a look that's filled with hatred. "I'm not thrilled with you either," she bites out.

"What'd I do?" he protests, looking confused.

She's not listening. No, our redhead is on a rant. "What is wrong with you guys? You," she points to me, "who the fuck bets fifty grand on a pool game? Oh wait, I know the answer. The kind of guy who has so much money that he'll spend a hundred and fifty million dollars on some kind of half-assed apology." Her coat flies across the room. "I just spent," she hisses, "eleven months with a guy who measured my worth by how much money I made. And you try to buy my forgiveness with an endowment to the university?" Her voice trembles with rage. "Do you know how angry that makes me?"

I open my mouth to cut in and tell her that I did *not* give the university the money as a gesture of apology, but she's whirled to face Sebastian. "And you." She points an accusing finger in his direction. "You thought my friend's restaurant wouldn't last six months? What kind of asshole would say that and crush her dreams? Now that you have two Michelin stars, do you think you can wander around the city and insult struggling chefs? You don't know anything about Piper's circumstances. How dare you."

"What are you talking about?" Sebastian blinks. "Is that Hell's Kitchen dive run by a friend of yours?"

"Yes." Her voice makes ice look balmy in comparison. "My roommate Piper."

"Ah." Sebastian digests that with an embarrassed look on his face. "Shit. I didn't know that."

Bailey isn't mollified. She transfers her glare to me. "A hundred and fifty million dollars?"

Her voice catches just a little, and I can tell she's really upset. "Okay." I hold up my hands. "Stop. Sit. Listen to me, please."

She settles down on a chair, a guarded look on her face. I open a bottle of vodka and pour the three of us a drink. "I shouldn't have said what I said the other day," I say quietly. "I'm very sorry. It was stupid and uncalled for, and it was a dick thing to do."

"You gave my school a hundred and fifty million dollars because you were sorry? Daniel, in the real world, people send flowers to apologize."

"I did," I run my hand through my hair in frustration. "Well, not flowers. It took a while to arrange, but the package should have been delivered today."

She opens her mouth to say something, then she shuts up. "Wait a second," she says slowly. "Piper did say something about FedEx. You sent me something?"

"I did."

"And the hundred and fifty million? Did that have anything to do with me?"

I have to be honest with her. "Yes." I put my hand up before she starts yelling at me again. "Please let me finish. I didn't spend any time thinking about the funding gap in liberal arts until I met you. Then I read the blog you kept while you were in Siberia, and I found it fascinating." I kneel in front of her and take her hands in mine. "The work you do is important. It deserves to be funded." I shrug. "The money for the endowment was already earmarked. I just suggested to my mother that we give it to the liberal arts school instead of the business school."

Her expression is still wary. "What did you send me?" she asks. "What was in the package?"

I gesture to the untouched drink in front of her. "Take a sip."

She drinks, and a look of startled surprise fills her face. "Daniel," she says softly. "What is this?"

I slide the bottle over her way. It's a bottle of Five Lakes, a small brand of vodka that's very hard to find outside of Russia. From reading Bailey's blog posts, I know that this particular brand is one of the things she misses about Siberia. It took all weekend to locate a dozen bottles in

Moscow and fly them to New York. After all that effort, FedEx just stuck a delivery notice on her door, and it's probably languishing in one of their pick-up centers. *This has to be the textbook definition of irony.*

"You found this in New York?"

"Moscow."

"This weekend?"

I smile at her. "Yes, Bailey."

"You read my blog?"

I can't quite make out her tone. Is she angry? "I did."

She digests that silently, then she turns to Sebastian. "Why did you eat at Piper's restaurant?"

He's been silent so far, watching the two of us. Now, he answers Bailey's question. "I have a very unstable chef at one of my restaurants, and I've been hearing good things about your friend's cooking. I thought I might eat there and look for a replacement at the same time, in a low-key kind of way."

She finally cracks a smile. A small one, but at least she's not frowning any more. "Sebastian, you do know that people recognize you, don't you? There's no low-key way for a two-Michelin-starred chef to eat in a restaurant in the city."

"I'm beginning to realize that," he replies. He takes a sip of his vodka and looks up. "Hey, this is good," he says to me. "Nice work, Daniel. Appropriate big gesture."

"Big gesture?" I stifle the urge to kill Sebastian as Bailey looks at us with a curious look.

"Daniel here," Sebastian teases, unabashed, "goes for the big, dramatic gesture."

Ignoring Sebastian's amusement, I give Bailey a serious look. "I screwed up, but it won't happen again. As multiple people have pointed out to me, I'm not the only one that stands to lose if this thing between us becomes public knowledge. That is, if you are still interested in pursuing it..." I hesitate, almost holding my breath waiting for her answer. I'm not the only one. Sebastian is waiting expectantly too.

She surveys the two of us. "Tell me what you want," she says finally. "This situation isn't typical for me. Billionaires and celebrities don't stumble into my world. Hot guys aren't interested in me, and as you already know, I don't have wild, crazy sex. I don't know how to navigate all of that."

I kiss the pulse that beats nervously in her wrist. She's not as calm as she appears. Neither am I. "I find everything about you fascinating, and I'd like to get to know you better."

"Me too," Sebastian says from his corner.

"Both of you at the same time? That wasn't a one-time thing?"

"Is that bad?" Sebastian asks, his words a challenge in her direction as I brace myself for her answer. There are a lot of women out there who think they want to try a threesome, and some of them even will. A longer commitment to something so unorthodox? That's a rarity. "Can you handle something outside the norm?"

She looks intrigued. "I'm a cultural anthropologist. Outside the norm is my bread and butter."

"Is that a yes?"

"No more big gestures, Daniel. If I do this, it isn't because of how rich you are."

"If I thought the reason you were here was my money, we wouldn't be doing anything."

She smiles. "Thank you for noticing. And Sebastian? Be nice to Piper."

"Yes ma'am."

It's far too early to talk about serious relationships or the future, or where this thing between the three of us is headed, but there's one thing I need to make clear. "While we are dating," I tell her, "I'd like us to be exclusive."

"What does that involve?" She examines her nails intently, and avoids looking at us. "There's three of us. If I sleep with Sebastian when you aren't around, am I cheating on you?"

A spike of unwarranted jealousy pierces through me at that image, and I force myself to suppress it. "No. I'm not going to lie to you and tell you that it doesn't bother me at all, but no. That's not cheating."

She bites her lower lip. As I see her teeth indent her flesh, I realize how much I want her. I can't wait to see her naked again. To see her spread out, open, ready for us.

"Okay." She looks at the two of us. "I don't really know how to be anything other than exclusive anyway."

Both Sebastian and I exhale with relief at the same time. My fuck-up wasn't the death knell to us. Now, I can't wait to see what happens next. I pick up the bottle of vodka and my glass, and gesture to the living room. "Follow me."

21

If I had a flower for every time I thought of you... I could walk through my garden forever.

— ALFRED LORD TENNYSON

Bailey:

I cannot believe I'm doing this.

There was, I can't lie, a lump in my throat when I realized what Daniel had done. Yes, getting vodka flown from Russia to New York was the act of a man with significant resources, but he couldn't have done it without learning something about me. Had he got me something shiny from Tiffany, I would have walked away.

He said he found me fascinating, and his actions have backed up his words.

Sebastian was always easier to forgive. His words about Piper's restaurant were cruel, but he clearly hadn't meant for her to overhear the conversation, and he had been there for a good reason.

And so I follow them to the living room, knowing full well that in a few minutes, I will succumb to the blazing attraction I feel.

There's one question I haven't asked either of them. *Where is this going?* I haven't asked because whichever way they answer, I'll be bruised. Even though I'm going away to Argentina for six months in the fall, I still don't want to hear them tell me that this is just a fling, and I'm not ready to confront the truth about why I feel that way.

THE LAST TIME I was here, I only saw Daniel's kitchen and his rec room. This time, he leads the way to the living room, with floor to ceiling windows on two sides, overlooking Central Park.

"Nice," I say, looking around.

That's an understatement. The room is huge, easily fifteen hundred square feet, but the furniture is arranged in a way to make the space seem friendly and cozy, not intimidating. The two walls that aren't windows are covered with artwork. I see a painting that has to be a Picasso, another that's clearly Salvador Dali. There's also a Star Wars movie poster on the wall, and one of those ubiquitous Keep Calm and Carry On posters. It's very eclectic.

"I'll give you a proper tour at some point," he promises. "But please, sit. Want a top-up of your drink?"

"Probably not," I reply, taking a seat on an ocean-blue stuffed chair. "I don't want to be too buzzed when we..." I feel the heat rise on my face, and my voice trails off.

"When we fuck." That's Sebastian. "Say the words, Bailey."

I lift my chin. "I don't want to be too buzzed when we fuck."

"An admirable goal," he agrees, crossing the room to sit down on the white couch that's perpendicular to me. I'm a little disappointed by that. I thought he'd sit on the arm of my chair, but instead, they are both giving me space. I don't want space. I want to be fucked.

Daniel lifts up his glass in a toast. "Cheers," he says simply. I wave my own glass in his direction and take another sip of the vodka, feeling the heat travel a fiery path down my body. Sitting here, having to pretend I care about small talk, when all I want to do is be bracketed between their hard bodies... *The anticipation is killing me.*

Sebastian leans forward and takes my hand in his own. His skin is callused from hours spent in front of the flames, and the contrast sets me shivering. His thumb glides over my palm, pressing down firmly. It's an erotic touch. My body reacts with a rush of wetness and I bite off my moan with difficulty.

"I want to hear you, Bailey." His blue eyes locking onto mine, his other hand moving to my wrist to hold me. "Each whimper, each moan. Don't hold back, baby."

He gets up to sit on my armrest, pulling me into his body for a kiss. His lips press down on me, insistent and forceful, and I surrender to the pleasure. One part of me wonders when Daniel's going to participate. Another part - *a bigger part* - likes the idea of giving him a show. He leans back on the couch, drink in hand, a half-smile on his face. His gaze stays on us.

He's enjoying watching us. *Game on.* I grab Sebastian's head with my hand, gripping the back of his neck, pulling him even closer to me. I don't stifle my noises of pleasure, the little moans, the soft gasps. It is such a turn on to know that Daniel is captivated by our display.

"You like being watched, Bailey?" Sebastian says into my ears, his teeth nibbling at an earlobe. His hand glides a caress on my chest, from my cleavage to my neck. "My little exhibitionist. Take off your top."

His hands are at my waist, plucking the fabric up and over my head. When my lace-clad breasts come into view, Daniel leans forward and takes another sip of his drink. His expression is hungry, and his eyes blaze with lust, but he remains in his seat.

Sebastian goes back to kissing me. His hands caress my breasts over the bra, but disappointingly, he doesn't make any move to unfasten it yet. Instead, he nudges me to my feet. "Your jeans are in the way," he mutters. "Let's get them off."

His big hands roam down my abdomen, and I flinch automatically. I don't have six-pack abs, or anything even close to them. Rolls of squishy flesh cannot be attractive.

Except Sebastian's kissing the same rolls of flesh, his breath heated, his stubble rasping against my skin, his hand pressed against my back to move me closer to him. His other hand works at the waistband of my jeans till they are undone, then he pushes them down my hips, kissing each bit of skin as it is revealed. "Ah fuck, those panties," he groans. "Soft, pretty pink. Just like your pussy."

I blush at his words, and Daniel chuckles from his spot on the couch. "I do like how you flush, Bailey," he says. "It's so much fun to corrupt the good girl."

"Please," I scoff, though I'm distracted by Sebastian's kisses, by the rub of his hard erection against my crotch as he stands back up. "I'm not really such a good girl."

Sebastian's teeth nip at my nipple through my bra, and I forget Daniel's words, though I feel every bit of his burning gaze on me. This is so hot. I'd have never thought I'd be so turned on by the idea of someone watching. His hand runs over my ass, and I tense, waiting for the spank that does not come. *Pity.*

I'm nudged back into my chair, and Sebastian pulls my jeans free, tossing them carelessly across the room. They land against one of the windows and slide to the floor, and I giggle. "I can't believe I'm making out in full view of Central Park," I confess. "I feel so naughty."

Daniel raises an amused eyebrow. "You little hussy," he scolds. "All the way down to your underwear before you even noticed the window." He leans back and unzips his own pants lazily. His erection springs out and I can't help it, I actually lick my lips. *I'm keyed up, okay?* They've had me wanting them ever since I saw them, and this is my first glimpse of cock. I want more.

My view of Daniel's dick is blocked off because Sebastian once again leans into me. His lips press on mine, nibbling and sucking on my lower lip. "Such a bad girl," he growls. "Can't take your eyes off his cock, can you?"

"No," I whisper, a thread of defiance in my voice. "I want to see. Take off your pants." I move my hands up his thighs, my fingers tracing the rock hard outline of his erection. "I want to touch you. Taste you."

A fire burns in his eyes. In an instant, my bra is off, and my wrists are pressed together behind my head. Sebastian uses the scrap of lace to bind my hands. "Keep them there," he orders. His fingers tangle in my hair, his grip tightening until little sparks of pain prickle at my scalp.

Oh my god. This is better than my dreams, even hotter than my most powerful fantasies. *This is real.* This is the hard press of his torso on mine. The ache in my shoulder blades anchors me, while his large hands boldly feel every heated inch of me and threatens to drown me in pleasure.

"Sebastian," I whisper. "Please…"

"Bailey begging," he says into my ear. "I like that."

His hands run up my bare thighs, inching slowly toward my core. I'm still wearing my panties, and my crotch is soaked, a fact that both embarrasses me and turns me on in equal measure.

"Fuck," Sebastian groans as his knuckles brush against the damp fabric. "You are so wet…"

"You make me wet," I say "Both of you. I want you."

"And you'll have us tonight, Bailey." Sebastian's blue eyes hold mine. "All in good time."

My legs part for him, unbidden. His fingers tease the edge where the fabric of my panties meet my skin, but he doesn't go further. Instead, he gets up and sits back on the couch, next to Daniel and lifts his drink up to his lips.

"Take off your panties." Daniel takes over.

"Are the two of you ever going to take off your clothes?" I pout in complaint. "Come on. I've been naked before, and I'm almost naked now. It's definitely your turn."

A smile grazes his face at that, and he gestures languidly to his massive, naked, throbbing, cock. "I'm not entirely clothed," he says. "Stand up, Bailey. Take off your panties."

Fine. They want a show. I can give them a show. I'm going to give them the best fucking strip tease I know how. Even if all I have to do is roll down a pair of panties to my feet and step out of them, and even if my wrists are tied together with a bra.

I stand up and stretch lazily, sucking in my stomach and arching my tits out toward them. Bringing my tied wrists in front of me, I push my breasts together with my upper arms. My nipples, I'm unsurprised to note, are erect nubs, hard with desire, aching for a touch from either of them. *Or from both of them.*

Moving slowly and sensually, I position myself so I'm in front of them, slowly sinking to my knees. "I want to suck your cocks," I murmur throatily, licking my lips. I'm so turned on that I'm not embarrassed by how brazen I sound. "I want to take you down my throat." I hold Daniel's gaze in mine. His cock is pulled out, and I reason that he's more likely to cave first. *Throw me down on the antique Persian rug and fuck the need out of me, Daniel.* "I want you to come in my mouth. I'll swallow every drop."

"Bailey," Daniel groans, throwing his head back. "What are you doing to us?"

"The same thing you are doing to me," I reply. I turn to Sebastian. "I'm burning up," I whisper. "Please don't make me wait."

"That does it." Sebastian sounds like a guy pushed to the edge. He pulls off his t-shirt, and his six-pack abs come into view, as does the ink on his bulging forearms. I want to lick each ridge of muscle. At the same time, I also want to run and cover myself, because he's in amazing shape and I have a bunch of excess weight to lose.

"What's wrong?"

"Umm," I flush. "It's a little intimidating to sleep with guys in perfect shape. Especially when I look the way I do."

"What do you look like, Bailey?" Daniel's voice is dangerous. "You are beautiful. Desirable. Warm and soft. Look at my cock."

I sneak a peek, and exhale, my throat dry with lust. He's so thick. So big and beautiful. I want to rub against it, and I want to nestle against Sebastian's rock hard abs, and trace out each line of his tattoos with my tongue.

Daniel and Sebastian are dangerous for me. They make me want too much.

"Enough with the bullshit." Sebastian moves in for the kill. One hand yanks up my bound wrists over my head. Another pulls my panties down, leaving me exposed and panting with lust. "The two of us can't keep our hands off you," he grits out. "Daniel's in the middle of a sensitive take over. I'm swamped with restaurant bullshit. And you are in the tenure window. Why do you question this chemistry between us?" His fingers pinch a nipple harshly and I gasp out as a painful pleasure radiates from that spot to the rest of my body. "Can't you tell how much we want you?"

He pushes me onto the couch, and I land with my face almost in Daniel's lap. A resounding spank lands on my ass. "Bailey," Sebastian says to me. "I want to fuck you hard and fast."

"Do it." I lean forward, licking my lips, and take Daniel's enormous head in my mouth. He groans as I maneuver my hands to clasp the base of his thick shaft. As best as I can, given my bound state, I pump and suck him, rewarded by the noises of desire he makes.

Behind me, Sebastian slaps my ass again, and my mouth deepens onto Daniel's cock. I hear the sound of a condom wrapper tear, then I feel Sebastian's cock nudge at my pussy.

This is actually happening. Sebastian is going to fuck me while I suck Daniel.

Two guys.

Two unbelievably hot guys.

Are.

Fucking.

Me.

At the same time.

As promised, Sebastian is not gentle. He thrusts into me

in one hard motion. His fingers dig into my curvy hips as he fucks me. I grind my elbows into the couch and sink my mouth even deeper on Daniel's cock. Blood rushes to my head, and I'm overwhelmed in the best possible way.

Pounding, burning, pulsing gnawing lust curls at me, tendrils snaking everywhere. There are fingers pulling on my nipples. Daniel? A knuckle rubs steady circles against my clitoris. I close my eyes and focus on the way Daniel's cock feels in my mouth. Harsh breathing fills the silence in the room, as does the slap of Sebastian's thighs against my body.

Each thrust stretches me. Each thrust sends an intense jolt up my body. Each muted groan of pleasure from them makes me even wetter. My orgasm is coiling up inside me, preparing to erupt, and when Sebastian grabbed my long hair and pulls, I lose it. With a shouted cry, I explode.

Through my haze of lust, I feel Daniel stiffen, then he is climaxing, and I eagerly swallow every drop. Sebastian's fingers dig deeper into my flesh, then he too is choking off a cry as he comes.

I collapse on the couch, limp and satiated. My head is on Daniel's lap, and I feel his fingers stroke my cheek. "Bailey," he mutters, untying my hands as I lie down, unable to move.

"Daniel," I reply, frowning at him through sleep-filled eyes. "You still have your clothes on."

His lips curl into a smile. "Will you spend the night?" he asks me. "With the two of us?"

My stomach growls right then, loud and long. I bury my face in my hands, unbelievably embarrassed by my body's betrayal. "Pretend that didn't happen," I whisper fervently. "Pretend I did something cool instead."

Sebastian laughs. "I think that's my cue to feed you, Bailey," he says, getting up and pulling his pants back on, but not before I get a good look at his dick. Even flaccid, he's impressively large. My pussy is going to be so tender tomorrow.

A smile breaks out on my face. "Let me see if I've got this straight," I tell them sitting up and reaching for my forgotten glass of vodka. The ice has melted and diluted the strong alcohol, but the taste of it still brings back warm memories of my time in Siberia. This was a very considerate gift. "You," I gesture toward Sebastian, "two-star Michelin chef, toast of New York's restaurant scene, are going to make me something to eat."

"That was the plan."

I turn to Daniel. "And once we eat something, we are going to sleep in your bed?"

"Well," Daniel laughs at my expression. "I was hoping we'd do this again, and more, before we went to sleep. If that's okay with you?"

I feel like Alice, falling down a rabbit hole. Up is down and left is right, and in Wonderland, hot billionaires are interested in me. But hey, as long as I'm immersed in fantasy land, I might as well enjoy the ride. "Oh, it's more than okay," I say. "That sounds pretty damn good."

22

Words are easy, like the wind. Faithful friends are hard to find.

— William Shakespeare, The Passionate
Pilgrim

Bailey:

Daniel Hartman's bedroom is, as I expected, large. A massive king-size bed rests against one wall. Another wall is covered entirely with floor to ceiling windows. Daniel draws the grey woolen drapes shut as we enter, and flicks on a couple of light switches. A soft glow fills the room from the two pendant lamps, hanging on either side of the headboard. My feet sink into the plush pile of a grey carpet, and I stifle a moan of pleasure.

Daniel notices. "It's just a rug," he suggests. "Come here, and I'll give you something else to moan about."

I don't reply right away, and Sebastian grins at me. "Cat got your tongue, Bailey?" he teases. "I didn't see you at a loss for words earlier when you were busy yelling at us."

At that, I have to laugh. "It's the red hair," I tell him. "All my life, I've tried not to be the hot-tempered redhead, but I actually enjoyed giving you guys a piece of my mind."

They both chuckle. The sex on the couch has dissipated some of the fierce tension between the three of us. The vodka has played its part as well, as has the excellent tomato soup and grilled cheese sandwich that Sebastian made us.

"Come here," I order Sebastian, sinking on the bed and leaning against Daniel. "I want to look at your tattoos."

He moves closer and I peer at them, my fingers reaching out to trace the ink on his skin. "A dragon and a phoenix?"

"Mmm."

"Is there a story?"

Daniel smiles at that. "There's always a story, Bailey," he says, his fingers stroking a path on my thighs. "Given your line of work, I thought you'd know that."

It takes difficulty to resist the urge to climb on top of him like a horny monkey. "I'm an anthropologist, not a journalist," I point out, realizing just an instant too late that mentioning the press around Daniel might not be a good idea.

He remains relaxed, and his hands don't pull away from my waist. "For work, I research the stories that bind us together. But for fun," my finger follows the flame of the dragon toward Sebastian's chest, "I ask hot naked guys to tell me about their tattoos."

Sebastian sits on the other side of me, and I feel his solid warmth at my side. "I got the dragon when I left home," he says. Something in his expression warns me against prying more. "And the phoenix six months after I opened my first restaurant."

"No tattoo for the Michelin stars?"

He shakes his head. "The tattoos," he explains, "are for

moments of personal clarity and growth. Michelin stars are great, but not tattoo worthy."

"You've had two moments of personal clarity in your entire life?" I tease, trying to ignore that Daniel's fingers are climbing higher on my thigh. "How old are you, Sebastian? You seem to be due for another."

He grins at that, then his smile fades. "What?" I ask him.

"I was just thinking about your friend," he says. "The chef at Aladdin's Lamp. Piper, isn't that her name?"

I stiffen. "Sheesh. Yes, I do want to hear that you are thinking about my hot roommate when we are naked in bed," I say, trying to bury the faint hurt under sarcasm. "Smooth."

Sebastian rolls his eyes. "I'm in bed with the woman I want to be with," he says impatiently, grabbing a handful of my hair and pulling me close to him to press a hard, passionate kiss on my lips. "I was thinking of her restaurant struggles," he clarifies when we pull apart. "I'd had already had the benefit of apprenticing under several leading chefs when I opened *Seb New York*, and the first six months were still insanely difficult. But Piper's fresh off culinary school, isn't she?"

I'm mollified by his kiss and touched by his concern for my friend. "Yeah," I confirm. "She had this crazy aunt who left her the restaurant in the will, but it came with a hundred different conditions. Piper's already sunk all kinds of money into the place."

"Would she be receptive to some help?" he asks. "I've some friends in the industry who are always looking for new ventures to invest in. They could give her some advice, if she's interested."

"What about you? Won't that hurt you if you send potential investors to Piper?"

He laughs. "Bailey, I have no shortage of people wanting to invest in me. Besides, my best friend is pretty fucking rich."

Of course. I slant a look at Daniel. "You guys have known each other for a long time, haven't you?"

Daniel nods. "Thirteen years." He shakes his head in mild disbelief. "That sounds crazy, doesn't it? Time flies by and you don't even realize it. I can still picture this skinny kid cooking in a greasy spoon."

"How'd you meet?"

Daniel rests his head on my shoulder. "Sebastian's parents threw him out of the house when he was sixteen," he says.

"Why?" I glance at Sebastian, shocked.

Sebastian looks uncomfortable at this foray into the past. "I couldn't sit still in class," he shrugs. "My mind leapt around during lessons. The teachers decided I was a trouble-maker. I grew up in a small town. Once you were labelled a trouble-maker, that was it. So I scraped up enough money for the bus fare, and ran away to New York."

I'm riveted. I've spent more than a few hours Googling the two of them but I've never heard this story.

Daniel continues. "So there's this sixteen year old kid in New York, and he works odd jobs in restaurants to earn money, and sleeps in a studio apartment that he shares with five other people, just to be able to afford the rent."

"I worked in a diner," Sebastian picks up. "One night, a bunch of rich kids come in." He grins, inclining his head at Daniel. "Including this one. By this time, I was nineteen and cooking during the graveyard shift, and anytime the owner wasn't around, I'd vary up the recipes just a little. A little more spice, a little more creativity. I wanted to get noticed. Create an opportunity."

"I ordered a grilled cheese sandwich," Daniel remembers. "I was expecting white bread and packaged cheese slices." He shakes his head. "Instead, I got a sandwich that had caramelized onions and real cheese, with a dipping sauce on the side that was about the best thing I'd ever tasted."

"The next thing I know, I'm getting invited to meet Daniel's parents." Sebastian smiles. "The rest is history. Real restaurant jobs, opportunities to learn from top-flight chefs. And when I was ready to open *Seb New York*, Daniel opened his purse strings."

I pull Sebastian in so he's leaning on me, and I'm held tight between them. His story has awed me. He's achieved so much in such a short time. Unlike Daniel, he wasn't born into money. Everything Sebastian has now, he's achieved with hard work.

The story also reveals a side of Daniel that I didn't know. Even when he was young, he'd realized he could use his money to help others. He didn't give Sebastian a handout - instead, he offered him a hand up. He was thoughtful enough and insightful enough to do that for Sebastian.

He's just done the same thing for me with the Hartman Foundation endowment.

"And look at him now," Daniel beams. "The best chef in the city."

Sebastian looks faintly embarrassed by that. "I'm not there yet," he says. "What'd you think, Bailey?" His big hand strokes my thighs lazily, and desire rises anew in me. "Daniel reached out and helped me when he didn't have to. Even with all the support I had, the first six months of running my own restaurant were among the toughest times in my life. I'd love to help your friend."

I think about Piper's sadness earlier today, about her

eyes, swollen from a crying jag. If Sebastian can help? If his friends can give her some pointers? I can't think of something that'd be better.

I kiss him, then turn to Daniel and kiss him too. "You guys are awesome," I tell them honestly. "What's the catch?"

Daniel grins lazily. "We might spank you a lot," he threatens. "And I have a plan for Wednesday's pool game."

"Really?" His voice has turned smoky, and I can tell that whatever the plan is, it involves sex. And I'm turned on by that idea. Who am I kidding? I'm turned on by anything these two guys propose.

He gives me a half-smile, but doesn't offer up any additional detail. Instead, he nudges my legs apart. "I want you now, Bailey," he says. "I want to sink into you. I want to pound you hard and make you cry out as you come."

I'm on board with this idea. There's a wooden side table on either side of the headboard, and Sebastian opens the drawer and pulls out a tube of lube. "Still on board with anal?" he asks me, with a wicked gleam in his eye.

"Now?" I squelch my little prickle of worry. So far, everything they've done has been amazing. I have every reason to expect that anal sex will be fantastic as well.

"Just my fingers for the moment," he says. "But soon, impatient one. Soon it'll be our cocks, one in your pussy, one buried tight in your ass. Would you like that?"

My nipples are bullets of need, my pussy is dripping with the proof of my desire. The answer to Sebastian's question is yes. Yes, yes and yes once again.

23

One may smile, and smile, and be a villain.

— WILLIAM SHAKESPEARE, HAMLET

Sebastian:

It feels amazing to wake up Tuesday morning with Bailey's soft body curled up between Daniel and me, naked and very tempting. Morning sex is phenomenal as well, and the simple pleasure of making her a plate of scrambled eggs makes me realize how personal the act of cooking is when you feed someone you care about.

She rushes away after breakfast, back to her apartment to get changed before heading to work. Daniel leaves as well, leaving me sitting at the kitchen table, filled with a sense of contented well-being, until I make the mistake of checking my email on my phone.

Then my good mood evaporates. A scathing review of Seb New York, a note from Helen that she thinks someone's stealing from *Seb II's* kitchens, and worst of all, Juliette's set up a meeting with the franchise investors at ten-thirty, and it's nine-thirty now. I'm going to have to hustle to get there on time.

I call her, wondering why I'm so reluctant to move this deal forward. Juliette's absolutely right - time is of the essence in these kinds of deals.

"I might be late," I warn her when she picks up. "I'm juggling multiple crises, Juliette. This is a horrible time for this meeting... Next time, give me a bit more of a heads-up."

"I admire you for making time for what you think is important," she says snidely. I frown for a second, wondering what on earth she's talking about, and then my attention is distracted by another incoming call. It's Katya, the restaurant manager at *Seb New York*. I quickly promise Juliette I'll be there, and switch to Katya, muttering a curse under my breath. Ever since I promoted Ben to be the sous-chef at *Seb II*, we've been lurching about from one crisis to another, and I don't have the time to baby my chefs.

Sure enough, Katya's calling about Ben. "Sebastian," she says when I pick up, "Ben hasn't shown up for prep."

"What the absolute fuck?" I swear into the phone, glancing at my watch again to confirm the time. Yes, it's still nine-thirty. If Ben doesn't show up soon, we won't have enough time to set up for the dinner crowd. "You've tried calling him?"

"Of course," she replies, sounding offended. "I do know how to do my job."

Damn it. Ben's either passed out from drinking or nursing a killer hangover, and I don't care which one. He's the sous-chef at a restaurant that has two Michelin stars, *and he's not at work.* Daniel's advice to fire him sounds increasingly attractive. "Okay, Katya. I'll be back to the restaurant as soon as I can, but in the meanwhile, can you call Helen? She'll figure out what to do."

Mentally, I resolve to give Helen a raise. Every restauranteur in the world is sniffing around my staff, and Helen can work anywhere she wants. The fact that she's still with me speaks testaments to her loyalty and friendship. I might have had shitty parents, but I've been more than fortunate in my friends.

AN HOUR LATER, I'm still trying to reach Ben as I wait with Juliette in a beige conference room in some nondescript office building in Greenwich Village. I've had to scramble to get here on time from Daniel's Upper East Side townhouse. As a result I'm wearing the same black t-shirt and jeans that I wore last night, and I'm not happy about it. Damn Juliette. It wouldn't have killed her to give me more notice. "I'm not too casually dressed, am I?" I ask, my phone pressed against my ear.

She shrugs. "It isn't your suit they are interested in."

Maybe. What Juliette interprets as a trivial question about dress code is actually a deeper question about fitting in. Daniel would have understood that, I realize.

I thought getting the first Michelin star would banish my feeling of inadequacy, but maybe the damage is too deep. For the first sixteen years of my life, everyone told me I was stupid and that I'd amount to nothing. My parents. My teachers. The career counselors. Nobody in my sleepy Mississippi town thought I'd do anything with my life.

The scars still haven't totally healed, not even after the second Michelin star. Maybe they never will.

Juliette lifts her head up. "Get off the phone," she hisses. "The investors are here."

There are four of them, all looking like they are cut from the same rich-guy mold. Custom-tailored suits, handmade shoes. Expensive watches on their wrists. One of them, an older man who looks about fifty, eyes the tattoos that peek out from under my sleeves with a look of combined revulsion and fascination. I'm definitely from the wrong side of the tracks.

Once introductions have been performed, Juliette's crisp voice slices through the small talk. "Gentlemen," she says. "Let's get started, shall we?"

The youngest guy gets up. "Chef Ardalan," he starts, leaning forward and looking intently into my eyes. He's trying to look sincere, but it just comes across as contrived. "Imagine this." He presses a button and the presentation starts on the screen in front of us. "A Sebastian Ardalan restaurant in every city in America."

I listen to the guy talk, disquiet growing within me. He's giving off a sleazy, timeshare salesman vibe, and while the presentation is flashy, it is devoid of substance and is a complete waste of my time. If I wanted to look at slick graphics and animations, I would have gone to see a big-budget Hollywood movie. What I want are detail and numbers, and there's none here.

When they are finished, I lean forward, searching for the right words of diplomacy. It's a lot easier in the kitchen. There, I say what I think, and the rules are much simpler. "Gentlemen," I start. "I appreciate the time you've taken to meet with me. This was a great presentation but before we can move forward, I do need to dive deeper into the details. How many restaurants? How much control will I have over the menu? Where will we source ingredients? I'm sure you can appreciate that I've built my reputation on having the highest standards about food quality and service. I won't risk sullying that."

I'm not naive. I know that a restaurant chain will have different food standards than Seb New York. I also know that not all mid-market restaurants are created equal. In some of them, you can tell that the owners take pride in the food they serve. Others? Not so much.

"Of course, of course." This is the guy who was horrified by the tattoos. "Why don't we set up a meeting in a couple of weeks with all the particulars?" He gives Juliette a meaningful look, but she ignores it. He plows ahead anyway. "Now, as we've discussed with Juliette here, we'd like some guarantees before we do a lot of upfront work. If we could sign a letter of intent?"

Earlier this morning, Daniel had warned me about this. "Sign nothing until a lawyer reads it," he'd cautioned me. Even though he thinks this deal is a terrible idea, he's still there to help.

I shake my head. "I'm sorry," I say, keeping a tight lid on my temper. "I cannot sign anything at this stage. If that's unacceptable to you, then we can part ways now. No hard feelings."

"No, no, of course not," the man splutters. "It was just a formality, like I told Juliette. We won't worry about it."

Then why'd you ask? I think, but I know the answer. They think I'm stupid. Even now, even after all these years.

"THAT WAS A DISASTER," I say flatly to Juliette when we are outside. "Ben's not at work and Helen's juggling two restaurants on her own. Juliette, I don't have time for flashy presentations." I exhale. "Let's face it, they weren't ready."

"Be a little patient," she snaps. "This is an incredible opportunity for you. These guys are chomping at the bit at a chance to partner with you."

"They had no specifics. How many restaurants were they thinking of opening? I have no idea. Will they be pricing to compete with Ruth's Chris or with The Cheesecake Factory? Guess what? I don't know."

"Stop it." Juliette holds up an irritated hand. "This was an initial meeting. You heard them. They'll get you specifics."

"And signing the letter of intent? Are you fucking kidding me?"

"Yeah, that was out of line," she admits. "I warned them that you wouldn't sign anything. But about the rest of it, I think you are expecting too much too soon."

"I disagree. Daniel always has details. These guys just weren't prepared."

"For fuck's sake, not Daniel again." Her voice is thick with exasperation. "Damn it, Sebastian. Have you ever wondered why Daniel doesn't like this deal? Maybe he's happy being the only billionaire in the room. You ever think of that?"

I can only shake my head in disbelief. "Not even for an instant. I've known Daniel all my adult life, Juliette. You could not be more wrong in your assessment."

If she's flustered, she doesn't show it. "This is an amazing opportunity," she says again. "It's my job as your business adviser to bring in these deals."

"Then do your job. Make sure they have facts and figures the next time we meet. Because Ben's fucking imploding, and I don't have time to deal with this bullshit. That's what I hire you for."

"You seem to have plenty of time for some things," she mutters sullenly under her breath. I'd stop to ask her what the fuck she's talking about, but my phone chimes. It's finally Ben. I pick up the line, preparing to give him a piece of my mind.

She stalks away to her car, and I let her. I don't have time to deal with Juliette right now. I'm too busy fighting other fires.

24

Ponder and deliberate before you make a move.

— Sun Tzu, The Art of War

Daniel:

"Mr. Hartman is in your office," my assistant Sophie tells me as I walk into work Tuesday morning.

I frown. My calendar's booked solid for the whole morning, which means that Cyrus high-handedly bumped someone. "Who got displaced?" I ask Sophie as I hang up my coat on the hanger and pour myself a cup of coffee from the pot she keeps in the area outside my office.

"Marketing. I can reschedule them to this evening, if you'd like?"

What I'd like to do is see Bailey again this evening, but I nod instead at Sophie. "Sounds good," I tell her. "And Sophie, don't let Cyrus bump people again, okay? It's rude and disrespectful."

"Yes Sir," she says. "I'm sorry."

"I'm not blaming you," I tell her. "I know how Cyrus can be. Just don't let it happen again."

I'm more than a little irritated. Ryan Communications hasn't yet accepted our offer, and they are trying to drag the deal out by nitpicking on a hundred little things. Cyrus spent all weekend in Kansas, playing golf and schmoozing the guys on their board. He better have results for me.

"I thought I told you not to ride roughshod on Sophie," I bite out as I walk in.

He waves his hand. "Forget about your secretary," he says. "I thought you'd want a status update from Kansas City."

I settle down on my chair and lean back, glaring at him. This fucking deal. If I was managing it, I'd tell Ryan Communications to accept our bid or we walk. But for some reason, Cyrus isn't willing to do that. "So give me one," I tell him.

"I talked to Brant Hollister," he starts. "You know him? He's the chairman of their board."

"Yes, I'm quite aware of who the crucial players are in this deal, Cyrus, thank you." I don't hold back the sarcasm. "What did Hollister have to say? When's the deal coming up for a vote?"

"They want guarantees."

"What kind?"

He avoids my gaze. "Since some of the payment is in Hartman stock, they want some guarantees on leadership. They don't think you are taking being the CEO of Hartman seriously enough."

I've heard variations of this line for months now. Cyrus has made no progress at all. "Cyrus," I say, my voice danger-ously flat, "this deal has dragged on for months. In the meanwhile, other, better opportunities have come and gone, and we've missed them because our focus has been on Ryan Communications. Here's a guarantee for you. If Ryan does not sign in three weeks, we walk. Is that absolutely clear?"

"Don't go ballistic at me," he grouses. "I'm just the messenger."

"No. You are not just the messenger. You are the Chief Operating Officer of Hartman, Cyrus, and you are not making any progress. I find myself questioning your judgment."

He stops dead in his tracks. "I'm your uncle," he says, his voice cold. "I taught you everything you know."

"Aren't you the one who always tells me to put the firm first?" I snap. "Well, I am. Get the fucking Ryan Communications deal done, Cyrus. Else, I assure you, there will be consequences."

When Cyrus is gone, I lean back in my chair and look absently out of the window. Normally, the view of the city invigorates me, but today I just have a headache. Last night, I counseled Sebastian to fire his sous-chef Ben. Right now, I have a feeling that I'm going to need to take my own advice.

"Hey Sophie," I press the button on the phone to talk to my assistant.

"Yes, Mr. Hartman?"

"Can you arrange a lunch meeting with my mother, please? As soon as she's available."

If it's time to fire Cyrus, I need to enlist help. As ridiculous as it sounds, I need my mother. After all, she is the biggest shareholder in the company.

25

I know not all that may be coming, but be it what it will, I'll go to it laughing.

— HERMAN MELVILLE, MOBY-DICK

Bailey:

The next two days are a blur.

Work is busy, but because I spent most of the weekend in my office, I'm done with my end of a paper I'm co-writing with Dr. Pierre Landrieu. Our topic is the adaptability of gender roles in isolated communities. My section is predominantly about my experiences in the Taiga, and requires no new research, just a re-read of the diaries and the blog I kept during my time there. Dr. Landrieu's section will include his experiences from his time in Patagonia. Pierre Landrieu is a star in my world - one of the pioneering voices in cultural anthropology, and I couldn't be more thrilled to co-write a paper with him.

I get several teasing messages from my girls about

missing Monday night drinking. Each one makes me blush. Gabby doesn't text me - instead, she calls and demands that we have lunch. "I refuse to be kept in the dark, Bails," she says.

We meet for lunch and I tell her everything, Daniel's stupid comment Friday night, the gift of vodka, which I finally picked up from FedEx, the Hartman Foundation grant to NYU, and finally, the proceedings of Monday night.

"So," I ask her when I'm done, "do you think I'm a fool?"

"Normally I'd give you grief for sleeping with Daniel after he acted like an asshole," she says thoughtfully. "But you know what? I'm tempted to give him a one-time pass. For some reason, Daniel Hartman is always in the tabloids. He's probably sick of it."

My heart sinks a little. Daniel didn't come across as a player, but I can't really trust my judgment about men. After all, I spent eleven months with Trevor. My instincts are horrible. "Is he always in the tabloids? What about?"

"That's the thing," she replies, taking a bite out of her egg salad sandwich. "He's never doing anything particularly newsworthy. He could be walking down the street, and he'd make the Post. He's dated some Hollywood actresses casually, but nothing that warrants this kind of coverage."

"Yikes. He's dated actresses?" I wince. "He's definitely slumming it then."

"Will you stop?" she demands. "You are beautiful and smart and accomplished."

"That's what they keep saying," I confess. "Sebastian and Daniel. They get very irritated with me when I'm insecure."

"In that case," Gabby announces, "I think I like them. It is immensely irritating when you put yourself down. So this wasn't a one-time thing?"

"I don't think so," I reply, crossing my fingers under the

table. "I mean, it definitely has an expiration date, how could it not? But hey, as long as they still want to do it, I'm game. They are so hot."

"That's awesome, Bails." Gabby seems genuinely happy for me. I wonder if she realizes she's not entirely over her own threesome. Even now, two months after the fact, there's a certain wistfulness in her eyes when she talks about Carter and Dominic. She's been hurt by men before, and she's wary for a reason, but because I care about my friend's happiness, I wish she'd try to find them. They were good to her, and she needs to date more men like that.

I'VE NEVER BEEN EXCITED about going to play a game of pool, but I'm almost giddy with anticipation by the time Wednesday evening comes around. Per Daniel's instructions, I get to the Maxwell Club early, which I can assure you almost never happens, but when I arrive, both men are already there waiting for me.

Thankfully, Juliette is nowhere to be seen. I haven't told Sebastian about my encounter with her in the bathroom last week. I'm not really catty, and I'm convinced that complaining about her will only make me sound petty and childish.

The guys smirk when they see me. "You're planning something," I accuse them with a grin as I walk up. "I can tell."

"Yup." Sebastian grins widely. "Come with me," he says, gesturing for me to follow him. "Daniel would like us to stay relatively inconspicuous," he mocks. "So he'll allow us a head start."

Daniel makes a rude gesture at Sebastian, and I stifle a giggle. Sebastian is unfazed. "Coming, Bailey?" he asks me.

After Gabby's revelation about Daniel attracting more than his share of tabloid attention, I've forgiven him for that stupid '*keep this out of the press*' comment. However, teasing him is fair game. "Of course," I tell Sebastian meekly. "You know me, I'm always obedient."

Daniel snorts. "We'll find out soon enough how obedient you are," he promises, sending a shiver of heat through me. I'm dying of curiosity, but I'm not going to give in and ask them what they are going to do. Biting my tongue, I follow Sebastian.

"Fascinating place, the Maxwell Club," he says conversationally, as we walk toward the restrooms. *Are we going to do it there?* I wonder. I'm not opposed to washroom sex on principle, though I'd prefer somewhere less germ-filled.

Before we get there, we stop in front of a door marked *Staff*. Sebastian waves a keycard at the lock, and the door opens. Another long corridor stretches in front of us. Sebastian seems to know where he's going. He takes my hand in his, and leads me forward.

"How do you know where to go?"

He chuckles. "Daniel told me. He has a signature line, as I'm sure you'll find out. *It's my business to know.*"

"Is it his business to know?" I grin. "I can't imagine how the back corridors of a private club in Manhattan concern Daniel."

"That's because you aren't using enough imagination," a smooth voice says from behind us. I jump and pivot around, but it's just Daniel, his brown eyes gleaming as he struggles not to laugh at me.

"You scared me," I accuse him. "Why do you know about the back rooms here?"

He links his arm in mine. "A few months ago, a reporter for the New York Times did a feature about this place on its hundredth anniversary. At that time, the club president offered a few of us tours of the back, including the closed off sections."

"Let me guess, it's really a sex club."

"Would you like it to be, Bailey?" he asks, his voice rich with amusement. "Do you want to go to one?" His eyes gleam.

"Do you fantasize about being on display in front of everyone, Bailey?" Sebastian prompts. "Is that it? You have a secret exhibitionist streak in you?"

"Is there a real sex club here?" There's a tremor in my voice and my footsteps slow down. I'm not sure I'm ready for that. Not just yet. Even though each word they utter causes the coils of lust in my core to tighten painfully, and even though my nipples are hard pebbles, poking out through my t-shirt.

"No," Sebastian admits. "Though it was interesting to watch your reaction."

I punch his arm. "Stop laughing at me," I tell him. "Else I'm going back out there and focusing on my pool game."

"Oh, you'll be focusing on your pool game tonight," Daniel says blandly. "In fact, it's to give you a little bit of extra incentive that we've brought you here." He stops in front of a door and waves his wallet at it. The lock turns green and he turns the handle. "Come on, Bailey," he invites. "Or are you afraid?"

"Of you?" I give him my most challenging look, and move into the room, with an exaggerated sway of my hips. "Definitely not."

The sparsely decorated room we enter looks like a disused conference room. There's nothing the slightest bit erotic about it, yet my eyes fixate on the table in the middle of the room, and I wonder if we are going to have sex on it.

"No, we aren't," Sebastian interprets my expression correctly. "But I like the way you think. Drop your pants, honey. We have a present for you."

The present is a glass butt plug. It looks intimidating and heavy, and I gulp. In theory, I'm game for anal sex. In practice? I can't see how this object is going to fit in my ass.

"Relax, we have lube," Daniel says. He notices that I'm still clothed. "Pants down, Bailey," he scolds. "We're running out of time. You need to practice your pool game."

"With the butt plug in me?" I squeak, my voice shrill. "Are you serious?"

"Absolutely," Sebastian says. "Daniel and I have been chatting about your game. There's nothing wrong with your mechanics. You just don't think you can win. So, today, we are giving you something else to focus on."

"A butt plug?" Though I remain skeptical, my hands are undoing the waistband on my jeans, and pushing them down to my knees, along with my panties. "The great secret to helping me at pool is to stuff a butt plug up my ass? How on earth did I fail to think of that?"

Smack. Daniel's palm connects with my ass in a stinging blow. Undoubtedly, this is punishment for the sarcasm. I turn to look at him, and find his eyes twinkling at me. "Want another?"

The stinging has faded into a dull prickle, but the gush of wetness from my core remains. *I liked that.* I liked the unexpected harshness of that slap. The slight sense of danger I feel turns me on. "Whatever," I say flippantly, knowing that I'll make him mad.

His lips curl into a smile. His palm connects harshly

once again with my bottom. "Bend over the table," he orders.

I obey, my breasts mashing into the cool glass of the tabletop, and Sebastian gently kicks my legs open wide. "You spread for us, do you understand?"

"If I feel like it." My words are airy, my body begs for another hard slap. I get one, but this time, Daniel's palm doesn't hit my ass. He connects with my pussy and I hiss in pain as a sharp ache radiates from the spot where I've been spanked.

Sebastian's hands steady me instantly, his fingers soothing me. "Let's get the plug in." He brushes away a strand of hair from my face, and his lips find mine. "You okay, Bailey?" he whispers. "It's just a game. It stops whenever you say so."

"I know." My voice is hushed. "I'm fine. It feels good to let go."

"There's always a safety net, sweetheart," Daniel's voice is quiet. "You won't fall. We won't let you."

Did Daniel just call me *sweetheart*? What the heck is that about? I want to stop and process that, but I feel the trickle of lube at my anus, and one of them inserts two fingers into me to prepare me for the plug.

My ass is still warm from my earlier spanks, my pussy already wet. When the two of them push the butt plug slowly and steadily into my anus, there's a burning stretch, but I'm still turned on.

"Are you trying to push a watermelon up there?" I bite out. "How big does this plug need to be, anyway?"

Sebastian enters my line of sight. "Bailey," he shakes his head, smirking. "You have seen my dick, haven't you? Trust me, you'll appreciate our consideration when it's time for both of us to take you."

A vision of them stretching my pussy and my ass with their dicks flashes in my mind, and this time, I can't keep back the moan. "Fuck, that's hot," I groan. "You guys are killing me here."

The plug keeps pushing against me, and finally, with a pop, it's seated in place, and my anus has closed around the neck. "There you go," Daniel pats my ass, as if pushing butt plugs into my butt is a commonplace occurrence for him. His hard, bulging erection proves that he's not quite as detached as he appears. "Get your pants back on. It's time to play pool."

"What?" My cry is plaintive. "You can't key me up this way and not get me off... that's not fair."

Daniel laughs. "Life isn't fair, princess," he points out.

"Says the billionaire," I retort sullenly.

Sebastian pulls me into his body. "Stop pouting," he mutters in my ear, his voice vibrating against me in a way that makes me want to grind my ass against his erection. "We'll get you off tonight. After you win."

I want to tell them that I have fingers and am perfectly capable of taking care of my own pleasure. But who am I fooling? I need Daniel and Sebastian to make me come. I want to be bracketed between their hard bodies.

The weight of the butt plug in my ass acts as a physical anchor, holding back my sassy retort. "Fine," I say instead. "Let's go play."

26

It's not the size of the dog in the fight, it's the size of the fight in the dog.

— MARK TWAIN

Bailey:

We have about an hour of practice time before Clark and Juliette show up, and I take full advantage. First, I order a couple of different appetizer platters, after making Daniel and Sebastian promise they'll share the food with me. "Didn't get a chance to eat all day?" Daniel asks me, looking bemused at the amount of food I've ordered.

"I like variety," I wink at him. It's fun knowing that I have a butt plug in my ass. It makes me feel quite naughty. "Are we going to play?" I ask them once I'm done ordering enough food to feed a small village. "Because I need to beat Trevor. He's a dickwad."

Though I've had other things on my mind since Sunday,

I haven't forgotten Trevor's mockery of my pool league aspirations. When I tell Sebastian and Daniel about the way he sneered, their gazes grow dark. "I'm going to look forward to the moment when you kick this guy's ass, Bailey," Sebastian says.

Daniel doesn't say anything, but I can tell he's pissed, and his irritation warms my heart. Yes, they have fifty grand riding on me beating my opponent at the end of season tournament, but it's more than that. I think they care.

As I play a friendly match with Sebastian, emotions take a backseat to lust. I'm very aware of the plug lodged in my ass. I'm terrified that it's going to fall out, so I keep my lower muscles firmly clenched and hope that it doesn't move.

Sebastian misses his shot and I move forward, chalking my cue. I'm about to bend forward when a low hum pulses through my body. I almost scream with shock, then I see the grins of amusement that both Daniel and Sebastian are trying to conceal. I walk over on shaking legs to them. "Is this thing on a remote?" I hiss out, careful to keep my voice low so the players at the adjoining tables won't hear me. "How am I expected to focus when I'm struggling not to come?"

"Poor Bailey," Daniel says to me. He wraps his arm around my lower back, and pulls me into his body. "What we are asking of you," he murmurs into my throat, "is so difficult. But you are going to win tonight, aren't you? You are going to rise to the challenge."

"We're in public," I mutter weakly. "Someone might be watching."

He releases me with a bemused expression on his face. "Would you believe I forgot?" he asks no one in particular. "I never forget." He shakes his head. "The effect you have on me, Bailey..."

"Make your shot," Sebastian says to me. "Forget the vibrations of the butt plug. Eye on the ball, and only the ball."

How? I want to scream. I can't tear my gaze away from the expression of naked heat on Daniel's face.

"Bailey," Sebastian says again, this time with a note of warning in his voice. "Play."

I draw in a deep breath. I'm shivering with pent-up lust and it takes real effort to pull away from Daniel and walk up to the table. As I move, I feel the weight of someone's stare on me. A prickling sensation of dread claws at my spine, and I look up, trying to find the source of my unease.

She's staring at me from the bar, her expression unreadable. Juliette.

Fuck. Are we in trouble?

THE FIRST CHANCE I GET, I nudge Daniel's side, pretending like I'm reaching for some hummus and pita bread. Sebastian's lining up for a shot at the eight ball. Normally, I'd be watching him play, but I have other things on my mind right now.

"Please don't freak out," I start nervously. Daniel's paranoid about his privacy, and I'm dreading his displeasure. "I think Juliette saw you kiss my throat earlier."

"Where is she?" His voice doesn't give anything away. Only a tightening of his grip on his glass betrays his tension.

"She was at the bar," I tell him. "She's not there now."

"Okay." His fingers lace in mine. "Thank you for telling me."

"That's it?" I ask in astonishment. "No scene? You aren't angry with me?"

He looks puzzled. "Why would I be angry with you?" he asks me, his brow furrowed. "It was my mistake, not yours." He shrugs. "Juliette is unlikely to go to the tabloids," he adds. "Sebastian will fire her in a heartbeat if she talks to the press. She's smart enough to realize that."

"You are pretty ruthless, you realize that?" I ask him, choosing a tortilla chip that is absolutely covered with cheese and munching on it. "You are talking about ruining someone's career."

"No," he corrects. "I'm not. I'm merely pointing out that every action has consequences. Wouldn't you defend yourself if you were attacked?"

I think about my quest to learn to play pool well enough so I can kick Trevor's ass at the end of season tournament, all because he'd lawyered up and demanded rent from me. My entire plan is about revenge, and my stakes aren't even as high as Daniel's. "I would," I say, grimacing. "I think I've just discovered I'm kind of petty."

He smiles at me. "I don't think you are petty, red," he teases. "But you know what they say about a redhead losing her temper."

"What do they say?" I try to glare at him, but I can't keep from grinning.

He winks. "I'll tell you tonight if you come home with us."

I laugh, forgetting about Juliette's stare as I flirt with Daniel. "I'm definitely coming home with you," I tell him. "You owe me an orgasm. Both you and Sebastian."

Sebastian walks up. From the look on his face, he's heard that last sentence. "Don't worry, Bailey," he whispers in my ear. "I always pay my debts."

27

It's no use going back to yesterday, because I was a different person then.

— LEWIS CARROLL, ALICE'S ADVENTURES IN
WONDERLAND

Bailey:

I barely pay attention to Clark, to the opposing team or to the games that unfold in front of us. As the evening goes by, Daniel and Sebastian have turned on the remote and made my butt plug vibrate too many times to count. Everything becomes a haze to me, and the only thing I can think of is that if I don't come, I will explode.

Finally, the final match of the night is played, and it is time to leave. As I'm putting on my coat, Juliette comes up to Sebastian. "I'll have proofs of your book for review tomorrow," she says. "Should I drop them off at the restaurant in the morning?"

"I'm not going to be there," Sebastian responds. "I'm

going to be meeting with suppliers tomorrow. Can you drop it off over the weekend?"

She shakes her head. "I'm not in town."

Daniel cuts in impatiently. "Why don't you drop them off at my place? I won't be at home, but Mrs. Nowak can let you in."

"Sounds good." She nods tersely at the three of us. "Have a good evening."

"You too," I say politely. I don't want to make an enemy of Juliette.

THE MOMENT we step into Daniel's mirrored foyer and the front door closes behind us, I'm sandwiched between their rock hard bodies. "All evening," Daniel's voice vibrates against my throat, "I've been thinking of you. Of the butt plug lodged in your ass. Of your wet, slick pussy."

My back is pressed against Sebastian's chest. His arms lock around my waist, keeping me close. My breathing comes faster and my heart pounds in my ribcage. We've had sex before, the three of us, but anal is new to me. Anticipation turns my nipples hard, and a tiny wisp of fear sets me shivering.

Daniel's hands slide down, infinitely slowly, down my forearms. "Do you trust us?" His voice is hoarse with his own lust, gravelly with need. "Or are you afraid?"

I look into his brown eyes. "Can I not be both?" I ask softly. "It'll hurt, won't it?"

Sebastian's teeth nip sharply at the soft skin at my shoulder, and intense desire shoots through me. "Did that hurt?" he asks.

"Yes."

"Was it good?"

Oh god yes. Who am I kidding? I want this. I want to know them in this most intimate of ways. All evening, the butt plug buried in my ass has been making me aware, needy. Now, adventure beckons and I'm ready.

Daniel kneels in front of me, pulling my jeans down so they bunch at my ankles. His broad palms rip my panties. "Hey," I protest half-heartedly, but he ignores my yelp.

"Spread your legs for me, Bailey," he orders. "I want to taste every inch of your pussy."

Sebastian's grip holds me up, thank heavens, because my body becomes boneless as Daniel's tongue plunges into my center. As his lips and teeth nibble, nip and suck, his fingers close around the plug that's embedded in my ass, and he pulls it out slowly.

I gasp as I feel my hole stretch to accommodate the widest part of the plug. He almost pulls it out of my body completely before pushing it back in. My entire body tingles, from my fingertips to my toes, and the only word I can use to describe the way I feel is *naughty*. I feel wicked and wanton, held against one man's chest while another man touches me so intimately, so possessively.

"You like that, Bailey?" Sebastian's voice is smoky. "Don't be coy. Look in the mirror."

Oh. The mirror. I'd forgotten about it.

I am transfixed by my reflection. My pale thighs are a stark contrast to the black fabric of my t-shirt. Sebastian's biceps bulge as he holds me still. Daniel's head is nestled between my legs, and I watch the powerful muscles of his back ripple under his shirt.

"Do you know what I see, Bailey?" His voice has taken on a ragged edge. "I see the way you bite down on your lip when Daniel's tongue circles your clitoris. I see the way you clench your fists when he plays with the plug." The cadence of his tone changes, and he issues a crisp order. "Pinch your nipples for me."

"Through my top?" I don't recognize the way I sound. Throaty. Breathless.

Daniel shoves two fingers into my wet pussy and I moan aloud. My hands move up to caress my breasts, feather-light touches that have only one purpose - to drive Daniel and Sebastian as wild as they drive me. My nails scratch my nubs and I hold Sebastian's gaze in the mirror as I squirm against his thickening erection. "Do you like that?" I whisper.

There's a blaze in his eyes. "Take off the shirt. Now."

Cool air wafts over my skin as I shed the garment. Daniel sits back on his haunches, his eyes locked on my body, and the instant the garment flies across the room, he continues his assault on my pussy.

"Put your hands behind your back." Sebastian isn't done with his instructions. "Touch my dick."

Gladly. I run my palms up and down his denim-covered shaft, while Daniel's tongue sucks and swirls and relentlessly and repeatedly brings me to the edge of orgasm. "Please," I pant out. All evening long, I've been one hair-trigger away from release. He has to stop torturing me.

I stroke Sebastian's dick, faster and faster in my own desperate race to my climax. "Bailey," he clenches out, "oh god baby, fuck."

'Oh god baby fuck' pretty much describes the way I'm feeling. My eyes are over-bright in my face, and just as Sebastian described it, I'm biting the edge of my lip, over and over, as Daniel's mouth, tongue, lips all feast on me.

Then a dam bursts, and wave after wave of the sweet release flow through me. I close my eyes and throw my head back against Sebastian's shoulder, and I surrender to pleasure.

Daniel keeps going. His tongue sweeps a long, lazy path along every inch of my slit. "Stop," I whisper, but he shakes his head

"We are just getting started," he chuckles. "But in the interests of keeping you warm, perhaps we should move this to the bedroom."

I hadn't realized I was cold, not until now, but I notice the chillness in the foyer when he mentions it. "I was otherwise distracted," I grin, reaching for my clothing. "Again, it seems as if I'm half naked and you guys are fully dressed."

"Don't bother about clothes, baby," Sebastian assures me, taking the bundle of garments out of my hand and holding it out of reach. "We'll be getting naked soon."

Fine. I can walk to Daniel's bedroom wearing a bra, a butt plug and nothing else. No problem, right?

It takes more courage than going to Siberia did.

When I'm talking to them, when we are shooting pool and drinking vodka, I can forget how good-looking they are, and how out of my league. It's a little harder when I'm half-naked, with all of the flab on display, and their bodies are sleek, muscled, chiseled perfection.

"Should you be thinking of anything other than sex right now, Bailey?" Daniel inquires politely as we climb the stairs. Crap. He's on to me. I can't allow myself to forget that Daniel's very good at reading me. They both are.

"No."

"Indeed. Perhaps another orgasm will help."

My pussy is puffy and swollen, and the thought of another climax fills me with mingled apprehension and anticipation. Since I don't like refusing such a kind offer - *come on, if a gorgeous guy that you like is volunteering to make you come, you accept!* - I just lower my lashes demurely. "As you wish," I say softly.

"What are you, Buttercup?" Sebastian pushes open the door to Daniel's bedroom.

"Wait. Guys watch the Princess Bride?" I turn toward Sebastian, surprised.

Neither of them reply. Daniel's dick is tenting his trousers, and Sebastian's bulge is clearly visible under his jeans.

They take off their clothes. Sebastian lifts his t-shirt over his head, causing the muscles around his abdomen to clench and ripple. Daniel throws the jacket over an armchair and moves to undo his cufflinks. I watch both of them, almost panting with lust. So hot. So very hot, and for the space of this evening, they are all mine.

There's a quiver in my stomach as I think about our very temporary fling. Nothing's been defined, nothing's been stated, but I know this can't last.

"Get on the bed," Daniel growls and I hop to it, glad to leave my gloomy thoughts behind. He's undressed fully while I was lost in thought, and he joins me, as does Sebastian. Hands unclasp my bra, and my breasts tumble loose.

We position ourselves so that I'm lying on the bed with Daniel behind me. Sebastian's on his knees in front of me, his cock jutting into my face. "Is this a hint?" I grin as I lean forward to take him into my mouth.

"Mmm," he groans. "Yes. Definitely a hint."

It is also a distraction. The mattress shifts as Daniel moves behind me, reaching for the lube on the nightstand. The butt plug is pulled out of me, and fresh lube coats my tight bud. "Relax," Daniel scolds. "Do you want to get spanked?"

I can't answer - Sebastian's cock is in my mouth. The answer is, however, yes. *I always want to get spanked.*

Sebastian's hand presses against the back of my head, keeping me in place. With his other hand, he's tugging at my erect nipples, pinching, pulling, and tweaking them till I'm half-crazed with lust. In the meanwhile, Daniel's fingers spread the lube all around my asshole. He pushes one finger in, and I moan around Sebastian's cock.

"You okay?"

I nod. The moan wasn't one of pain - the butt plug has done its job, and I've grown accustomed to its girth. Daniel kisses my shoulder. "Good girl," he says softly, adding another finger and twisting them in me. "Relax. I promise it'll be good for you."

I'm not tense, I want to retort. Though I've climaxed only minutes ago, I'm painfully aroused once again.

His fingers leave and I hear the sound of a condom wrapper tear. I instinctively tense up, until I realize what I'm doing, then I force myself to relax. I have nothing to stress about. Daniel isn't going to hurt me.

"Good girl," he says once again. Sebastian's hands tangle in my hair and caress my cheek, while Daniel's thick cock nudges at my anus. He pushes into me the same way he pushed the plug in earlier - slowly and steadily. I feel stretched, and it's an odd feeling, but it isn't painful.

"Oh," I say through the mouthful of cock. "That's not bad."

'That's not bad' is an understatement. Daniel gives me some time to get used to him, then he pulls out almost completely, and slides in again. This time, I can't hold back my moan of pleasure.

Sebastian pulls back, and his dick leaves my mouth with a *pop.* "Are you okay?" he asks with a shade of concern.

My nails dig into Daniel's 1500 thread-count Egyptian cotton sheets. My face contorts with the lust that's rampaging through my blood. "Yes."

"In that case..." he says with a grin, "get your mouth back on me."

I'm happy to. In the oral-sex balance sheet, I'm solidly in the red, and I too believe in paying my debts.

"Fuck, Bailey, you are so tight, sweetheart," Daniel grinds out, his fingers digging into my hips. "Oh god, I'm not going to last very long here."

I pull away. "In that case," I tell Sebastian bossily, "you should get in there. I think I was promised a dick in both my pussy and ass tonight."

They start laughing and Sebastian kisses me with passion. "So very demanding." He obligingly reaches for a condom and shifts so he's in front of me.

Daniel's grip tightens around my waist, and he flips me so that he's lying on his back and I'm resting on him. His dick is still buried in my ass. It's an impressive feat. I'd normally have something snarky to say, but I'm enjoying the way he feels in me far too much to risk ruining it.

"She's soaked," Sebastian marvels. "You like this, don't you? I've never seen you as wet as you are right now." He rolls on the condom and moves so he's in the space between my knees. "Hold still," he instructs, holding his cock in his hand and swiping it up my slit.

My legs are in the air, spread wide apart. "Stop teasing," I choke out, as Daniel's thumbs run maddening circles over my tender nipples. "Don't make me beg."

"If you insist." Sebastian's hands hold my thighs apart, and his dick thrusts into me.

Hard.

Nothing held back.

Long, powerful, unforgiving strokes.

Exactly the way I want it.

I whimper and moan, twist and flail. I'm full - so filled by their hard cocks. When one of them pulls out, the other pushes in, and just like that, they have a rhythm going. In and out. Faster. Harder. More.

The heat rises, molten lava waiting to spill. Their breathing is harsh and labored. Sebastian's eyes stay on me, Daniel's fingers run over my body. "Not going to last," one of them clenches out. Which one? I can't tell. It could have been Daniel. It could have been Sebastian. It could have even been me.

We aren't three distinct people now. The boundaries have dissolved in this moment. We are overwhelmed by our desire, by the rising pressure as we tumble toward our climaxes. Then I reach my personal point of no return. My nails dig into Sebastian's back, and every muscle tightens as my orgasm rips through me.

They aren't far behind. I hear muttered curses, then their grip on me tightens, and the pounding doubles in frequency. They come within seconds of each other, and we all collapse on the bed in a sweaty, sated heap.

"I DON'T THINK Juliette likes me," I say thoughtfully, when the fog in my brain clears enough that I can form words.

Sebastian shakes his head. "It's not you, it's me. She's been working with some investors who want to set up a restaurant chain, and I went to meet with them yesterday, but it was a waste of time. She thinks I should give them another chance."

"I didn't think you needed outside investors." I'm almost

too tired for conversation, but this is interesting. "You know, because of your resident billionaire."

"Resident billionaire," Daniel snorts. "You have such charming names for me, Bailey. This isn't the sort of project I'd invest in."

"Why?"

"He doesn't approve of it," Sebastian answers. He doesn't sound annoyed by Daniel's failure to invest in this project.

"Why?" I ask again.

Daniel shrugs. "Sebastian works too hard."

I roll my eyes. "Pot calling the kettle black much?" I ask him.

He smiles. "Fair enough," he concedes. "Everyone in this room is guilty of that particular sin. It's easier to tell your friends that they should relax than it is to take your own advice."

I snuggle into their bodies, and pull a pillow over my head. "I'm taking your advice," I say, and my voice comes out muffled. "I'm going to sleep."

"Goodnight, sweetheart," Daniel says, affection tinting his voice. Okay. This is the third time he's called me sweetheart. Seriously weird.

28

You're entirely bonkers. But I'll tell you a secret. All the best people are.

— LEWIS CARROLL, ALICE'S ADVENTURES IN
WONDERLAND

Daniel:

My mother's social life is a lot fuller than I think it is, so it isn't until Friday that we manage to have lunch. She's picked a cafe where the smell of incense hangs thick in the air, and every server has multiple piercings. In the custom Armani suit I'm wearing, I feel very out of place.

"You could have warned me," I tell her with a grin, knowing that she's secretly amused by my discomfort. "I would have worn my Bob Marley t-shirt."

"Do you own a Bob Marley t-shirt?" she asks with interest.

"I have hidden depths, mother," I tell her. "You'd be surprised."

She laughs. "It's more likely to be you than your sister," she says, launching on her favorite rant. "Seriously, that girl and her stuck-up fiancé."

"Mom," I say patiently. "Leave Sue be. She likes Graham well enough, and that should be all that matters for us." I can't bring myself to believe that Sue could love Graham. He's young and ambitious, and wants to go into politics. He's very... straight-laced. "I didn't ask you to lunch to discuss her."

"No," she agrees. "Tell me about the other girl. Did you apologize? Did she forgive you?"

My mother likes to know what's going on in our lives, and I should have known I'd get an inquisition today. The last time I saw her, we'd had lunch with the president of NYU, and we were too busy discussing the details of the Hartman endowment for my mother to quiz me. Not today. Today, she's looking for answers.

I find myself strangely reluctant to talk about Bailey. "It's fine," I tell her. "I don't want to get into details."

She ignores my words with practiced ease. "What's her name?" she probes.

"Bailey." My mother is like a bloodhound on a trail. When she starts her line of questioning, my sister and I have learned to fold early. It's easier that way. "She's an assistant professor at NYU. She teaches Cultural Anthropology and she's up for tenure this year in a severely underfunded department."

"Ah." She tries to hide her smile. "That explains the grant to NYU's Liberal Arts departments. I should have known from the grand gesture that you were wooing someone. Remember Natalie?"

"It wasn't a grand gesture," I say automatically, wincing as I remember the Natalie episode, as my family likes to call it.

One evening when I was sixteen, I was trying to plan a romantic evening for the girl I had the hots for, and I'd asked JP, the family butler, to set up a fireworks show. He'd tried to protest about the expenditure, but I was a teenager and I didn't listen. When the bill came in, I found out my fireworks display had cost thirty thousand dollars.

I smile at the memory of how pissed my father had been. "I thought dad was going to have a coronary."

She laughs fondly. "He was not happy with you," she agrees.

"That's an understatement," I note dryly. "He told me I was burning money, yelled at me for an hour, and then grounded me for a month."

"You would have been in worse trouble had you not stood up for JP. When you told your dad that JP was not to blame, and you'd accept your punishment, but he wasn't to take it out on JP, I think your dad almost cried."

"You've never told me this."

She smiles. "You were a teenager who'd just spent thousands of dollars on fireworks," she replies. "Your father was proud of you that day. He thought your heart was in the right place."

My father died seven years ago, and I still miss him. Hearing the muted sadness in my mother's voice, I know she does too. They met when she was twenty-four and he was twenty five. She was a poster child for the seventies, and he was the son of a billionaire. It shouldn't have worked, but it did. My parents are the reason I believe in love.

"Why haven't I met Bailey?"

Because I'm in a pretty unconventional relationship, and

I'm not sure what my mother will think about it. Heck, I'm not even sure what I think of it. Originally, it was all about physical attraction and nothing else. But the more time the three of us spend together, the more I'm coming to realize that what we have together transcends sex, and that terrifies me.

I settle for a half-answer. "I'm not dating her," I reply. "Besides, you hated the last woman I introduced you to."

"Megan," my mother says in distaste, referring to a very short-lived relationship, "was not good for you. However, I didn't interfere, did I?"

"No, you didn't," I say fondly. My parents have always left me to live my own life, and have only offered advice if I've asked for it. "A point in your favor."

"I agree," she says. "So why aren't you dating her?"

Bloodhound.

"Invasive discussions about my personal life are not the reason we are having lunch," I tell her. "I wanted to talk to you about Cyrus."

She frowns. "Why?" she demands. "I was quite looking forward to my meal. Why ruin it?"

The waitress finally ambles over to us and hands us menus. It's a pretty laid back place, evidently, and things like serving us food doesn't seem to be too high on her priority list. I glance at the offerings briefly and order a lentil salad. My mother orders something with kale in it, which makes me shudder. Not even Sebastian can convince me to eat kale. "It's good for you," my mother says, looking at the expression of mild revulsion on my face.

"If you say so," I tell her and wait for the waitress to walk away before continuing my conversation. After the Piper incident, I'm a lot more careful about paying attention to my surroundings. "So, Cyrus."

"Fine," she sighs. "Tell me about Cyrus."

I quickly fill her in on the Kansas City project, and Cyrus' abysmal lack of progress over it. "I might have to fire Cyrus if this deal doesn't come through."

She raises an eyebrow. "That seems extreme, coming from you."

"It isn't just this deal," I explain. "Cyrus is rude and high-handed to the employees. He treats my admin like dirt. He's just not pleasant to be around. He's exhausting my reservoir of good-will.

"You want to know if I'll back you up, if it comes to a board vote."

I roll my eyes. "I expect you'll back me up," I tell her. "What are you going to do, vote against your favorite child? I just thought you'd appreciate a heads-up. Besides," I look dubiously at the salad that the waitress has just deposited in front of me, "having lunch with you is always an interesting experience."

She chuckles. "I love both you and Susan equally," she says loyally. "Of course I'll vote in your favor. But it would look better if you have the rest of the board on your side as well."

"I'm working on it," I tell her. "Half the board are grand-dad's old golf buddies, and they are ready to believe that I'm letting down the good name of the Hartmans."

"Yes," she says dryly. "I've heard a few of their grum-blings. *'It's the mother,'* Alison Strauss said once when she was talking about you. *'You can tell by the breeding.'*"

"Alison Strauss is a miserable old hag," I tell her. "You aren't bothered by her, are you?"

She shakes her head. "No, Danny, how could I be? This has been my reality for the last thirty seven years." She looks sad. "When your dad was alive, the two of us could laugh about it. But Graham's family thinks I'm from the wrong side of the tracks too. It just gets old, that's all."

I can't imagine Graham in this place, but I can absolutely see both Bailey and Sebastian here. Sebastian will want to say hello to the chef. Bailey will order every single thing on the menu, because she likes variety. They'd both fit in perfectly, because they both have a certain kindness and grace and an innate desire to make everyone around them feel comfortable.

The realization strikes me out of the blue. I'm starting to fall in love with Bailey Moore. For the first time, I can see the glimmerings of a future that involves something other than running the family firm. I don't know her very well, and we haven't spent a lot of time together, but sometimes, *you just know.*

"Hey mom," I say. "You know our Sunday family lunches?"

She raises an eyebrow.

"In a few weeks, once this stupid Kansas City deal is over, I'm bringing Bailey *and* Sebastian to it."

Sebastian has come to lunch many times, he won't be a new addition to the gathering. But she hears the emphasis I've placed on the words *Bailey and Sebastian*, and her eyes widen as she processes what I've left unsaid. You have to hand it to my mother. She's not slow on the uptake.

I realize I'm holding my breath as I wait for her to react, but I shouldn't have been nervous. She starts chuckling, then, unable to contain her mirth, her chuckles turn to helpless laughter. "Oh dear," she says, wiping the tears away from her eyes, "The expression on Graham's face is going to be priceless." Her hand rests on top of mine. "I cannot wait."

29

Whoever receives friends and does not participate in the preparation of their meal does not deserve to have friends.

— Jean Anthelme Brillat-Savarin

Sebastian:

The next two weeks are idyllic.

Juliette's off my back for the time being, since her investment consortium still hasn't provided me with the numbers I'm looking for. "I'm following up all the time," she assures me. I nod, secretly grateful that her relentless focus is being turned to someone else.

At the restaurants, Ben seems to have settled down, and Helen reports that she's whipping the line cooks into shape at *Seb II*. Our Yelp reviewers seem largely positive, and night after night, our tables are fully booked. The second Michelin star is doing wonders for our bottom line.

"I'm making you richer," I quip to Daniel as we watch Bailey play pool on Wednesday night. In a few short weeks, her improvement has been amazing. Today, she's circling the table, her movements confident, looking for her next shot. Such a difference from the timid mouse who was afraid of her breasts grazing the table. Fuck me, those gorgeous tits are a weapon. The poor guy playing opposite her can't keep his eyes away from them.

Bailey walks over to us, interrupting my dark thoughts about her opponent's eyes and where he can put them. "Which ball should I aim for?" She frowns. "I don't want him to run the table if I miss."

Per pool league rules, Bailey can use two *'advice'* breaks. Daniel's paying more attention to the game, so he responds. "Try for the green," he says. "Even if you miss, the cue ball is going to be in a terrible position for his follow-up shot, and you'll get another go."

"Devious," she quips. "This is all very *'Art of War'* material. No wonder you two are so good at it."

"Sun Tzu has nothing on us," I agree. "Now, get back in there and kick ass, Bailey."

She gives us a mocking bow that reveals a breath-taking amount of cleavage. My dick stirs instantly and I can tell she knows the effect she's having on me, because when she straightens, her eyes are locked on my crotch. "Brat," I accuse her. "Go play."

She wins in pretty convincing fashion, and she's delighted by it. It's the first time she's won every single game in a match. Once we are done toasting to her success over a shot of vodka, we wait out the rest of the games. Clark is melting down as usual because he's playing a woman, and Juliette's standing off to one side, typing something into a phone. She's been acting weird, Juliette, but I'm too involved in my own life to get fussed about it.

"You staying over tonight?" Daniel asks her.

"Only if you let me grade." She gestures to her laptop bag, bulging at the seams. "I have to get some of this stuff done tonight, and you two have a way of distracting me from work."

"We'll keep our hands off you," I promise solemnly.

She rolls her eyes. "That," she says, her lips curling upwards into a smile that she tries to hide, "is a lie."

"Nope," I laugh. "I promise to keep my hands off you, but I make no guarantees about you keeping your hands off me."

"Vain much?" She looks around and steps closer to us. "It's true, I can't keep my hands off you." Her face flushes. "I'm becoming some kind of nympho."

"You are a tiger, Bailey." Daniel starts to touch her before he remembers he's in a public place and checks himself. "Always responsive, always ready."

"Always wet," I add, teasing her. "It's very flattering."

She goes beet-red, then she laughs good-naturedly. "I blame you two for that. I used to be a normal person before we met."

She's joking. As mushy as it sounds, we are all better people around each other. Daniel works less, and seems to be happier for it. I don't lose my temper quite as readily. Bailey accepts she's a beautiful woman.

Because there's three of us, two can always entertain each other if the third is working, and no one's left resentful. I'm a chef - working long hours is always going to be part of my life. More than that, I work evenings and weekends, and that's always made dating difficult. It's an odd thing to voluntarily be in a ménage, but strangely, it's working better than any relationship has ever worked in my life.

~

"You hungry, Bailey?" I ask her, when we get to Daniel's place. We shared a plate of appetizers at the Maxwell Club, but she probably forgot to eat all day, immersed in her work. We are stretched out on the couch, Bailey sitting between the two of us. *If only she didn't need to correct papers...*

"I'm starving," she admits, "but don't get up. You've been in the kitchen all day. I can fix myself something. Daniel usually has ingredients for a stir-fry or something." She rises to her feet. "Come on, billionaire boy. You can help me."

"Billionaire boy?" Daniel snorts. "Geez, that's a flattering nickname."

I rise to my feet as well. "This I have to see," I announce. "Daniel Hartman cooking. Have you ever turned on a stove burner by yourself?"

He looks embarrassed as he leads the way to the kitchen. "Probably," he says defensively, "though I can't remember when."

"You're joking, right?" Bailey eyes Daniel with open astonishment. "You are an adult. How do you manage?"

"Restaurants," he admits sheepishly. I'm getting quite a kick out of watching Daniel squirm. It happens so rarely. "Take out. And Sebastian cooks whenever he's here. You know. Billionaire stuff."

"We are fixing this now," she announces. "Don't worry, Daniel. I'll teach you."

Unsurprisingly, Daniel's not terribly inept. Bailey slices the vegetables and Daniel tends to the stove, and in about fifteen minutes, the stir-fry is ready. They skip making rice - it's too late for carbohydrates.

They both turn to me with expectant faces when I taste the food, and I stifle a laugh. "It's not bad," I tell them. I wink at Bailey. "You, I might hire. This guy, on the other hand..."

"This guy owns half your restaurants," Daniel retorts with a grin. "Okay, how about an hour of work before we go to bed? I do have some emails to read and respond to."

"I'm surprised you held off as long as you did," I say over my shoulder, as we head back to the living room. Daniel used to be like Juliette, huddled over his phone when he wasn't playing pool. Nowadays, he actually puts his phone away when he gets to the club, and doesn't reach for it until we are done for the evening. *A definite improvement.*

Bailey pulls out a stack of papers to grade. "No fooling around," she warns us sternly, as we settle on either side of her. "I need to get this done."

"How's the writing going?" I ask her. She's working on a paper with some kind of anthropology super-star, but she's been unimpressed with the experience so far. From the sounds of it, she's doing all the heavy lifting and her co-writer is coasting on his celebrity.

She makes a face. "Don't ask. He was supposed to send me twenty pages. Instead he sent me two paragraphs. Two paragraphs of rambling text with not a single source. Kill me now."

Daniel shakes his head. "Poor Bailey." He pulls up his laptop and starts typing. "Seb, you going to be bored while we work?"

"Can you guys concentrate if I watch TV?"

They both nod. "In that case, I'm good."

We all do our own things for a while, and it feels extremely intimate. Daniel's fingers tapping away at the keyboard, Bailey's pen scratching at the papers she's correcting, with the sound of Sports Centre in the background. I'm tired from an extremely long day at the restaurant, and my eyes are beginning to shut, when I hear Daniel clear his throat.

"Bailey?" He sounds hesitant. "There's a big company gala coming up next week. Would you like to come?"

I look up. Daniel has been more relaxed in the last couple of weeks, but as far as I know, all the restrictions about not courting publicity still apply. His deal is moving along at a steadier pace now that he's lit a fire under Cyrus, but it's not done yet.

Bailey looks surprised as well. "Really?"

He looks uncomfortable. "I don't like that fact that I have to hide you," he says. His wave encompasses me as well. "What the three of us share is important to me." He makes a face. "I have an obligation to my company and I can't acknowledge you publically as my girlfriend until this deal falls into place. But I would like you to be there."

"And you?" Bailey's looking at me. "Are you going to be there as well?"

"Daniel's assistant Sophie likes me," I grin. "I get invited every year."

She stiffens at that, and I put my arm around her. "There's only one woman I can't take my eyes off," I scold her softly. "Only one woman that matters. You should know that."

"I still can't believe it," she says. "I mean, come on. You two are among the city's most eligible bachelors."

"That sounds like the Post talking," Daniel replies. "If *'eligible'* is a calculation of our net worth, then yes, I guess we are very eligible. But we work all the time, and we'd probably make terrible boyfriends. I don't think you could drag Sebastian into a dance club, even if you dangled a third Michelin star in front of him. I mean, look at us now. One of us is working, the other has no energy to do anything other than watch Sports Centre."

"That's a lie, baby, don't listen to him." I wink at Bailey. "I have plenty of energy for what matters." I put my hand on her thigh and move it up toward her sweet, *sweet* pussy, and she giggles and brushes my hand away.

"I have papers to correct, Sebastian," she says sternly. "About this party," she says to Daniel. "When is it?"

"In a week. Saturday night. It's at the MOMA," he adds persuasively.

She rolls her eyes. "Of course it is." She gives the essay she's reading an A, then looks up. "Are you sure this is a good idea, Daniel? I'd love to go, but I don't want to put your deal at risk. Is it worth it for something that has an expiration date?"

I sit up at that. "What do you mean, has an expiration date?"

She doesn't meet our eyes. "Look, you guys have a bet to win and I want to beat Trevor. What we are doing is nice, and I'm really enjoying myself. But is it real?"

Daniel has gone still on the other side of me. "What do you mean, is it real? What are you talking about? You think we are here right now because of the stupid bet?"

"Look at me," I order Bailey, and she reluctantly listens. "Here's the only question that matters. What do you want? Do you want us to have an expiration date?"

I can't breathe as I wait for her answer, but she doesn't leave us hanging for long. "No," she whispers. "I really don't want this to end."

Though her words are exactly what I want to hear, I can tell from her expression that there's something she's not telling us. I exchange a glance with Daniel. I wonder if he knows what's going on.

30

I would rather walk with a friend in the dark, than alone in the light.

— HELEN KELLER

Bailey:

"So," Wendy looks expectantly at me. "Tell us everything."

I've missed the last three Monday night drinking sessions. The first week, I'd missed it because I'd left, filled with a sense of righteous indignation, to tell Daniel Hartman exactly what I thought about his stupid endowment. The last two weeks, work has been a bitch and I've had to work late every evening to keep my head above water. The midterm assignment of the undergraduate Introduction to Cultural Anthropology class is to write a twenty-page paper. I've been reading about the cultural impact of Miley Cyrus, twerking, and Lady Gaga's meat dress all weekend. I'm very up-to-date on pop culture right now.

In my absence, the girls couldn't get their curiosity sated. It's Monday night again, and I'm around, which means it's time for the drinking and the inquisition. Four sets of eyes are staring at me, waiting for me to describe the last few weeks of my life. Normally, there'd be a virtual set of eyes as well, but Miki texted earlier, saying she couldn't Skype in.

"Okay, what do you know so far?" I ask. I'm not entirely displeased about being ambushed for details. Daniel's request for me to attend his company party has confused me, and our discussion about whether our relationship's expiration date has set my head spinning. I need the collective wisdom of the women in this room.

"No, no, no." Piper's in her customary place at the rocking chair, Jasper curled up on her lap. "That's a delaying tactic. Out with it. Tell us everything."

"Where should I start?" I sigh. "I'm having a threesome with two ridiculously hot guys."

"Yes," Wendy's voice is impatient. "We know. Daniel Hartman and Sebastian Ardalan."

"Right. And you guys know about the bet?"

"What bet?"

"I thought I told you," I frown at Gabby. "Daniel bet Clark fifty grand that I'd win my tournament game at the end of this season. Also, no offense, Gabby, but your friend Clark's a dick."

She grimaces. "Trust me, Bails, Clark Ellis isn't my friend. He's just a co-worker."

"They bet on you?" Wendy looks intrigued. "Are you mad at them?"

"No way," I laugh. "Are you kidding me? I want to beat Trevor, remember? They are giving me a ton of coaching."

"No doubt," Katie interjects slyly.

"I meant with my pool game," I blush, and the girls all

laugh at me. I flip them off and drink some of the delicious mojitos that Gabby, our resident mixed-drink genius, has made.

"You've been seeing them for a few weeks now," Katie continues. "Where does this go?" Katie's the most practical one of us. Trust her to ask the question.

"Glad you asked," I sigh. "I don't know." I tell them about being invited to Daniel's company gala. "What does it mean?"

"Why don't you ask them?" Wendy suggests.

"I did. I asked if there was an expiration date to the threesome, and they said no."

Piper wolf-whistles from her corner. Jasper starts at the noise, looking indignant and preparing to jump off and seek a quieter corner for his nap. Then he stretches slowly, and settles back down on Piper's lap. Piper shakes her head at his antics. "Cat," she mutters in mock irritation. "So let me get this straight. You are in a threesome and it's a proper relationship? What's that like?"

"Surprisingly normal." I blush. "Well, aside from the sex, of course."

Wendy chuckles. "Tell us about the sex, Bails," she sing-songs. "Leave no dirty detail out."

"I'm not going to kiss and tell." I grin at Wendy's sigh of disappointment. "But Daniel and Sebastian are so hot that they've replaced most of the regulars in my mental slide-show of masturbation material. Sorry, Clooney and Pitt."

"I know." Katie fans herself. "I saw Sebastian Ardalan's new cookbook in the stores the other day. The cover stopped me dead in the tracks."

"Why?" Wendy asks.

"Because he's bare-chested in the photo," Katie giggles.

"He's all muscled and ripped and hot, and the book's called Heat."

"Don't forget the tattoos," Gabby grins. She's seen the cover too. "I couldn't get a clear look at them in the picture. What are they, Bailey? You'd know, wouldn't you?"

I make a rude gesture in her direction. "He hates that cover," I tell them. "His agent made him do it." I frown. "She's creepy. I don't like her. Do you know she's already warned me away from him?"

"What?"

"Yeah. She followed me one day to the bathroom and told me to stay away from Sebastian. She told me that he had a brief period to take advantage of the Michelin star, and I was a distraction."

"The bitch." Gabby sounds incensed. "What did the guys say when you told them?"

"I haven't. It's not that big a deal, really. She just shoots me these death glares from time to time. I'm a big girl. I can handle Juliette."

"If you insist." Gabby doesn't sound convinced. Then her expression turns mischievous. "And then there's the hundred and fifty million dollar gift. Have you guys heard about that?"

"What?" Everyone shrieks again, and three sets of heads swivel to me.

"Thanks, Gabby," I say dryly. "That was really helpful. It wasn't a gift, you guys. It was an endowment to the NYU." I fill them in on the details, and once again, they hang on my every word. We all have dating adventures to discuss from time to time, but a threesome is still outside the norm.

"You're frowning," Wendy points out. "Why?"

"I don't know," I sigh. "They are so out of my league, you know. And the threesome thing, is that really practical?

Besides, in a few months, I'm going to Argentina. I just feel like I'm setting myself up for a world of hurt."

Katie snorts. "Bailey, you went to Siberia for a year. I wouldn't exactly describe you as practical. Does it really bother you that this isn't very conventional?"

I think about it. "I don't think so," I tell them. "I guess I'm just kind of pinching myself. They are really gorgeous, they are really nice, and they want me. It feels unreal, you know? I keep waiting for reality to kick in." I down the rest of my mojito and Gabby helpfully refills it. An empty glass rarely stays that way on drinking night.

"You know," Gabby says. "As much as I distrust all guys on principle, I have to acknowledge that good guys exist. I mean, Adam's amazing."

"Yes he is," Katie agrees smugly. "I have impeccable taste."

Gabby shakes her head, a smile on her lips. "And from the sounds of it, Daniel and Sebastian seem pretty good too. Don't be so eager to find a problem, Bailey. Listen to your instincts. Do you think you can trust them?"

Last week, Sebastian had bought me a piece of jewelry, a silver and amethyst bracelet he said he found in a Tibetan shop in SoHo. "You don't have a lot of amethyst," he'd said as he handed it to me. "I thought I'd rectify that."

I think about that bracelet right now. It hadn't been an expensive gift, but it had been a deeply personal one. As had the vodka. Sebastian and Daniel are both ridiculously wealthy, but the gifts they give me show they pay attention to my needs. My desires.

"I can absolutely trust them," I say firmly. "By the way, Madam Pot Calling the Kettle Black, have you ever tried to find the guys in your own ménage situation? Carter and Dominic?"

She flushes, and I know I have her. Gabby won't admit it, but she can't forget her one-night stand. "No," she replies. "I haven't, and I'm not going to. It was just a one-time thing. Not all guys are good and trustworthy, Bailey. Some of them are jerks. Just like Trevor was."

I want to push her on this, but I notice the expression on her face, and I back off. Gabby is, unusually for her, looking close to tears. Piper notices too, and changes the topic.

"Talking about good-looking guys," she leans forward and fixes me with an accusing look. "Tell me about Wyatt Lawless and Owen Lamb."

I give her a puzzled look. "Who are they?"

"Two guys who've eaten at my restaurant every day for the last two weeks," she replies. "Every *single* day. I'm not at the front of the house all the time, so it took me a few nights to realize it. Then last night, they offered to become my partners."

Oh. These must be Sebastian's friends, and shit, I forgot to mention our conversation to Piper. "Okay, don't be mad," I tell her. "I yelled at Sebastian for upsetting you, and he felt so bad that he said he was going to talk to a couple of his friends about your restaurant."

Piper gives me a peculiar look. "Bailey, do you know who these guys are?"

"Not a clue. Should I know?"

"I guess not, you don't work in the industry. Lawless and Lamb are legendary. They have something of a Midas touch. Their restaurants are very popular."

"That's good then, right?" I ask nervously. I can't make out if she's mad at me or not. "You aren't irritated with me for telling Sebastian?"

She shakes her head. "No, of course not. You did what you thought was a good thing."

"So what's the problem?" Katie asks. "They are good at what they do and you need help. Do they want too much money? Or equity?"

"It isn't that." Piper doesn't meet our eyes. "They just rubbed me the wrong way, that's all."

Wendy's been fiddling around on her phone during this conversation. She whistles as she looks at her screen. "Is this them?" she asks, handing her phone to Piper. "Seriously, what am I doing wrong with my life? The only guys I meet are smarmy lawyers. Bailey finds two studs, Gabby decides to hook up and voila - she finds a couple of hotties, and now you as well?" She shakes her head and gulps down her drink. "Life is *so* unfair."

"Pictures can't reveal personality," Piper retorts. "These two are smug, self-satisfied and annoying as all fuck. You can have them."

We exchange glances. Piper sounds entirely too heated, and it appears that Sebastian's friends have got under her skin. "You don't have to work with them if you don't want to," I assure her. "Do you want me to ask Sebastian if he knows anyone else who can help?"

"No," she replies. "I'll suck it up. These guys are really good."

"And really hot," Wendy adds, her eyes still on her phone. She sighs. "You have no idea how long it's been since I kissed someone, let alone anything else."

I survey my friends. Apart from Katie, who is happily married with twin girls, we are all single. Dating in New York City is tough. Women outnumber men by a significant margin, and it's really hard to meet someone even a little nice. I'm not surprised at Wendy's statement.

"So, how's the pool game going?" Katie asks. "Are you getting good enough that you are going to beat Trevor?"

"I don't know if I'm going to be ready for that," I admit. "But I *am* getting better. In the last two weeks, I've won both my matches." I grin. "Clark hates it. I can tell he's getting nervous about the money."

"Shouldn't have made the bet then." Gabby doesn't sound sympathetic. "Asshole."

"You have to beat Trevor, Bailey," Wendy leans forward, swaying slightly. "I'm having a shitty week with clients. Rich men cheat around on their wives, then try to contest the pre-nup. They hide their assets, pretend they are broke and do everything in the world to avoid meeting their obligations." She sounds earnest and more than a little drunk. "Do it on behalf of women everywhere, Bails. Kick Trevor's ass in that final game. Make him pay."

31

You cannot swim for new horizons until you have courage to lose sight of the shore.

— WILLIAM FAULKNER

Sebastian:

Of course my respite doesn't last. Tuesday morning, Juliette emails me with a more detailed proposal from the investors that want to open up a restaurant chain with my name on the door, and it is a disaster.

"This can't be right," I mutter aloud.

Katya, who is tallying up the proceedings of last night's register, looks up. "Sorry, Chef, did you say something?"

I shake my head. "These numbers can't be right." The projected profitability on these restaurants seems too high, and the amount of money they've set aside for food and labor doesn't match what I know from experience. Yes, we do spend more on locally sourced and organically grown food at my restaurants. But I've worked in other kitchens as well, and there's not a single restaurant in the country that can cut their food expenses down to ten percent. Food's typically a third. If you spend a hundred dollars on a meal, then the ingredients should cost about thirty bucks.

Not, as these guys have projected, ten dollars.

Even fast food restaurants spend more on food. I frown and scroll down. Labor costs at my restaurants are thirty-seven percent, which is on the high side for the industry, but I believe in paying my people well - I was dirt poor for far too many years to be otherwise. This proposal has labor costs at twenty five percent, which is closer to a fast food operation than a sit-down restaurant.

They've allocated fifteen percent for marketing, and ten percent for executive wages.

This stinks. This stinks like the porta-potties after the chili cook-off at the Hattiesburg County Fair.

I call Juliette and don't bother with pleasantries. "Did you look at this thing before you sent it to me?"

"No, I'm looking at it right now." Her voice is distracted as she absorbs the pertinent facts. "Oh, this seems off."

No shit, Sherlock. "That's an understatement," I say sarcastically. "Juliette, these numbers are a joke. Either these guys have no clue what they are doing or..." I stop talking as a more sinister notion occurs to me. "Fuck. These guys don't give a shit, do they?"

I'm kicking myself as they speak. I should have realized this at once. Low food costs, low labor costs? They are going to use my name to get customers through the door, and they are going to give them the most indifferent dining experience that they can get away with. That explains the high marketing costs - they won't get many repeat customers, and will constantly have to find new ones. Of course, the executives will get handsomely rewarded for their cost-cutting.

This isn't the way to build a sustainable restaurant. This is frozen meat, sourced in countries with dubious food safety standards. This is hiring college kids and working them to the bone for minimum wage.

This is the antithesis of everything I've stood for in my entire life.

"I don't want this deal."

"Sebastian, don't be hasty." Juliette's voice is edged with frantic worry. "Listen, I agree, these aren't good numbers, but it's just an initial proposal. Let's meet these guys and express our concerns, and they can work on them."

"Juliette, I don't think I care enough. You know what? Daniel was right about this deal. It's too much to take on, especially when my focus should be here."

"Please," she snaps. "That's not what this is about. This is about your precious threesome with Jessica Rabbit."

I hold back my angry retort with difficulty. I've just realized that Katya's sitting right next to me, and though she's making a valiant effort to look like she's not listening with bated breath to this conversation, she is. "This isn't about Bailey," I grit out. "This is about you finding the wrong partners for this deal, Juliette. I'm not interested in working with someone whose values are so diametrically opposed to mine."

"I'll call them," she says. "I'll be in touch."

I hang up, shaking my head. It'll take her a while to realize I'm not playing ball, but she'll get the message eventually.

Katya clears her throat once I'm off the phone. "Umm, Chef, I didn't mean to overhear your conversation..."

"But you heard every word." I wave it aside before she

can start to apologize. "It's not your fault, this office is the size of a shoe-closet."

"Yeah," she agrees. "I guess the rumor mill was right. You are going to leave us to run a mass-market chain."

"It's by no means a done deal, Katya, as you probably heard."

She bites her lip and doesn't look at me. "Please don't go, Chef. Ben's insane. He'll drive this place into the ground." She gulps. "I've been working the front for five years. I've worked crazy hours, day in and day out because I believe in what we are doing here. We care about food. We care about people." She looks unhappy. "Ben doesn't give a shit, Chef. I hear the talk from the line cooks. He does the bare minimum at prep. He's disorganized, he's messy and when you are not here, he shows up reeking of alcohol."

"Really? No one's said anything."

Her fingers play with her hair in a nervous gesture. "The staff won't complain about Ben to you, Chef. They don't think you'll support them against him."

I give her an astonished look. "Why?"

She squares her shoulders. "In for a penny, in for a pound, right?" she asks. "You didn't fire Ben when he was a lazy line cook. You promoted him to sous-chef when he wasn't ready, and when his kitchen was floundering, you put Helen in charge of *Seb II* so you could pay him personal attention."

Fuck. She's right. She's absolutely correct.

I've been living in the past. Something about Ben reminds me of my struggles during the early days in Manhattan, and so I've overlooked many instances of bad behavior that should have got him fired. Heck, even Daniel has told me to get rid of him.

This franchise deal is another example. I wanted so

much for there to be a restaurant with my name on it in Hattiesburg. I ached to go back and fix the wounds of the past. And in my relentless focus on what's behind me, I've failed to appreciate what I have. A loyal staff, some of whom I've known since I moved to the city. Two profitable restaurants, a rarity in Manhattan. A best friend, Daniel, who is about the most amazing partner that I could ever ask for, and a woman, Bailey, who has, in a very short period of time, become one of the most important people in my life.

I have everything, but I've been too lost in the angst and in my own perceived inadequacies to notice.

I sit up, and it seems like a weight lifts off my shoulders as I make a decision. "Katya? Those rumor mills are wrong. I'm not going anywhere."

A smile breaks out on her face, wide and delighted. When I see it, I know I've made the right choice. I belong here. This is my home.

32

Sometimes the questions are complicated and the answers are simple.

— Dr. Seuss

Bailey:

Before I have a chance to prepare, it's the Saturday of the party.

The apartment is quiet. Since it's Saturday, Piper's still at work. She muttered something unflattering about Lawless and Lamb this morning as I was heading out the door, and I'm going to take it to mean that the partnership is going as well as can be expected. Well, as well as it can when you place three extremely passionate and stubborn people in a room.

I'm vacillating between a black floor-length dress and a black knee-length dress when the doorbell rings. I open it to find a young man holding a garment bag. "Ms. Moore?" he asks me politely. "I have a delivery for you."

"I'm not expecting anything," I say stupidly, then my brain makes the connection between the formal event tonight and the garment bag. *Billionaires at work again.* Since yelling at the delivery guy is rather pointless, I sign for the parcel and offer him a tip. He declines politely — *it's been taken care of, Ms. Moore, but thank you,* - then leaves. I'm left holding a surprisingly heavy garment bag.

My phone rings as I walk toward my bedroom. I glance at the display. *Sebastian.* "Did I not tell you two to stop buying me things?" I ask him crossly, not bothering to say hello first.

"You did," he laughs. "We didn't promise to listen. Bailey, have you opened the bag yet?"

"No, the guy just dropped it off."

Daniel's voice cuts in. Sebastian must have me on speaker phone. "You want to play a game tonight, baby?"

Heat runs through me at that question. "A game?" My voice is breathy. I sound like I've just run a marathon.

"Open the bag," Sebastian orders.

My breathing catches as the sight of the rich violet colored fabric that comes into view, and I reverently pull the dress out. It's a deep purple silk gown. It's possibly the loveliest thing I've ever seen in my life. There are shoes to match, and a purple lace bra, but no panties. My lips curl into a grin. "No underwear?" I tease them. "Surely that's a bit cliché?"

"Clichés are popular for a reason," Daniel says, his voice rich with amusement. "Your lack of underwear will be addressed in a moment. Do you see a black pouch among the stuff?"

I root around the mess on my bed until I find the bag Daniel's referring to. "I just did," I tell them. "I'm almost afraid to see what's in it."

"Don't be boring, Bailey," Sebastian scolds. "Open it."

I unzip the bag, and I have to laugh. I'd been mentally bracing myself for jewelry, the expensive kind, the kind I didn't want, because I'm much more comfortable wearing the pieces I buy for myself when traveling the world. But the bag opens to reveal something far more interesting. A pair of black silk panties, except the crotch has been replaced by a string of pearl-like beads.

My breath catches at the idea of the beads slipping between the folds of my pussy, pressed up against my clitoris, caressing me and shifting in me with each move I make… "You shouldn't have," I giggle into the phone, my voice high with arousal. "A girl can get used to this."

Daniel chuckles. "That's why I like you, Bailey. No false coyness from you. Now, both Sebastian and I are quite happy to volunteer to help you into the panties, if you'd like."

I roll my eyes. "Daniel, it's a pair of panties. I can manage."

"Ah, she breaks my heart with her refusal," he replies, laughing.

"Are you going to be good and wear the dress, Bailey?" Sebastian growls. I notice he doesn't say anything about wearing the sex toy panties. He's correctly assuming that I have no objection to them.

"What's wrong with my clothes?"

"How many black dresses were you trying to decide between?"

"Two, damn it," I admit, chagrined at how well they already seem to know me. "Fine, I'll wear your dress." I realize how ungracious I sound, and I wince. "It's a very lovely dress," I say, my voice softening in apology. "Thank you. It was very kind of both of you."

"A car will be by at eight to pick you up," Daniel says. "We'll be in it. And we'll be checking if everything's on properly."

"So wear those panties unless you want to earn a spanking, honey," Sebastian advises.

I'm so turned on that I cannot breathe. The idea of them making me lift up my dress in the car so that they can examine me almost makes my heart stop in my chest. And their threats of a spanking? I can't stop imagining me bent over one of their laps, panties rolled down to my knees, being punished for failing to follow their very precise orders.

They must know where my thoughts are — I'm practically panting with lust into the phone. "Bailey," Daniel gives me one last instruction. "Don't masturbate. Wait for us."

"Is that another order?" I sass at them, though I fully intend to obey. "Will I get punished if I don't listen?"

"You absolutely will," Daniel assures me. "And you won't like it, so I suggest you do as you are told."

The total dominance with which he says those words turns me on even more. It is going to be a herculean task to keep my fingers to myself while I slip those panties on.

At that thought, my face heats in embarrassment. I'm going to be wearing a sex toy during one of Daniel's work functions? How very awkward.

How very naughty, my inner rebel reminds me, and I grin widely. Hey, it's not my work event. If Daniel wants to play sex games at his company party, I'm happy to indulge.

THEY'D SAID there would be a car for me. When I heard the knock on the door, I assume it's the driver, but no. It's the two of them, and Sebastian is holding a bottle of champagne.

"Aren't you late for your own party?" I ask Daniel. "And aren't we all too old to get pre-drunk?"

"Hello to you too, Bailey," he replies with a twitch of his lips. "You look lovely in that dress."

"I agree," Sebastian says. "Invite us in, honey. This isn't pre-drinking. This is celebrating."

I step aside. "What are you celebrating?" I ask them, heading into the kitchen to find some champagne flutes.

Sebastian pops the cork expertly and pours the shimmery liquid into three glasses. "I'm going to turn down the franchise deal."

"Seriously?" This has been so important to him. "You were so enthused about it. What made you change your mind?"

We clink glasses and I take a sip. The bubbles tickle my throat and it feels very sensual. Add in the string of pearls that rub against my clitoris every time I move, and I'm incredibly aware of my body.

"I wanted the idea of it more than the real thing," he replies. "So many nights, when I was cooking at one lousy restaurant after another in the early days, I dreamed of going back home one day and proving everyone wrong." His lips turn into a grimace. "It's a dreadful thing to live in the past."

"And what prompted this revelation?"

"I couldn't tell you," he says frankly. "A feeling has been growing within me that this is the wrong thing to do. Then on Thursday, I saw the details of the proposal, and it was garbage. Juliette keeps saying that the terms can be reworked, but I don't want it to be."

"How has Juliette taken the news?" I can't see her

approving of Sebastian's decision, and she doesn't strike me as the kind that is going to roll over and play dead.

"She's still arguing with me." He dismisses her with a shrug. "Whatever. She'll come around soon enough."

"Sebastian," I say, my voice earnest. She'd followed me into the bathroom and told me to stay away from Sebastian, all because he kissed me. In the face of outright defeat, I can't imagine what she might do, but I know it won't be pretty. "I wouldn't underestimate Juliette."

He tosses the champagne back and refills our glasses. "I don't want to talk about Juliette," he says. "Not when all I can think of is pulling up your dress to check if you are wearing a very sexy pair of panties. I'm going to taste you, Bailey. I'm going to get you keyed up and aroused, and tonight, every time I turn and look at you, I'll know you are hot, swollen and ready for my dick."

Daniel bares his teeth. "When the party is over tonight, Bailey," his hands caress the curve of my butt. "I'm going to take your ass while Sebastian pounds your pussy. Would you like that?"

I dismiss thoughts of Juliette from my mind, focusing instead on the two desirable men in front of me. "Yes," I whisper, moving so I'm standing between their rock solid bodies, "I would like that very much."

33

'Tis a secret: none knows how it comes, how it goes. But the name of the secret is Love!

— Lewis Carroll, Sylvie and Bruno
Concluded

Bailey:

I've retreated to a quiet corner of the crowded bar. The party is in full swing and everyone appears to be having a blast. There's a band playing, people are dancing and strolling among the artwork, all while sipping at their wine and beer. The museum security people must be having a coronary at the thought of damage to their Van Gogh's and Picasso's.

Daniel walks up to me with two drinks in his hand, extending one to me. "I noticed you were empty," he says with a smile, gesturing to the glass in my hand. "Having fun?"

"I'm a little intimidated by the conspicuous consumption on display," I reply with a wink. "Also, I'm uh, distracted."

"Mmm." His gaze moves over me like a heated touch and goosebumps rise on my skin in response. The beads starts to vibrate against my pussy, and I almost spill my drink, startled. "Steady there, Bailey," he grins.

"How?" I ask weakly.

"There's a remote, of course. The range isn't great, but it works well enough when I'm up close to you."

He's standing a safe distance away, and no one looking at us will think that we are having anything other than a casual conversation. Daniel's extremely good at managing his image.

As the waves of pleasure thrum through my body, I realize that's not the only thing he's good at. He's very skilled at torturing me as well. I'm too proud to beg him to stop, and I definitely don't want to orgasm in front of an audience of hundreds. To take my mind off the vibrations at my core, I ask him something I've been curious about. "Has everyone in your family always been so driven? Cyrus looks a little scary."

The beads stop buzzing. I'm not at all surprised that Daniel's glowering uncle can put him off sex. "Talking about Cyrus, where is he?" Daniel wonders aloud, scanning the room, then his attention switches back to me. "Sorry, Bailey. He's due to make a speech soon. To answer your question, the lesson we learned from early childhood was that the family firm is the only thing that mattered. We are merely guardians of its legacy." He smiles tiredly. "It's a wearying concept for a child."

"You have a sister, right? Does she work at your company as well?"

He shakes his head. "Susan was supposed to marry

well and produce babies. She's dating the most boring guy in the world, so I'd say that she's doing her part." He sips at his drink. "I'm being dramatic. I had a wonderful childhood, we both did. My father did his best to shield us from the family obligations. We only had to listen to lectures on our duties as Hartmans when we visited my grandparents."

"Cyrus seems all about duty."

He grimaces. "Yeah, well, the apple didn't fall too far from the tree there. Cyrus is a spitting image of my grandfather. My mother can't stand him."

"Why was your father different?" I ask. "How come he was immune to the family pressures?"

He smiles. "The oldest reason in the world, and one I understand too well," he says lightly. "He met a woman that mattered more than obligations." His eyes linger on me till I squirm with discomfort. He can't mean me, right?

Silence stretches between us. "Families are funny things," Daniel says finally. "You think that you are free of their influence the moment you move out, but that's not really ever the case, is it? I work at the family firm, even though Cyrus persists in acting like my nanny. Sebastian almost made the biggest mistake of his career because he can't forget how little support his parents gave him." He gulps down the rest of the drink. "What about you, Bailey? Do you get along with your parents?"

"This is," I remark to no one in particular, "about the strangest conversation I've ever had when I'm about to come."

He laughs at that, long and hard. People turn around and gape discreetly at their boss. Across the room, I spot Cyrus in a far corner, deep in conversation with Juliette. They look up as I notice them, and both of them frown in my direction, though I can't bring myself to be bothered. So they disapprove of me. *Big fucking deal.*

When Daniel's done with his mirth, he flashes me a devious smile. "As much as it would be enjoyable to watch you come right now," he says, "I much rather keep you keyed up for later."

"Asshole," I say without heat. "Yes, I get along very well with my parents. My dad was a freelance photographer and my mother was a painter. They gave me wanderlust."

"Is your quest for tenure a search for the stability you didn't have growing up?"

That's a very perceptive question, but I don't know why I'm surprised. Daniel pays attention. I laugh uneasily, and his hand comes out and rests on my forearm. "I've made you uncomfortable," he says, apology in his tone. "I didn't mean to."

"You know too much about me already," I admit. "It's intimidating."

"It's not meant to be." He takes in the room around us, the glitz and the glamour, the expensive gowns and suits, all the trappings of wealth. "Look at this place," he mutters, stepping closer to me. "There's hundreds of people here. Yet I can let my guard down around only two of them."

One of those people is obviously Sebastian. And the other? Is he really talking about me? "Why?" I whisper. There's a tremble in my voice that I try to disguise. "Why me? I'm not gorgeous and thin. Look at the women here. Any of them would fit better in your world."

"Why do women always think that gorgeous is the same thing as thin?" he asks exasperatedly. "I don't see how an extra ten pounds makes you any less interesting or accomplished or fascinating."

"Ten?" I snort. "Try thirty."

He shakes his head. The pearls comes to life again and I shiver as lust hums through my body. "I've seen you naked," he says softly. "You are beautiful and perfect. And if you put yourself down again, I will punish you and you won't like it."

The intensity increases and I whimper. I can barely stand, I'm so close to the edge. I'm afraid someone's going to look at me and reach the obvious conclusion. My pussy is damp, my cunt lips slippery with desire. "Turn it off," I beg. "I'm going to come."

"Will you behave?"

"Okay," I whimper. "No comments about how I need to lose weight."

"And none about how you don't fit in my world," he prompts.

"Fine. Please, Daniel..."

The vibrations stop. "What were we talking about?" he asks smoothly, not missing a beat.

"Family," I reply weakly. I'm struggling to focus my thoughts, which are drifting about my head like tendrils of fog on a cloudy night. "You were saying something about how you and Sebastian were controlled by family expectations." His words come back to me. "Was it really going to be the biggest mistake of Sebastian's career? You must be pretty relieved he walked away then."

He lifts his shoulder in an elegant shrug. "I always trusted him to make the right decision."

"You did?"

"Of course, Bailey. And I trust you the same way. You were uncomfortable the other day when we talked about expiration dates. Will you tell me why?"

Sebastian walks up to us at that moment. I'm grateful for the distraction. I still haven't told them that I'm going away in September. No matter how much we'd like to pretend otherwise, that'll be the end of us.

Then Daniel's words register.

I trust you.

And I know what I have to do.

"I have something to say." I take a deep breath and look up at both of them. "I've been avoiding telling both of you, but in September, I have a six month research project in Patagonia. That's why I was so reluctant to talk about long-term stuff the other day."

Sebastian looks puzzled. "I know you are going to Argentina. Why does it matter? Are you not allowed to fly home for an occasional weekend?"

I gape at him. "How do you know about my trip?"

Daniel clears his throat. "I told him," he says. "I didn't realize it was a secret. Your department chair mentioned it to me during one of the meetings we had to discuss the Hartman endowment."

Of course. "It's your business to know things, right?" My tone comes out bitter.

"Bailey," Daniel mutters. "I'm sorry. I didn't mean to upset you. Yes, it's a long journey and we won't be able to see each other as often as we are able to now. But surely you didn't think that would mean the end of our relationship?" He grimaces. "You are looking at two fellow workaholics." His fingers link in mine.

"You're okay? There's no need to pick between Patagonia and you?"

"Why on earth?" Daniel asks. "Wait. This was a concern in a previous relationship?"

I nod. "In Siberia," I confess. "I didn't want to end things with Ivan, but he couldn't contemplate the idea of a long-distance relationship, and he wouldn't consider moving. It was very clear that my only option, if I wanted to stay with him, was to give up my career."

"We aren't him." Sebastian's voice is steady. "I let my past go this week, Bailey. Can you do the same?"

Juliette's still glaring at us. Earlier this evening, in my apartment, I told Sebastian to be careful of her, but now, I'm the one not listening to my own words, *because I've suddenly seen hope.* This doesn't have to end. I don't have to choose between a relationship and my career. I can have both.

A waiter carrying a tray of champagne passes by, and I flag him down. He sees Daniel standing next to me and immediately beelines toward us. "A toast?" I suggest, lifting my glass of champagne in the air. "To a future, rich with possibilities?"

We drink to that, and Daniel waves the waiter away. "I'm more interested," he whispers with a wicked gleam in his eyes, "in the very immediate future. Once Cyrus is done with his speech, shall we head out of here?"

My pussy is slick with desire. "I thought you'd never ask."

34

You know you're in love when you can't fall asleep because reality is finally better than your dreams.

— Dr. Seuss

Daniel:

I find Cyrus before I head out. He's been avoiding me in the office, and he's dragging his feet on keeping me updated on the Kansas City deal. "You didn't return my call," I tell him pointedly. "Where are we with Ryan Communications?"

"I'm working on it," he replies evasively. "If there's any news, I'll let you know."

No. I'm his boss. He might have been my mentor once, and I might have needed his guidance in the early days. But no more, and this shit isn't going to cut it. "You're out of time, Cyrus," I tell him flatly. "I warned you about this. You had three weeks to get the Ryan Communications deal done, and I've seen nothing." I exhale and paste a bland smile on my face as a group of people from Operations walks by. Once they are out of hearing range, I continue. "On Monday morning, I'm going to ask for your resignation."

"You can't do that," he blusters. "You think the board's going to allow you to get rid of me?"

"I have the votes I need." My voice is confident. "You don't think I'd threaten you if I can't back it up, do you?" I shake my head. "You better hope that Wayne Ryan is willing to work the weekend, Cyrus. Because Monday morning, I want to see one of two pieces of paper on my desk. Either a deal waiting for me to sign, or your letter of resignation."

Not waiting for him to respond, I turn and walk away.

I've made my move. *It's time for Cyrus to make his.*

"WHAT WAS THAT ABOUT?" Bailey asks in the car as we drive back to my place. "You were glaring at Cyrus."

"Was it that obvious?"

She places her hand on my arm. "Not really," she says. "I have the benefit of knowing how you feel about him."

"I don't want to talk about Cyrus, not now. Right now..." I give her a meaning look, "I have other things on my mind. Spread your legs for me. Put one leg over my thigh, and the other over Sebastian's."

She complies, blushing. "The driver?" she asks. "What if he sees us?"

"The partition is up," I point out. "He won't be able to see anything." I grin at her. "However, it isn't soundproof, so keep your voice down."

She's wearing her hair down tonight. It cascades in shiny, lustrous waves down her shoulders. I bend down and kiss a spot at the base of her neck that I know drives her insane. She shifts and presses the back of her hand against her mouth, stifling her moan.

Sebastian's hands are on her dress, hiking it up. "All evening," he mutters, "I've been looking forward to unwrapping this parcel." The fabric inches up and exposes her creamy thighs, and her legs fall open to reveal the softness between them. I gulp. Seeing that ivory white string of beads, nestled against the fiery red of her neatly trimmed pussy hair makes me instantly hard.

It had been something of an impulse to ask her to the company gala, and I'm very glad I did. Keeping her a secret doesn't sit well with me. If she needs me to be discreet about our threesome because of her career, then I'm happy to comply.

However, had it not been for this Ryan Communications deal, I wouldn't have felt the same need myself. If my dad were still alive, he would have loved Bailey. I've already told my mother about her. I'm not embarrassed about the unconventional nature of our relationship - I can't live my life according to the expectations of other people.

I'm glad she told us about her trip. Things feel different between the three of us now. Deeper and more meaningful.

Sebastian pulls something out of his pocket with a grin on his face. I smile when I see what it is. A blindfold.

Bailey's eyes widen. "In the car?"

"I think you'll enjoy yourself more if you aren't stressed about who might be watching," he says smoothly.

"You have such interesting theories, Sebastian." Her voice has a trace of sarcasm in it, but there's a healthy measure of lust as well. She's an adventurer, our Bailey. She reminds me of a sky-diver, hesitating at the door of a plane before jumping into mid-air.

"So many protests," I scold her. "When we all know you want this. Close your eyes."

She laughs. "I do want it," she says. "The two of you have a bad habit of keying me up in public. I expect you to make up for it."

I move her hair out of the way and Sebastian fastens the blindfold. "Can you see anything?"

She shakes her head. "No," she says.

"How does it feel?" I move my hand up her thigh, and watch her shiver. Sebastian cups her chin and kisses her, while I run my finger over the string of pearls. She whimpers. "Daniel," she begs. "Don't tease me."

"How do you know who it is?" I ask her.

"The two of you kiss differently," she confesses, her cheeks pink. "And you touch me differently. I can tell you apart."

"Really?" Sebastian sounds intrigued, and the two of us exchange looks. "Let's test this theory out."

"Test it out on my clitoris." Her hands move toward her pussy. "Else I'm going to have to take care of myself right now."

Oh, the idea of watching Bailey masturbating is very tempting, but that's just too much sass from her. "Hands above your head," I order. "You don't need to take care of yourself when the two of us are here, honey. We've got you."

Sebastian's fingers tug at the beads, moving them aside so he can rub a thumb over her clitoris. "Fuck," she groans. "Sebastian."

Okay, that's two out of two. I feel a silly smile break out on my face at the idea of her being able to recognize my touch.

We test her, the two of us, and sure enough, she's right. She knows who we are, every single time. She's also biting her lips back to keep from crying out, and her nails dig into her palms. "Damn it, I need to come," she pleads, and Sebastian relents. His fingers push into her pussy, and his thumb strums at her clitoris. I kiss her and I feel her moan into my mouth as she climaxes.

It's Saturday night, and traffic is heavy. We take advantage, making Bailey orgasm two more times, till she finally pushes our hands away. "No more," she begs. "I'm too sensitive." She removes the blindfold and rests her head on Sebastian's shoulder, reaching out to link her fingers in mine. "I had a really good time tonight. Thanks for inviting me."

She's sleepy and sated, and as I hold her hand, a rush of affection floods through me. Despite my confrontation with Cyrus, I agree with her. I had a really good time tonight as well.

35

Supreme excellence consists of breaking the enemy's resistance without fighting.

— Sun Tzu, The Art of War

Daniel:

On Saturday, I'd dared Cyrus to make his move.

On Monday, he answers.

I check my messages when I wake up and there's one from Sally in Corporate Affairs, who manages my media presence for me. "CALL ME ASAP," the subject says, and there's an attachment.

My heart starts beating faster. Sally isn't prone to outbursts of drama. I get out of bed and move to my laptop, while I dial her number on my phone. My computer's being slow, so it isn't till she answers that I'm able to open the attachment.

Then I see the headline in one of the tabloids, and I stop breathing.

'*New York billionaire in secret three-way tryst!*' it screams, but that's not what causes fear to clutch at me.

It's the picture underneath, one of Bailey, Sebastian and I. Her hair obstructs her face but I would know her anywhere. She's in her bra and panties, bent over a pool table, and I'm standing behind her, cupping her ass. Sebastian's in the picture as well. He's shirtless, and he's about to make a shot.

I remember the evening well. It was two weeks ago, and Bailey had been teasing Sebastian about being distracted by her cleavage. *If I play against either of you in my bra and panties,* she had laughed, *I'll win.* So we bet on it and Sebastian had promptly lost the game, much to Bailey's delight.

The photo has been taken in my apartment.

In the background of my mind, I give silent thanks that her face is hidden. This isn't about her - she's an innocent victim in a battle between Cyrus and me.

My mind is working at light-speed. Someone's been inside my apartment to plant a camera in the game room. Cyrus is involved somehow, I'm sure of it. After all, he's the only one who has something to gain if my personal life is in the news.

"Daniel," Sally says on the line. "You've seen the picture."

"I have."

She gulps. "There's more. Sophie will be calling you as soon as she gets in, but your board has convened an emergency meeting for tomorrow. They are going to question your fitness to lead the company."

Sally is well-connected to the gossip mills. "Tomorrow morning? That soon?"

"Mr. Strauss is going to cut short his vacation in Florida

and fly back this evening," she says. "We pay for his car service."

"Thank you, Sally. Any recommendations to manage this?"

She clears her throat. "Don't come into the office - there's a horde of paparazzi at the door. Stay out of sight until the board meeting."

I nod. Her advice is sensible, and I'm going to take it, but not until I get some answers. Because that photo was taken in my apartment, and if there was a camera in the game room, there is much more than one photo of the three of us. The pool table has been a prop in many games, and not all of them involve a cue ball.

This photo obstructs Bailey's face. The others won't. Worse, there could be video. This is serious.

My next call is to Stone Bradley, who runs a private investigation firm that I've used in the past. He picks up on the first ring. "Stone, this is Daniel Hartman," I say. "Sorry to wake you so early."

"I was up," he says. "And I saw the tabloids. You want to find out who took that photo?"

"Yes. And I need the answer by tomorrow morning."

"I'll do what I can." His voice is calm. "We can discuss my fee when I deliver results. Who would have motive to do this?"

"My money's on my Uncle Cyrus. I threatened to fire him on Saturday night."

"Okay, that's a place to start. I'm assuming the game room is in your place? I'll be there in twenty minutes."

I HESITATE before making my next call. I need to talk to Bailey and Sebastian. I was the person that was paranoid about publicity, and ironically, I'm the person who has broken their trust. Now, they are caught up in my battle with Cyrus, and I hate that I've put them in the middle of this.

Bailey doesn't have tenure. If her name gets revealed, her job is at risk. Sure, I could wave my magic wand and the university wouldn't fire her because a hundred and fifty million dollars is a lot of money, but she'd still be the subject of scrutiny and whispered gossip among her colleagues.

And though Sebastian has posed bare-chested for his book cover, he prefers to avoid the spotlight, letting his food do the talking for him. Still, a scandal like this is probably good for Sebastian. In his business, the only bad publicity is when a restaurant fails a health inspection.

Bailey. I need to call Bailey first. She has more to lose.

Before I can dial, the phone rings in my hand. I pick it up before my brain registers the caller. It's my Uncle Cyrus. It takes effort to keep my voice calm and collected, but against all odds, I succeed. "How can I help you, Cyrus?"

"I saw the tabloids," he says, his voice dripping with false sympathy. "I thought I told you to keep things quiet, Danny."

My mother calls me Danny when she's either feeling very fond of me, or very exasperated with me. *Cyrus does not get to call me that.*

"The board's convened an emergency meeting," he continues. "I thought you should know."

I don't tell him Sally's already informed me. I just wait for him to proceed, to tell me why he's really calling me. His next words reveal his true intent. "This might be the time,

Danny, to think about what's best for the company. If I were you, I'd resign."

"Would you?" My tone is cool.

"I would indeed," comes the too-quick reply. "This isn't just about you. Think about the employees of Hartman. When the stock price plummets, that's their future that you are playing dice with."

Please. Wall Street gives a fuck about only one thing. Earnings. They wouldn't give a shit if I were caught fucking a goat in the middle of Penn Station, as long as Hartman hit or exceeded their quarterly earnings target. The corporate world is not America's morality police.

No - this is just Cyrus, trying to play on my love for the company that my dad gave his life for. This is Cyrus wanting my job.

Then he plays his trump card, and all the fight leaves me. "And think about the girl. Bailey Moore, right? How would it look for a professor without tenure to be photographed in such a compromising position? The university trustees will be exceedingly displeased."

"How do you know who she is?" My voice is very quiet.

He clears his throat. "She was at the company party on Saturday, wasn't she?" I can hear the lie in his voice. "Someone introduced us."

How far will Cyrus go? I think I've just received my answer. He'll ruin Bailey's life, without hesitation, in order to become the CEO of Hartman.

If he was responsible for the camera, and I'm certain he is, he has photos and videos of Bailey.

I was going to fight, and I would have won. It would have been ugly, but I would have prevailed. But I can't do it without destroying Bailey's life.

The world is a cruel and unfair place. People will give Sebastian and me a free pass. *Boys will be boys, and all that.* Bailey, however, will be branded a slut and worse. I can't let that happen. I care far too much about her.

36

One of the deep secrets of life is that all that is really worth the doing is what we do for others.

— LEWIS CARROLL, THE LETTERS OF LEWIS
CARROLL

Sebastian:

I'm fast asleep when Daniel calls, and it takes several rings of the phone to pull me out of my slumber. When I see who it is, I pick it up, but my eyes stay closed. It was a late night at *Seb New York,* and I want to catch up on sleep. "Dude," I protest into the receiver, my voice thick with fatigue. "It's far too early for a phone call."

"There's a photo of you, Bailey and me on the front page of the Post."

Okay. That wakes me up. I drag myself up to a seated position and wipe the back of my hand over my eyes. "Tell me more."

"We're shirtless, she's in her bra and panties, and the photo was taken in my game room."

I'm wide awake now. This is bad. This is very bad. Every time I see Bailey's round ass bent over the pool table, my dick hardens. The three of us have had sex a countless number of times in that room.

"Stone Bradley's on his way over."

I know Stone. Daniel's used him before. He's smart and discreet, and he gets results. "I'm coming over as well."

"Be careful," he advises. "The front of my building is swarming with reporters."

"I'll figure out a way." Daniel's building has a back entrance. If that doesn't work, then I'll just brave them. I pause, not sure if the next question is going to be a sore point. "How's Bailey taking this?"

Daniel groans. "I can't reach her. Her phone's going straight to voicemail. I'm stuck here. I can't go find her and talk to her, and before you suggest it, neither can you. The paparazzi are going to be wondering who Bailey is. We can't lead them to her."

Damn it, he's right. I definitely don't want Bailey associated with this mess. In my business, any publicity is good publicity, but Bailey's in academia and it's not the same in her world.

"I'm going to keep trying her," he continues. "I don't know what else to do."

I can hear the hopelessness in his voice. "I'll see you in thirty minutes," I tell him. "And we can tackle this shit together."

37

Go wisely and slowly. Those who rush stumble and fall.

— WILLIAM SHAKESPEARE, ROMEO AND JULIET

Bailey:

Had I stopped to think about it, I would have realized that there had been warning signs. Dr. Landrieu was late with his work. A couple of weeks ago, he'd presented a synopsis that had been light on facts, and when I'd asked him for his list of sources, he'd been evasive.

I didn't question it because he's famous and tenured and I'm just a lowly assistant professor.

I've been busy hanging out with Daniel and Sebastian, being distracted by amazing sex, gourmet meals and my steadily improving pool game. For the first time in my life, I've placed my personal life ahead of work.

Monday morning, when I get to my office, I realize my distraction has come with a price tag. There's a message from the Smithsonian Press in my inbox. I open it, absently thinking that their paper review process has become quite fast, only to be greeted with a shock.

I'm being accused of plagiarism.

My heart hammers in my chest as I scan the contents of the email. The peer review process raised some red flags. Further inquiry found entire sections of our paper without merit, with no underlying facts to back up our assertions. And most damningly, the subject of our research is too similar to some pioneering work that the University of Buenos Aires has been doing. A professor there is alleging that his work has been stolen.

Of course, the paper has been rejected, but that's the least of my troubles. Right now, my department chair is probably receiving an email questioning the ethics of his department. Tomorrow, the president of NYU will get a memo, and as soon as he gets it, I will be fired. Even though my work is rock-solid, and even though Landrieu committed the crime.

I bury my head in my hands and give in to complete, total despair. I don't hear the knock at first, then it's repeated again.

I lift my head up to see Sameer at my door, his face radiating concern. "Bailey, is everything okay?"

"No," I whisper. I bring up the email on the screen and wave him toward it. "Everything's not okay at all."

TWO HOURS LATER, my office is crowded with people. Sameer's there, holding a mug of tea, his expression somber. Steve Ashworth, the department head is there. And so is a woman called Peggy Wilkerson, who is, as best as I can tell, a lawyer from the University administrative office. For a brief moment, I wonder if I'm being fired now, until I reason that if that were the case, Steve and Peggy would have made sure to kick Sameer out.

"I didn't do this, Steve," I say for the first time. When I say those words aloud, a cloud seems to fall away from me. "This email is talking about plagiarism in the Patagonia section. That's not me. That's Pierre Landrieu."

"I know, Bailey," Steve starts to say, then Peggy nudges him and he closes his mouth. I guess the university can't acknowledge that I'm innocent in case I turn around and sue them when they fire me.

And they will fire me. NYU hates scandal, and plagiarism is a cardinal sin in our profession. I'm good at what I do, but in the larger scheme of things, I'm an easily replaceable assistant professor, while Pierre Landrieu is a superstar who has his tenure. As Trevor has pointed out, people with liberal art PhDs are working in his fast-food restaurants. The university will have no trouble finding a replacement.

But I won't go out without a fight, because this is unfair.

"There's going to be a review," Steve mumbles, looking everywhere but at me. "We'll discuss the matter with the Smithsonian Press and with Valentin Perez in Buenos Aires. I'll keep you posted."

"What about Dr. Landrieu? Aren't you going to talk to him?"

"Yes," he blinks. "We'll talk to him too."

This is bullshit. The fact that they are not even trying to talk to Pierre Landrieu, possibly the only person who can prove my innocence? They've already made their decision. *I'm getting fired.*

Steve and Peggy take their leave, and Sameer remains behind. "This blows," he says frankly.

"Yeah, well, what do you do?" My voice is gloomy. "You heard them. They've made up their minds to fire me."

"Fight this, Bailey," he urges, patting my shoulder. "Write letters. Petition people who have influence. Take this public. What the university is doing is wrong and unfair. Don't let them get away with it."

I don't reply. I'm in shock as I watch him leave my office. My life feels like a house of cards, all tumbling down. I can't believe how quickly Steve must have agreed to fire me.

I grope around in my purse for my phone. Usually, Daniel, Sebastian and I message each other multiple times a day, a fact that caused no end of giggles at the last Drinking Pack night. When I glance at the screen, it's dead. Crap. My battery must have run out, and I haven't noticed. A sudden, overwhelming urge to talk to Daniel and Sebastian washes over me. They can't fix this situation - no one can, but when I'm with them, I feel cared for.

There's a spare charger somewhere in my clutter. I hunt around for it, when a thought strikes me. A thought I'm tempted to dismiss right off the bat.

Petition people who have influence, Sameer said. Who has more influence than Daniel Hartman? NYU has a hundred and fifty million reasons to listen to him.

Part of me doesn't want to do this. I'd like to do this on my own. Maybe I should trust in the system and let the review process work.

I'm many things, but I'm not naive. In the real world, Dr. Landrieu is famous and world-renowned, and I'm an assistant professor. It's going to be far more convenient if I take the fall for the plagiarism. After all, who's going to fight for me? Sameer? He has a kid and he doesn't have tenure. He'd be stupid to interfere.

Steve? The university administration can exert a lot of pressure on the head of my department. Delayed funding, slower hiring, inconvenient class schedules. Steve will know not to mess with the powers-that-be.

No. If I want to keep my job, I have only one option. Though I've made it explicitly clear that I want nothing to do with his money or his influence, I need to ask Daniel for help.

When I first met them, I would have hated to ask for a favor, but things are different now. My relationship with Daniel and Sebastian has deepened. We are no longer at the point where I'm worried that they are trying to impress me with their money and their power. I trust them.

I plug my phone into the charger and wait somewhat impatiently till the battery has enough juice for me to be able to power it up. As I start dialing Daniel's phone number, I see missed call after missed call. Fifteen in all, all from Daniel.

There are more than a dozen text messages as well, and I open one of them. 'Bailey. Please trust me. Whatever happens, I will fix this.'

What's going on?

38

There is a stubbornness about me that never can bear to be frightened at the will of others. My courage always rises at every attempt to intimidate me.

— JANE AUSTEN, PRIDE AND PREJUDICE

Bailey:

Of course, I call Daniel right away, not bothering to listen to his voicemails. The text message he sent me was very mysterious, and I don't do well with mystery.

He picks up on the first ring. "Bailey," he says. His voice is cautious.

"What's going on?" I ask him. "You can't have heard about this already." Daniel is freakishly well-informed, but even he can't already know about my troubles.

"Heard what?" he asks. "Have you listened to any of my messages?"

"No, I thought I'd call you and you could fill me in." I grimace. "I don't really remember my voicemail password."

He chuckles. "Ah, Bailey, I love you." There's a smile in his voice as he says those words, and it feels like someone has draped a warm blanket, fresh from the dryer, all around my heart. It feels pretty damn good.

His next words wipe that feeling away. "Have you looked at the Post?"

"No, I've had rather an eventful morning," I reply. "Should I?"

His voice is taut with tension when he replies. "Yes, you really should."

"Damn." That's all I can bring myself to say after seeing that picture. Just damn.

"I'm so sorry I let this happen, Bailey." There's misery in his tone. "This is my fault. I've failed you."

"Whoa there, Mr. Overreaction," I snap. "Slow it down. Did you leak this photo to the tabloids?"

"Of course not."

I glare at my cell phone, my own troubles forgotten for the moment. Maybe if I have more time to think about it, I might become angry with Daniel. Right now, I'm more concerned about the impact this will have on his Kansas City deal. He's been working so hard.

"Then the person that leaked the photo is the one I'm angry at, not you." My voice softens. "Daniel, I trust you. We'll deal with this, Sebastian, you and me. Together." I laugh, though there's not much humor in my tone. The stress of the morning has brought on a mammoth headache.

All I want to do is swallow some aspirin and crawl into bed. "Your news is kind of stealing the thunder from mine."

"What's going on?" His tone becomes alert. "You said I couldn't have heard already. Heard what?"

"Dr. Landrieu plagiarized huge sections of his research from some professor at the University of Buenos Aires, and I'm being cast as the scapegoat." I try and fail to keep the bitterness from my voice. "The university is reviewing my case now. I'm expecting to be fired tomorrow."

"Fuck," he swears. I can picture him so clearly on the other end of the line. His eyes closed, his expression tired. All I want to do is snuggle next to him, comfort him and be comforted. "I'll make a call," he says finally. "I'll put a stop to that."

"It's not too much to ask?" I don't want him to think that I'm with him for his contacts or his money. Most of the time, I can fight my own battles. Sometimes though, I need a little help.

"No, Bailey," he says with exasperation. "God, you are the most maddening woman. I call you, fully prepared for you to never want to see me or hear from me again because of the tabloids, and you are asking me if it would be too much trouble to call NYU on your behalf?"

"Well, if you put it like that." I take a deep breath. "How's Sebastian handling this? And can I come over?"

"He's here. He's not thrilled, of course, but he's managing. The notoriety won't harm him. It's you I'm concerned about. And as much as I want to see you," his tone softens, "coming over is a bad idea. The entrance to my house is crawling with paparazzi, waiting for another whiff of scandal."

"Why is it okay for Sebastian to come over and not me?"

"His face is in the photo, honey. Yours isn't, and I'd like to keep it that way."

"Oh," I pause. "Okay, that makes perfect sense. I thought I was going to get some sexist reason."

He laughs. "When this is over, you'll meet my mother, and you'll understand how much trouble I'd get into if I ever dared to insinuate that the rules are different for women."

Sure, there's a photo of us in the tabloids. Right now, I don't care. Not when Daniel just said he wanted me to meet his family. "You want me to meet your mother?" I ask out aloud, needing to confirm what I've heard.

"Of course. I'd have taken Sebastian and you already to Sunday lunch, except I was trying to stay out of the tabloids, remember?"

"Oh. And your mom will be cool with our thing...?"

"Ménage, Bailey. Or threesome, if you prefer." He sounds amused.

"I can't say those words out aloud in a sentence that has mom in it," I reply. Then I groan. "Shit, if you are going to tell your mom about me, I have to tell my parents about us too at some point."

"I've already told her." He sounds puzzled. "I told her weeks ago."

Oh. I don't know what to do with that revelation, so I focus back on the conversation at hand. Looking at the photo on my screen again, I notice something that has so far escaped my attention. "Daniel, this was taken in your game room."

"I know. The place is being swept for bugs now."

"Who could have planted it?"

"My money's on Cyrus," he admits. "He more or less threatened to leak some more pictures if I didn't resign as

CEO." He hesitates. "I think I'm going to do it, Bailey. The next photo could reveal your face, and I can't risk it."

My first, instinctive reaction is to tell him to fight. He can't give in to Cyrus' blackmail. Then I stop and consider the consequences of what would happen if naked photos of me end up in public circulation.

My colleagues would whisper about my personal life. If I do get tenure, everyone will assume it's because I'm sleeping with the billionaire who gave the university one hundred and fifty million dollars. And my parents? Yikes. I don't even want to think of their reaction.

Then I think about Daniel and Sebastian.

Daniel defended me against Clark before he even knew me, betting on me to succeed. He's spent hours patiently coaching me, helping me practice shot after shot. Yes, he said one horrible and hurtful thing, but after that moment, he's done everything to make amends.

Sebastian looks like a bad boy with his ripped abs and his tattoos, yet he's cooked dinner for me more times than I can count. When I forget to eat, lost in research or engrossed by corrections, it's Sebastian that reminds me to stop for food.

I'll be lying if I told you that being in the public eye this way doesn't bother me. Of course it does. I'm human, and this is a horrible, disgusting invasion of our privacy.

But when it comes down to it, I care more about Sebastian and Daniel. And I can't see a version of the future that doesn't have them in it. I love them. As insane as it is, I love both of them, and I want both of them in my life. For a long time. Forever.

My decision is made. When I speak, my voice is firm. "No. You can't give in to Cyrus. Fight back, Daniel."

He makes a noncommittal sound, and I fear he's already

made up his mind. "How could Cyrus have planted the camera anyway?" I ask him, to keep him from making any rash decisions. "Has he visited you lately?"

"No," Daniel says, sounding frustrated. "If I could prove it was Cyrus, I could fight back, but I have nothing. The only people who have visited are you and Sebastian. And my housekeeper, of course, but she's been with me forever."

"And Juliette..." I say slowly, remembering something. "Remember? A few weeks ago? Juliette needed to drop off the proofs of Sebastian's cookbook, and you told her to drop them off at your house?"

"That's right," he says slowly. "I'd forgotten about that. Hang on, Bailey, let me get Sebastian on the line. Talk to him while I go alert Stone." I hear him call out to Sebastian. "It's Bailey," he explains.

"How are you doing, Bailey?" Sebastian comes on the line and asks me, his voice concerned.

"I'm fine, I think," I tell him. "It hasn't sunk in yet. I've already had quite the morning."

"What happened?"

I fill him in on the happenings at the university, and he swears softly. "That sucks."

"Yeah, Daniel's going to make a call for me," I tell him, wishing I was there in person with them. "I decided I'm not too proud to ask for help."

"Good girl," he says approvingly. "Ah, here's Daniel. Let me put you on speaker phone."

"Did Bailey fill you in about Juliette?" Daniel asks.

"No," Sebastian sounds puzzled. "What's Juliette have to do with this?"

Daniel quickly explains our discussion and Sebastian whistles. "You think Juliette planted that camera?" he asks. "I can't see her doing something like that."

"You guys. Listen to me," I interrupt both of them. "She's already warned me away from Sebastian once." I tell them about the bathroom incident. "She's obsessed with Sebastian's career. And Daniel," my voice rises with excitement as I remember something else. "She was talking to Cyrus at your party for the longest time."

"Really?"

"You didn't notice?"

"No," he says. "They don't really know each other."

"Well," I insist, my voice stubborn, "they appeared to be as thick as thieves. I know what I saw."

"I'm not doubting you," he says at once. "Not even in the slightest. I know how eager Juliette is to get this deal done." His voice is grim. "I just didn't think she'd stoop to this level."

To be honest, neither did I. Yeah, Juliette's ambitious and intense, but I didn't think she'd resort to leaking photos of us to the tabloids. For starters, the plan makes no sense. Sebastian isn't going to be more cooperative if this photo is front page news.

"I'm going to sort this out," Sebastian promises. He hasn't said anything for a while. "Bailey, if Juliette did do this..." His voice trails off. "I'm so sorry."

"Will you stop?" Exasperation tints my voice. "God, you are just as bad as Daniel. Stop blaming yourselves for things that Cyrus and Juliette did. I'm not annoyed at the two of you. I'm saving my anger for the people that caused this situation."

There's silence on the other end of the line for a long time. Finally, Sebastian speaks, his voice very quiet. "We don't deserve you, Bailey," he says. I hear a phone ring in the background, and Sebastian picks it up. "Helen? What's going on?" he asks. "Bailey, I have to take this call. Talk to you later?"

"Bye," I tell him. "Daniel, you still there?"

"I am," he confirms.

"You said you loved me earlier." My heart is in my throat as I speak, but I have to know. "Was that a slip of the tongue?"

"Of course I love you, silly." His voice softens. "Though it's a rotten time to tell you that."

A smile breaks out on my face. He loves me. One down, one to go. Now, I just have to confirm that Sebastian feels the same way. Because there's three of us in my version of happily-ever-after, and I'm not going to settle for anything less than both of them.

"I love you too, billionaire boy," I reply. "Now, go fix this. And if it turns out Juliette planted the camera, I will punch her."

"Stop calling me billionaire boy," he grumbles, though there's a smile in his voice. "I hate that nickname."

39

It seems to me that our three basic needs, for food and security and love, are so mixed and mingled and entwined that we cannot straightly think of one without the others. So it happens that when I write of hunger, I am really writing about love and the hunger for it, and warmth and the love of it and the hunger for it... and then the warmth and richness and fine reality of hunger satisfied... and it is all one.

— M.F.K. FISHER, THE ART OF EATING

Sebastian:

Helen's voice is pitched high and her words tumble out. "Chef, thank god. You have to get down here."

Helen manages the pass at *Seb New York* with complete calm. I've seen her deal with missing line cooks, burnt meat, overcooked fish, and she's unflappable. "What's wrong?"

"There's been a fire at the restaurant." Her voice is strained. "The kitchen's destroyed."

"A fire?" Every muscle in my body is suddenly rigid. There's a tingling in my fingers and a tightening in my chest. It's difficult to breathe. "Where? How? What happened?" I'm putting on my coat as we speak, and Daniel eyes me with concern as I pace toward the door.

"At *Seb New York*," she confirms my deepest fear. My restaurant. My precious, *precious* restaurant. "The firemen are here now, and they think some spilled oil caused it. Ben was in the kitchen, and they've rushed him to ER." Her voice catches. "They don't think he's going to make it."

I clutch at the phone, my knuckles white. This is my fault. This is all my fault. Ben has shown up drunk to work, and I've failed to send him home, even though the kitchen is a dangerous place for someone who is inebriated. I should have fired him so he couldn't have hurt himself. I was going to fire him after my conversation with Katya on Thursday. Now, it's too late.

"I'll be right there," I tell her. *What have I done?*

"WHAT'S THE MATTER?" Daniel asks when I hang up. He's put on his jacket on as well. "I heard the word *fire*."

"In the kitchen at *Seb New York*," I say. I notice he's following me. "What are you doing?"

"What does it look like?" he asks me with a frown. "I'm coming with you."

"Daniel, there's a wall of reporters outside the door, and you said that Sally told you to keep a low profile."

"You came here," he says. "You braved the wall of reporters." He gives me a half-smile. "It's time to return the favor. Sebastian, I've listened to Cyrus all these years, and to what end? Cyrus doesn't care about me. He just cares about becoming the CEO of Hartman." He shakes his head. "What's really important is this. Us. You, me and Bailey."

"What about the reporters? The Kansas City deal? The meeting with the board of directors? Or are you going to give in to Cyrus and resign?"

"I don't know." His smile is strangely carefree. "Right now, I don't have any of the answers. Let's go deal with the fire. Once that's done, I need to call the president of NYU and tell him that I'm not going to stand by and watch them fire Bailey in order to sweep their little plagiarism problem under the table. Then, we talk to Juliette. The other stuff - Cyrus, the board of directors, the Kansas City deal - all of that can wait." He looks me in the eye. "People matter more than a job, Sebastian. I think it's time I proved that."

I slant him a look. "You sure about this? I don't want you to regret it."

"I'm positive." He sounds completely confident. "Hartman and Company is not my life. I don't think I could look myself in the mirror if I didn't help you."

This is the Daniel Hartman who extended his hand to help a nineteen year old runaway from Mississippi. On impulse, I hug my best friend. "I'm glad you are coming," I tell him. "It would be good to have a friend at my side. Thank you."

As we brave the horde of reporters, shouting questions at us, asking us if we have a statement for the press, I wish one thing. Though I know that it's right to protect Bailey from all of this ugliness, part of me is selfish.

The three of us are a team. We belong together. As I head to face the destruction of the restaurant that I've worked so hard to build, an essential piece of me is missing. I wish Bailey could be with us.

Daniel:

It doesn't take us long to get into my car and head to *Seb New York*. The street outside is crowded with fire trucks, ambulances and police cars. We open the door and hurry out, Sebastian making straight for Helen. When she sees him, she throws her arms around him and breaks down.

Sebastian's face is white with shock as he pats her back, and I've never felt more helpless in my life. In order to be somewhat useful, I head to the person who seems to be in charge, a big fireman who looks to be in his fifties. "I'm Daniel Hartman," I introduce myself. "Sebastian's a little occupied at the moment." I wave in Sebastian's direction. "Can you fill me in?"

"Sure thing, Mr. Hartman," the guys says. "My name is Neil Williams. Our crew was the first to respond to the call."

"Who called it in?"

"The florist next door," he says. "The call came in shortly after eleven."

"*Seb New York* isn't open for lunch." I frown. "In fact, they aren't even open Mondays."

"They aren't," he confirms. "The woman who is the emergency contact said the same thing. Katya something?"

"Katya Marinova," I tell him. "She's the restaurant manager. So, what happened?"

"As best as I can tell, the fire was caused by an oil spill. In restaurants, it's usually deep fryers."

"And Ben? I heard he's injured."

"He's badly burned," Neil Williams confirms, his face sober. "More than that, he inhaled a lot of smoke. An ambulance took him away. The cops could probably tell you which hospital he's in."

No matter how many times I've urged Sebastian to fire Ben, he doesn't deserve this. No one does. The poor guy. "And the damage to the premises? Is it safe enough to enter?"

"Absolutely not." His voice is stern. "A crew will have to come in and verify that there's no structural damage. Until they've given the green light, no one should enter the place."

"Fair enough." I've no desire to risk anyone's life. Enough damage has been done today. I shake his hand. "Thank you for your help."

"No worries," he says. He hesitates, about to say something else. "You're the billionaire on the Post this morning, right? My wife reads that rag."

Damn Cyrus and Juliette. "I am." My voice is curt.

He raises his hands. "I just want to tell you how wrong I think it is." He frowns. "They have no right to be in your business that way."

"Thanks." I'm about to add something else, when I see a person I very much want to talk to. Juliette. "Mr. Williams," I look at the fire chief, "will you excuse me? I need to catch up with someone."

I'm having the morning from hell. We all are. At the university, Bailey's worried about being fired. Sebastian is comforting his staff, most of whom are in tears. Juliette didn't cause either of these two things, but if she was responsible for our picture in the tabloids?

I'm not in the mood to be kind.

Approaching her, I take hold of her elbow. "Juliette," I tell her, my voice simmering with barely-contained anger. "Can we talk?"

40

All you need is love. But a little chocolate now and then doesn't hurt.

— CHARLES M. SCHULTZ

Bailey:

I go through my day on autopilot. At three, I give up on the grading and head back home. Piper's sitting on the couch, smothered under a pile of blankets, and Jasper's fulfilling his role as paperweight, sitting on her stomach, looking smug. "You're back early," she says. "How come?"

"I might be getting fired." I sit on the other end of the couch and draw the blankets over me.

"What? Why?"

I tell her the whole sorry mess. Her eyes get wider and wider as I relate all the events of the crazy day - the plagiarism accusation, the photo in the tabloid, Daniel's phone call, the 'I love you' declaration.

"Wow," she says when I'm done. "That's a pretty eventful day. All I had to do was listen to Wyatt Lawless and Owen Lamb tell me that my menu was disorganized and scattered."

"Ouch," I say sympathetically. "I hope you told them where to stick it."

She dismisses her partners with a wave. "Forget them," she says. "I'm certainly planning to. So, your guys said '*I love you*.' What happens now?"

"Only Daniel said it," I clarify. "I still don't know what Sebastian is thinking."

She snorts inelegantly. "Sebastian Ardalan is a chef, Bailey. He's been cooking meals for you? Packing your lunch? Making breakfast? The man loves you." Her eyes soften. "We cooks tend to show our love with food."

I think I'm going to cry. If that's true, that's probably the sweetest thing I've ever heard. "You think?" Jasper stretches and lurches toward me, deciding that my lap resembles his next bed. I scratch him behind his ears.

"I do," she says. "Are you stressed about your job?"

"Yeah," I confess. "I love them, Piper. I really do. And I think that Daniel should fight back." I sigh. "Still, I'm not looking forward to having my naked pictures all over the Internet."

Piper gets up. "Where are you going?" I ask her.

"To put the kettle on," she tells me. "Unless you want hot chocolate instead?"

That sounds amazing. Not as good as being snuggled between Daniel and Sebastian, but it's a pretty close second. Jasper's warm body in my lap helps as well. I feel slightly better. "Yes please," I tell her.

We start spiking our hot chocolate with tequila and peppermint schnapps when Gabby comes over. She's the only one of our gang who can make it tonight. Wendy's working and Miki's been scarce lately. I think her marriage is falling apart, but she won't talk about it.

The three of us are a sad bunch. I keep glancing at my phone to see if I've heard from Sebastian or Daniel. Gabby's distracted by something as well, though she insists she's fine. And Piper's still steaming about the criticism of her menu.

Then, Piper flips on the local news, and we discover that a fire has destroyed most of Sebastian's restaurant. When I see that, I've had enough. I don't care about the tabloids. I don't care about Cyrus' threats or Juliette's conspiracies. All I care about is being with the men I love.

I rise to my feet, displacing Jasper, who jumps to the ground with an indignant yowl. "Fuck this shit," I announce. "I'm tired of being miserable here. I'm going to find them."

I text Daniel and Sebastian. *I'm coming over. Don't try to stop me.*

Daniel replies back within seconds with instructions, because that's the kind of thing he does. *The Plaza, room 221. Want me to send a car?*

Subway's quicker, I type, a smile breaking out on my face. *See you soon.*

"You have to go see about a boy, Bailey?" Piper giggles, wildly misquoting Good Will Hunting.

I wink at Gabby and Piper. Now that I know I'm going to be seeing Daniel and Sebastian soon, I feel so much better. "Not one boy, ladies. I have to go see about *two* of them."

41

The greatest victory is that which requires no battle.

— SUN TZU, THE ART OF WAR

Sebastian:

"I'm so sorry," she says as soon as I open the hotel room door. "I just saw the news about your restaurant on TV."

I draw her into my arms and hold her, taking comfort in the feel of her softness, the smell of her hair, the sweet and trusting way her head rests on my shoulder. "I missed you," I whisper. "What a fucking day."

We stand there for what feels like hours. Finally, I disentangle us gently, and lead her in. "You hungry?" I ask her automatically.

She smiles at that and she hugs me again. "What's that for?" I ask, surprised. "Not that that wasn't very nice, because it was."

She shakes her head. "Piper said something to me," she

says mysteriously, taking off her coat and tossing it on the back of a couch. She looks around the spacious living room, takes in the three doors leading off it. "Two bedrooms and a bathroom?" she guesses. "You guys don't know how to do low-key, do you?" Where's our resident billionaire?"

Her voice is fond, not mocking. "He's on the phone with Stone Bradley," I answer. "He's the investigator."

She sits on the couch, and pulls me down with her, resting her head on my shoulder again. "Are you okay?" she asks softly. "I know how much that place meant to you."

"Yeah..." I hold her hand and it feels like home, sitting next to her, talking about our day. "We were lucky. No one except Ben was around."

"Ben, your problem sous-chef?"

I nod. "I don't know what he was doing there," I say. "When I was starting out, I would go in on the days I didn't have to work and try to teach myself new techniques. Maybe he was experimenting with a new recipe..." I swallow, thinking of Ben's frail body in the hospital. "He's been badly burned," I tell her. "He was in a forced coma when we visited, but the doctors think he's going to make it." I close my eyes and tighten my grip on her hand. "Had it been any other day of the week..."

Her hand, the one that isn't tight in mine, strokes my back. "You're a good person, Sebastian," she says softly. "What about the restaurant itself?"

"Closed for a minimum of six weeks." I exhale. "We'll work through it. We always do." I bring her hand up to my mouth and touch the soft skin with my lips. "I love you."

Her eyes twinkle. "I know. Piper told me."

I'm confused by her words, but not interested enough to sort it out. It's enough that she knows how I feel. "Clever woman, Piper. I hear she's driving Lawless and Lamb crazy."

"Is she? She won't give me any of the good gossip." She strokes my cheek. "I love you too, you know."

The tightness eases in my chest. "That's good," I tell her. "That's really good."

THERE ARE days when the sex between the three of us is heated and explosive and raw. Today's not that day. The sex is sweet and sensual, slow and tender. When I part her thighs and taste her, her breath catches. "Sebastian," she whimpers. "Oh god yes."

Daniel lowers his mouth over her lush breasts. I see a flash of his teeth as he nibbles at that erect nub, and her reaction makes my dick ache. She pushes her hips against me. "More..." she begs. "Don't stop."

"I'm not planning on it," Daniel replies.

Me, I'm enjoying the taste of her too much to break away. She tastes sweet and salty and right. Her body quivers when I peel back her hood and trace a tiny circle over her clitoris. "I'm going to come," she gasps as I repeat that stroke, over and over. I can feel her tense, her muscles tightening as she nears her climax. Her hands grip tightly at my hair, and she pushes my mouth deeper into her pussy.

Her face distorts with pleasure as she comes, but I don't let up. "Once more," I tell her, my voice muffled by her pussy.

"I'm good with that," she exhales, and both Daniel and I chuckle. That statement is pure Bailey. She likes her orgasms, my fiery redhead, and she's not afraid to ask for them.

"Switch with me," Daniel tells me. "I want a taste too."

We trade places. I move up the bed and kiss Bailey

deeply. I've never told a woman that I love her. Work has kept me busy, and my restaurants have been everything to me. Today, on a day when *Seb New York* has almost been destroyed, I feel the warmth of Bailey's body next to mine, and the fire doesn't seem to matter as much. Those three simple words - *I love you* - seem to bind us closer, deepening the intimacy between us.

She tries to wriggle away from Daniel's mouth, her pussy sensitive as a result of her first orgasm. This is typical Bailey as well, and Daniel and I exchange grins. She wants the orgasm, but she'll try to writhe away from it. "Stay put, sweetheart," I tell her, pinning her in place with my leg.

"Fuck, fuck, fuck," she throws her head back on the pillow, her red hair a contrast against the pristine white of the sheets. "Daniel, please..."

Her body trembles and shivers as she comes with a moan. It's too much. I need to be inside her right now, and from the look in Daniel's eyes as he lifts up his head, he feels the same way.

Grabbing a condom from the side table, I roll it on and ease myself into her hot pussy. She's wet and tight, her sex swollen from her two orgasms. The sensation is bliss. Pure, unadulterated bliss.

Daniel positions himself behind her and pushes in her asshole, after the application of generous amounts of lube. She groans as we both fill her. "This," she gasps, "feels so good."

Daniel kisses the back of her neck, pushing her curls out of the way. My palms graze over her erect nipples, and she hisses in pleasure and rakes her nails down my back. "Tiger," I accuse her with a smile.

She starts to say something in reply, then Daniel nibbles at the curve of her shoulder, and she loses her train of thought, throwing back her head in a gesture of complete abandon. "Bailey," Daniel mutters. "You are so beautiful."

It's been the day from hell. As my lips meet hers, it all fades away. In the softness of her body, in the sweet sigh of pleasure she makes, in the sheen of sweat on her skin as she rocks between us, I come home. As she writhes against us, I know I can't last much longer. I'm going to come, whispering her name, kissing her skin, touching her and holding her.

This is love, and it's the only thing that matters.

"I FORGOT TO ASK EARLIER," she says, once our passion is sated, her voice heavy with exhaustion. "Did you guys ever talk to Juliette?"

Daniel's playing with a lock of her hair, winding it around his fingers and releasing it, then winding it up again. "Yeah," he says. "We talked to her."

"And?" She props herself up on an elbow and looks at him. "What did she say?"

I think back on our conversation with Juliette. It had been unexpected. I thought she would deny what she did, but she had confessed to everything. Cyrus had lied to her and he'd used her. She'd given him the photo, but she swore to us that she didn't know he would leak it to the press.

Though I'm furious, I think I believe her story. Of course, our business relationship is over. I won't work with someone I can't trust, and whether Juliette intended harm or not, she should have never gone behind my back.

"She confessed that she planted the camera," Daniel says. He shakes his head. "Cyrus gave her the idea. He's been grooming her for weeks, insinuating that Sebastian would be much better off without either you or me holding him back."

"Oh." She bites her lower lip as she thinks that over. "She gave Cyrus the camera?"

"No, thank heavens." This is the bit I'm most grateful about. "Cyrus promised her that he'd just use it to scare Daniel into ending the threesome, but she grew uneasy with the plan." I frown. "She's a little too comfortable with the idea of blackmail, Juliette. I don't like that."

"She didn't trust Cyrus, I take it?" she asks.

Daniel shakes his head. "No, she didn't. She just gave him the one photo with your face obscured. Cyrus knows who you are, unfortunately, but at least there aren't any photos. Or worse, video."

"What happens now?"

Daniel exhales. "There's more to the story. Have you ever wondered why I'm in the press all the time? I'm a CEO, not a celebrity. I might be rich, but in New York City, there are at least two dozen people richer than me, and they never get photographed. Stone Bradley figured it out. Cyrus has been selling me out to the tabloids all along. He's been paying the paparazzi to trail me." He looks grim. "He could never move directly against me. I have enough votes on the board. This way however? If he portrays me as an irresponsible playboy, and if he can blame the failure of the Ryan Communications deal on me?"

She hisses. "Suddenly, your board reconsiders. Damn it. What are you going to do?"

"Expose him. Juliette's agreed to tell her story to the board tomorrow."

"Is that going to be enough?" Her voice is skeptical. "It's her word against his, isn't it?"

"Stone's looking for evidence," Daniel says. "The board

meets in the morning. If he's found something by then, I'll use it. If not, Juliette's the best that I have."

We're all silent as we each contemplate the next day. Daniel's going to be in the fight of his life to protect his company from Cyrus. Bailey has her hearing at NYU to contend with, and I have to go deal with the aftermath of the fire.

Tomorrow's going to be another long day, but no matter what, I know we'll all be just fine. Because today, we all discovered something really important. We can handle anything the world throws at us. As long as we are *together.*

42

I love you as certain dark things are to be loved, in secret,
between the shadow and the soul.

— PABLO NERUDA, 100 LOVE SONNETS

Bailey:

I'm so used to staying over at Daniel's that it takes me a
few minutes the next morning to register I'm somewhere different. The usual morning aroma of coffee is
absent, as is the sound of Daniel clattering around in his
kitchen, trying to make breakfast, until Sebastian mutters a
curse and swings out of bed to help him.

I'm at the Plaza. That's the good news.

The bad news is that today's the Day of Judgment for all
three of us. Daniel meets his board. I have my review with
the university and at some point today, Sebastian will meet
the safety experts and the insurers and find out how long
it'll take for *Seb New York* to reopen.

Sebastian strolls into the bedroom, his hair damp from a

shower. A towel rides low on his hips and I openly lick my lips. I'm not looking forward to today, and staying in bed and having sex with Sebastian seems like a much better plan.

"Don't you dare," he warns as he realizes my intent, though from the gleam in his eyes, my horniness isn't *entirely* unwelcome. "Come on. Out of bed with you. Don't you have a meeting with your university president this morning?"

"Yes," I groan, pulling the covers over my head, muffling the sound of my voice. "I would like to skip it entirely."

Daniel enters the room, holding a cup of coffee. He's fully dressed - he's wearing a gray suit with some kind of darker weave running through it, a light shirt and a purple tie, and he looks good enough to eat.

With a grin, he waves the cup in my direction, and I emerge out from under the covers to glare at him. Damn it, that coffee smells really good. Good enough that I want to get out of bed for it. "That's not fair," I accuse him.

"But it's remarkably effective," he replies. "Come have breakfast with us before I have to take off. Is the tie too much, do you think?"

With a start, I realize Daniel's nervous. Most of the time, Daniel's in perfect control. He's smart, he's well-informed, and he's entirely too self-assured for his own good. When he plays, he plans on winning. He doesn't make bets he thinks he can lose.

Today's situation is different. Anything can happen, and by the end of the day, he could be forced out of his own company. If it happened to Steve Jobs, it can certainly happen to Daniel Hartman.

"The tie looks great," I reassure him, swinging out of bed and taking the cup of coffee from his hand. "Stop worrying.

You've made the company too much money for the board to fire you."

"We'll see." His tone is deliberately neutral. "Half the board are cronies of my grandfather, people who still resent my father for marrying my mother. Cyrus might not be what's best for Hartman, but he's one of them and I'm a wild-card."

"A wild-card who's in a threesome." I wink at him, hoping to tease him out of his grim mood. In the back of my mind, I wonder if he's called NYU on my behalf, but I don't bring it up. I don't want to nag. If he's remembered, that's great. If he hasn't, I'll deal with the consequences.

"What time is your meeting at the university?" he asks as we sit down.

"Ten-thirty," I mutter, not looking at them. I don't want to think about my academic career going up in flames. Only a few days ago, I was sitting on top of the world. I had two perfect guys, they were supportive of me going off to Argentina for six months, and my pool game had improved by leaps and bounds. Now, it feels like a guillotine hangs over my head.

The table is crowded with dishes - scrambled eggs, bacon, pancakes, toast, fruit and more. I raise an eyebrow at the spread. "Hungry this morning?" I ask as I reach for some toast.

"I thought you liked variety, Bailey," Sebastian winks. He's the most relaxed person in the room. He fills his plate with scrambled eggs and adds two slices of bacon.

Daniel's more like me - he can't eat either. He's just pretending to munch on a piece of toast. "I haven't forgotten about your meeting," he says. "I'm going to call the president on my way into work. I promise you, it'll work out."

"Thank you." I lace my fingers in his. "I know you have

other things on your mind."

"There's nothing more important than you, Bailey," he says lightly. "You should know that by now." He puts down the toast onto the plate and rises to his feet. "I have to go," he says. He leans down and presses a kiss against my lips. "I'll be in a board meeting the same time you have your review, so I won't be able to call you. Text me as soon as you know something?"

I put my arm around his neck and draw him into a deeper kiss. "You too," I say when I let him go. "I'm almost as nervous about your board meeting as I am about my job." That's a lie - I'm far more nervous about Daniel than I am about the university.

Sebastian rises to his feet and the two of them exchange a hug. No words are spoken between them - they've been friends long enough that no words are necessary.

"Are you nervous?" I ask Sebastian once Daniel has left.

"I'm terrified," he says. "All last night, I kept dreaming about Daniel's stupid board meeting. This is my fault, you know. Juliette works for me."

"You didn't make her give Cyrus that photo," I tell him. "And I didn't plagiarize from Valentin Perez. Other people did. The situation sucks, that's all."

"True." He finishes the rest of the food on his plate. "Want me to walk you to NYU and lend you moral support?"

I beam at him. "Would you do that? What about the restaurant?"

"My meeting with the insurers is not till one," he replies. "I can do both."

"Thank you," I say again.

Yes, this is a pretty grim day, but my heart lightens as I realize something. I don't have to face it on my own.

43

*Victorious warriors win first and then go to war, while defeated
warriors go to war first and then seek to win.*

— SUN TZU, THE ART OF WAR

Daniel:

Never bring a knife to a gunfight, they say. Unless Stone Bradley's come through with evidence that Cyrus has been selling me out to the tabloids for years, I'm about to do just that.

"Mr. Bradley's waiting for you in your office, Mr. Hartman," Sophie says to me as I walk in. "And Ms. Kincaid is there as well."

I close my eyes to conceal my relief. Though I didn't tell Bailey last night because I didn't want to worry her, there's always been the possibility that Juliette wouldn't show. Thankfully, she's here, keeping up her end of the bargain.

"Thanks, Sophie."

She smiles up. "You'll beat this, Mr. Hartman," she says. "I have complete faith in you. And there's coffee in your office, and I ordered bagels and cream cheese."

"Don't worry, Sophie, I'm not going anywhere." As I open the door to my office, I hope I'm not lying. If there's ever a time for Bradley to earn the exorbitant fees he charges, it's now.

Juliette's looking out of the window with a coffee cup in her hand. Stone's pretending to be engrossed in reading his newspaper, but he's subtly checking out her ass. I roll my eyes, and he grimaces, abashed at being caught.

"Daniel," Juliette exclaims, turning in my direction as she hears the door open. "I'm so sorry. Last night, I couldn't sleep at all, thinking about what I've done." She pauses and straightens her spine. "Never mind, the way I feel isn't your problem. I'm here to try and fix what I did."

"I appreciate that." I'm not lying. Without Juliette, I'd have nothing to offer the board in my defense. But is Juliette's testimony enough? Or does Stone have something more for me? "Stone? Have you found anything?"

He grins. "I struck gold. There's a problem when you ally yourself with paparazzi sleazeballs, Hartman. These guys would sell their grandmothers out for a story. I waved some cash in front of them, and it wasn't too hard to get them talking. Cyrus has been paying for reporters to stalk you and he's been dropping some serious dough so that the editors of the tabloids will run your mug in their paper."

Stone Bradley sounds confident in his claims, but accusations aren't going to be enough for today's meeting. "I need proof."

He hands me a folder. "And I have it. Printouts of emails from your uncle to the editor of the Post. Communication between the photographers and Cyrus. Bank transfers. And much more."

"He used a traceable email address?" I'm aghast. "How dumb is he?"

"Cocky, maybe," Stone shrugs. Juliette's listening to our conversation with keen interest. "Perhaps he thought he'd be above suspicion."

He would have had cause to think that. I'd always muttered curses about the tabloids, but I'd never wondered why they followed me around. I was too busy running my family company to pay attention to that. Cyrus almost got away with it. *Until he involved Bailey.*

I flip through the contents, my relief growing as I read each damning bit of evidence. "This is good stuff, Stone."

"I told you I'd take care of it," he replies.

Stone's earned his arrogance. He had twenty-four hours to track all of this down, and he's come through in spades. "My bill will be in the mail," he adds.

I laugh. "No doubt." I stick out my hand and shake his. "Thank you for your help, Bradley. I really appreciate it."

"No worries," he says. He pulls a business card out of his wallet and hands it to Juliette with a wink. "Call me, Juliette. Let's do lunch."

When he departs, Juliette looks at me with a confused look on her face. "Did he just ask me on a date?"

I chuckle. "His timing could use some work. Then again, maybe he just believes in seizing every opportunity."

She rolls her eyes, though she does tuck away the card in her bag. "What time is the board meeting?" she asks.

I glance at my watch. "Fifteen minutes," I tell her. "You want a bagel?"

"No thanks," she says. "I'm so nervous I'll throw up if I eat."

We wait in silence, each of us lost in our own thoughts. Had she not involved Bailey, I would feel sorry for Juliette. Cyrus fed her a bunch of lies and half-truths, and she fell for it. But she did involve Bailey, and there's no forgiving that, not by me.

Once upon a time, I would have said that Juliette and I were friends. Not anymore.

∼

I WALK into the boardroom on my own. Juliette's waiting in my office, and Sophie will bring her in at the right time. First, I need to assess the lay of the land.

My mother's sitting at the long conference table, as are the rest of the board members. Cyrus is present too, barely concealing his smugness under a somber look. I ignore him for the present, and give my mother a questioning glance.

She rises to her feet and inclines her head toward the coffee. I follow her and pour myself a cup. "I would have come to your office," she says in a low voice. "But I wanted to get a sense of what you are going to face."

"And?"

"This could go either way," she whispers. "I think Cyrus has something up his sleeve."

"I know what it is," I reply. "Ryan Communications voted last night to reject our deal." That piece of news was in my email this morning, but I hadn't shared it with either Sebastian or Bailey. The two of them are worried enough for me. I didn't want to make it worse.

She draws in a sharp breath. "That's not good."

I nod. "He's not the only one with an ace up his sleeve, mom," I tell her with a small smile. "We're about to find out if the board gives a shit about ethics, or if they care only about pedigree."

Vincent Strauss rises to his feet, giving my mother a disapproving look as he does so. My mother, who is practiced at ignoring these slights, doesn't react. Inside me, something hardens. If I prevail today, I'm going to clean house. Cyrus needs to go, and so does half this board. These guys are here because of their connections, not because of their ability. In the last few years, they've been more an obstacle than a help as I've grown Hartman, but I've held off from making any waves because of some misplaced sense of family obligation.

Cyrus did something important when he betrayed me. He made me realize that I'm not required to protect these people. They are going to regret pissing me off.

"Shall we get going?" he asks in his paper-dry voice. "I'd like to open by making a statement."

Vincent is the Chairman of the Board, and there's no dissent around the room. He clears his throat. "Daniel Hartman," he addresses me with a definite tone of disapproval. "This board has kept silent as time and time again, you've dragged the good name of this company through the tabloids. But this latest episode," he emphasizes that word with disfavor, "has cost us an important deal. Cyrus has made me aware that Ryan Communications rejected Hartman's offer last night. It is my considered opinion that your appearance in the paper yesterday was the direct cause. I'm going to recommend to my colleagues," he nods at his cronies around the table, "that we seek your resignation, and continue forward under more stable leadership." His gaze rests on Cyrus.

It's time to go on the attack. I rise to my feet. "Thank you, Vincent," I gesture for him to sit, a deliberate and patronizing gesture. I have no desire to be conciliatory, not anymore. I don't get angry easily, but my blood boils as I survey all of them. "It is customary," I continue, "to be allowed a chance to defend myself. Let's start with the picture in the Post, shall we?"

I press a button and the photo of Bailey, Sebastian and I fills the screen that covers one wall of the boardroom. "When I saw the photo, I was furious. Then I realized something that made me even angrier." I glance around the table, holding each of their eyes in my gaze. "This photo was taken in my home."

A couple of people sit up at that. Everyone in this room is united in their need for public discretion. But a man's home is still his castle, and I'm not the only one unwilling to put my personal life under a microscope.

"I didn't put that camera there, I assure you," I continue. "And if I didn't, who did?"

"I don't see how this matters, Danny," Cyrus interrupts, his voice tense. "The reality is that the damage has been done. We have to find a way today to move forward."

"Indeed." My agreement surprises him. "We do have to move forward, and more importantly, we have to clean house. Hartman has a long and prestigious reputation. Our company does not need to be tabloid fodder, right?"

My mother looks at me with narrowed eyes. She probably thinks I should be highlighting the results that I've delivered as CEO, and without Stone's evidence, that's exactly what I would have done. However, the documents he's uncovered for me offer a better way.

"That's right," another gray-haired member of the board says, leaning forward. "Am I to understand, Daniel, that this means you are offering us your resignation?"

"Oh no," I reply, my tone steely. "No, it isn't my resignation that's going to be on the table today." I reach forward and punch in Sophie's extension. "Sophie, can you ask Juliette Kincaid to come into the boardroom, please?" I take note of Cyrus' sudden paleness with grim satisfaction.

Let the bloodbath begin.

44

No, no! The adventures first, explanations take such a dreadful time.

— Lewis Carroll, Alice's Adventures in
Wonderland

Bailey:

"Then what happened?" I lean forward, totally engrossed by Daniel's recounting of the day's events.

"The board voted unanimously to ask for Cyrus' resignation," Daniel replies.

"And Juliette?"

He gives me a sidelong look. "I was going to talk to you about that," he says. "She offered to quit the team."

"She can't," I exclaim. "Or you'll lose your bet."

Sebastian rolls his eyes at that. "Yes," he says dryly. "Daniel Hartman is going to notice losing fifty grand in a bet."

"I don't like losing," Daniel reminds him mildly. "Although in this case, I'm more concerned about what Bailey thinks." He looks at me. "It's your call," he says. "The way the brackets are set up, if we win, we'll meet Trevor's team in the finals. If Juliette quits the team, we can't replace her, and we might not make the finals."

"Oh no," I tell him grimly. "You tell her to show up tomorrow night and play her heart out. Fuck, I'll tell her to show up. She owes me. I need to beat Trevor."

Both Sebastian and Daniel chuckle. "That's what I thought you'd say," Daniel grins. "She'll be there." He shakes his head ruefully. "Remind me never to piss you off, Bailey."

"And the restaurant?" I turn to Sebastian. "When can you re-open?"

He grimaces. "Six weeks, as predicted," he says. "Still, the damage wasn't as bad as I'd feared." He shrugs. "It's not a terrible thing for the team to take a break," he adds. "We've been working our fingers to the bone to get the second star."

"They'll still get paid?"

He nods. "I'd be crazy to do anything else," he replies. "My competitors were salivating at the idea of my team being out of work." He snorts. "They were hoping to poach my staff. Not going to happen."

"And Ben's pulling through?"

He nods, though this time his expression holds sadness. "His hands are damaged," he says quietly. "His career as a chef is over." He sighs. "It's probably for the best. It takes skill and temperament to cut it in a kitchen. Ben had the skill, but he couldn't cope with the stress."

"What's going to happen to him?"

"I'm paying for rehab," Daniel cuts in. "Then, after that, if he's better, we'll find him a job."

They are both such good people. I feel really lucky that they are mine.

"You still have to tell us about your review meeting," Sebastian points out. "Your '*I didn't get fired*' text message was a little short on the details."

I make a face as I think about the meeting. "I was a bit anti-climactic," I tell them. "I had a speech rehearsed about ethics and morality and all that stuff, but I didn't get a chance to use it. They just told me I wasn't getting fired, and that was it."

"What are they going to do about the plagiarism?" Sebastian asks. "Are they going to fire Landrieu? Or reprimand him?"

"Who can tell?" I'm a little disillusioned. "Does the university have enough balls to create a hue and cry about Landrieu's work? I doubt it. They were transparently grateful that I was going to spend the next semester on leave in Argentina, and there was no mention of my tenure window."

"You don't think they'll offer tenure?" Daniel's voice is sharp.

I shake my head. "Don't interfere," I warn him. "Not this year they won't. They'll need to wait for this to fade away." I grimace. "Still, I didn't get fired today. That's a win, right? You take what you get. I was disappointed during the meeting, but I got over it." I grin at them. "I have other, more interesting things to distract me."

"Do you?" Daniel's voice is amused. "You mean things like pool practice? Stone has assured me that the game room is free of any recording equipment. Want to play?"

I bound up. "I love games," I say eagerly. "Let's go."

EPILOGUE

I'm a great believer in luck, and I find the harder I work the more I have of it.

— THOMAS JEFFERSON

Bailey:

July, the day of the tournament...

During the regular season, pool league is a fun, social activity for all except Clark Ellis, who really takes it far too seriously. Team captains match beginner against beginner, and expert against expert. Everyone stays challenged that way, and people can hone their game against equally skilled opponents.

The rules are different when it's tournament time. Now, the objective is to win at all costs. As a result, when your opponent is a seven, the highest skill rank attainable in the American Poolplayers Association, the strategic response is to counter with a two or a three. Because of the handicapping system, the player who is a seven needs to win six games to win the match, and the lower-ranked player needs to just win two games to prevail.

I'm a three now. Trevor's still a seven. I just have to win two games.

Juliette had come up to me the Wednesday after the great tabloid debacle, and she'd apologized quietly. After that, she's stayed away from us, merely showing up, playing without saying a word and leaving. I feel a little sorry for her, to be honest, and I'm tempted to tell Daniel and Sebastian that it's time we all buried the hatchet.

Trevor's team walks over. These guys - and they are all men, there's not a single woman among them - have a definite swagger as they approach. Trevor gives me a snide look. "I'm surprised your team got this far, Bailey," he calls over, his voice cutting through the noise. "But it ends here."

His team fist-bumps each other and exchanges high-fives, while I exchange a dry glance with Daniel and Sebastian. *It ends here.* Seriously, who talks like that? Do they think they are in a Quentin Tarantino movie? We are in Yonkers, for crying out aloud, in a sports bar located in a strip mall. Glamorous, this isn't.

I would normally be a bundle of nerves by this point, but Daniel and Sebastian have taken steps to prevent it. And by steps, I mean a butt plug buried in my ass, and a vibrator nestled against my clitoris. Then there's the red lace bra and panties they've made me wear under my black dress. The sexy lingerie and the toys, not to mention the multiple orgasms I had in the car on my way over here, have all left me too blissed out to be nervous. Tense? Not me. I'm a deep pool of relaxation.

Clark goes up first, and Trevor puts up Peter, the only

guy on their team who isn't a complete jerk. Even though I should be rooting for my own team, I'm secretly not too heartbroken when Peter beats Clark. Clark's a jerk. I'm never going to want him to win.

Next up is a player from Trevor's team called Frankie. He's listed as a five, but that's a garbage rank. I've seen Frankie play, and he's almost as good as Trevor. I whisper my disbelief to Daniel and Sebastian, and Daniel nods, unsurprised. "I've heard Trevor's team does this," he says. "They win as many games as it takes to qualify for the tournament, and then they start throwing games to lower their rank."

"That's cheating," I say indignantly.

He doesn't look concerned. "We can take them, Bailey. I have complete confidence in you."

Juliette is selected to play against Frankie. She's a four. Sebastian walks up to her to warn her about Frankie's true skill level, and I turn to Daniel. "Are they talking again?" I ask him, indicating Sebastian and Juliette.

He shakes his head. "Not really."

"Well, they should. His cookbook is still a New York Times bestseller. That was all Juliette's doing."

"She involved you," he responds with a half-smile. "Neither Sebastian nor I find forgiveness easy."

I think both of them are wrong, and it's time to let this go, but for the moment, I hold my peace and watch Juliette play. She's on fire today. She's hitting the ball cleanly, she's making smart, strategic decisions, and best of all, she's in Frankie's head. He thought he was playing against a *girl*, and it would be an easy win. Juliette's proving him wrong.

I cheer loudly as she wins her first game. "Go Juliette," I yell, drawing a glare from Trevor. I refrain with difficulty from flipping him off, and instead do a fist-bump of solidarity with Juliette. She looks surprised, but grateful. "Thanks, Bailey," she says. "One game down, three to go, right?"

"You've got this. Frankie's spooked, and he gets worse when threatened, not better."

Sure enough, Frankie's level of play drops off in the second game, much to Trevor's disgust, and Juliette wins again. Frankie manages to hold on in the third game, but then he drops the next two. Juliette's won her match.

One-one.

I'm somewhat relieved and somewhat disappointed. Both Daniel and Sebastian rarely lose, and they will win their games. It won't matter whether I win or lose after that. It'll matter to Clark, obviously, because of the bet, but it won't matter in the scheme of the tournament.

Sure enough, Daniel makes quick work of his opponent. And then something unexpected happens.

Sebastian loses his match by a hair.

It's all up to me now. And the butterflies in my stomach are back in full flutter.

THE THEME SONG from '*Chariots of Fire*' plays in my head as I walk to the center of the room, under the spotlight. Trevor walks forward, almost in slow motion. The coin toss to determine who breaks seems to take an eternity, then the quarter lands face up on the felt. Heads. I'm breaking.

"You've got this." Sebastian's voice is low and certain next to me.

"Did you throw your game?" I demand. "Did you set this up?"

"I don't know what you are talking about," he says

blandly, watching Daniel rack the balls for me. "Why does Trevor look so pleased about the coin toss?"

"He thinks I can't break," I chuckle. "He's about to find out he's wrong."

The vibrator buzzes against my clitoris right then, and I almost drop the chalk I'm holding in my hand. I glare around, trying to decide which one of them is the culprit. One of them has the remote. When I find out which one...

The buzzing stops. "Go on," Sebastian smiles wickedly. "It's time to show Trevor what you can do."

Can a girl who just started playing pool a few months back beat an expert? Not every day. Not even most days. Some days, however, the planets line up just so.

Trevor underestimates me. I can see him laughing with Frankie, rolling his eyes as I bend down to break. At the right angle, you can see my bra. From the way Trevor suddenly swallows, I know he's caught a glimpse of red lace.

You called my breasts cow-like, asshole, I think, and the resulting surge of anger powers my break. I hit the cue ball with a resounding thwack, and it speeds toward the rack. Balls scatter everywhere, and two balls roll into two pockets. "I'm playing solid," I call out calmly as I walk around the table, chalking my cue. Trevor gapes at me, and behind him, his team falls silent. They've seen me play before. They thought the tournament was theirs.

Not just yet. Not if I have anything to do with it.

My best chance is to win quickly. I have to be careful not to give Trevor an open shot, because then he's capable of running the table. My shot selection needs to be strategic. If I'm not sure I'm going to sink a ball, I need to position the cue ball in such a way that Trevor can't, either.

I've been practicing. Interspersed with hot sex and even hotter spankings, I've been working hard on improving my game. I've never been as good as I am in this moment. I've never felt as confident.

"Go on Bailey," a familiar voice yells out. "You show them, girl."

I turn around, and a huge grin covers my face. Not only do I have Daniel and Sebastian rooting for me to succeed, but I also have my own personal cheering squad. The Thursday Night Drinking Pack - or the four of them that live in New York - Katie, Gabby, Piper and Wendy - have all made the trek to Yonkers to watch me play. "Miki sends her apologies," Wendy tells me. "She was going to try for a flight, but bad weather derailed her plans."

"She was going to fly out to New York for this?"

"What could be more important than watching you win?" Gabby asks matter-of-factly.

Tears form in my eyes. I'm about to answer and thank them all for their constant, unwavering support, when Trevor interrupts with an impatient look on his face. "If the peanut gallery is done, Bailey, perhaps you can get on with it."

You want to get on with it, you jackass? Let's get on with it.

I'm on fire as I play. My focus is completely on the table. I'm seeing the balls more clearly. It feels like time has slowed down and my awareness has tunneled to this game. Even the feel of the butt plug and the vibrator can't distract me from my mission.

Today, I'm going to win on the behalf of all long-suffering women who put up with men that don't treat them right. Today, I'm going to pay Clark back for his disdain by making sure he loses his bet. I'm going to reward Daniel and Sebastian for their steadfast faith in me.

It takes five games. I win the first. Trevor fights back and wins the next three, but by the time the fifth game begins, he's become cocky and complacent, and he makes a mistake.

And I pounce. I run the table. I win the match.

There's noise in the background. Wendy, Gabby, Katie and Piper are throwing back shots and cheering loudly in celebration. Clark's looking ashen at the thought of paying Daniel fifty grand. Trevor is stunned, and his palm, when he shakes my hand, is cold and clammy. Behind him, his team looks disappointed, and Frankie's just punched his fist into the table. Ouch. That looks painful.

That's the background. In the foreground, Daniel and Sebastian are beaming, and I can tell how proud they are of me. I walk up to them and draw them in for a hug. "Tell me," I whisper so that only they can hear me. "What kind of games should we play next?"

Sebastian's hand runs over my butt in a possessive gesture. Daniel's eyes twinkle. "I don't know," he says. "Let's go home and find out."

Thank you for reading Bailey, Daniel, & Sebastian's story! I hope you love them as much as I do.

THE MENAGE IN MANHATTAN SERIES

WANT MORE? *Piper's story - The Heat - is next.* Read on for a free extended preview, or check out the other books in the MENAGE IN MANHATTAN SERIES.

The Bet - Bailey, Daniel, & Sebastian
The Heat - Piper, Owen, & Wyatt
The Wager - Wendy, Asher, & Hudson
The Hack - Miki, Oliver & Finn

DO YOU ENJOY FUN, light, contemporary romances with lots of heat and humor? Want to read *Boyfriend by the Hour (A Romantic Comedy)* for free? Want to stay up-to-date on new releases, freebies, sales, and more? (There will be an occasional cat picture.) **Sign up to my newsletter!** You'll get the book right away, and unless I have a very important announcement—like a new release—I only email once a week.

A PREVIEW OF THE HEAT BY TARA CRESCENT

CHAPTER ONE

If you can't stand the heat, get out of the kitchen.

— HARRY S. TRUMAN

Piper:

Bad news always comes in threes, my Aunt Vera used to say. Judging from the day I'm having, she was right.

The first blow comes from my restaurant's landlord. "Ms. Jackson," Michael O'Connor wheezes into the phone. "I'm afraid I'm going to have to increase your rent."

My heart sinks to my toes. I've been dreading this moment ever since I took over *Aladdin's Lamp* in early January and discovered the lease was going to expire in five months.

Mr. O'Connor is a nice older man who lives above the restaurant, and he seems to have had a soft spot for my Aunt Vera, from whom I inherited the place. But property developers have been sniffing around, and I know he's been getting offers.

"How much?" I ask, my fingers crossed as I hope for the best.

"Three thousand dollars a month," he responds. His voice softens with sympathy. "I'm sorry, Piper. I know that's a steep increase..."

"But it's still below market rate," I finish. "I understand, Mr. O'Connor."

He promises me the increase won't take effect for another month and he hangs up.

Of course, I can't afford three thousand extra dollars. I'm already struggling to stay afloat. But there's nothing I can do, so I get dressed and trudge toward the restaurant. If I'm lucky, we'll have a larger lunch crowd than normal.

I'm not lucky — the place is almost empty. I don my chef's hat and apron and take over from Josef, the surly Lebanese man who loosely functions as my sous-chef. The reason I say loosely? Josef has a pretty serious alcohol problem, and doesn't show up to work on any kind of regular basis.

Not for the first time, I wish I could fire him, but Aunt Vera's will forbids me from doing so. I'm not allowed to fire any of the existing staff unless I can give them a year's salary as a severance bonus. I'm stuck with Josef, who fails to show up to work every third day, and Kimmie, who chews gum in front of the customers. My only useful employee is the waitress I hired a month after I took over. Petra is a gem.

"I've made the lentil soup," Josef says, wobbling a little as he speaks. Great, he's drunk already. I make a mental note to taste the soup before I send it out, when my cell phone vibrates in my pocket.

I look at the display and grimace. It's my mother. Cue the second disaster of the day.

"Darling," she exclaims when I answer. "Are you sitting down?"

This is Lillian Jackson's standard greeting when she has some piece of gossip to give me. "No mother," I reply. "I'm working."

She huffs dismissively. My mother thinks *Aladdin's Lamp* is a hobby of mine, and one day, I'll get tired of playing chef, go back home to New Orleans, and marry some suitable young man from the right family. Trying to get her to take what I do seriously is a waste of time, and I don't even try. "What's the matter?" I ask, hoping she'll get to the point quickly.

"Your cousin Angelina is getting married," she responds. "Piper dear, this is going to be hard for you to hear, so I thought I should be the first person to tell you. She's getting married to Anthony. You remember Anthony, don't you? Your fiancé?" Her breath catches. "Piper, I'm so sorry, honey."

"Ma, I'm fine." *So much drama.* Anthony and I went on five dates before he proposed in front of the entire family on Christmas Eve, knowing I'd be pressured into saying *yes.* My break up with him was the topic of gossip for my mother's friends for months.

Kimmie's come in with a ticket, and she gives me an impatient look. I need to get working on it. I can't afford to chase away the small handful of customers I have. "Anthony and I are old history," I tell her. "I'm very excited for Angelina. Listen, I have to go, okay? Some diners just walked in."

"Your father and I are very worried about you, Piper," she pronounces, ignoring my feeble attempt at ending our conversation. "We're coming up to see you."

My heart sinks. Oh God, more family interference. "You are?"

"Yes dear." Her tone is firm. "We've already bought our airline tickets. We're coming this weekend."

"Ma." I exhale in annoyance. "I work in a restaurant. I can't take the weekend off, you already know that." I've said this to my mother a million times. She never listens.

"Don't be ridiculous, dear." She dismisses my concern with an airy laugh. "Of course you can. You're in charge, aren't you? You can do whatever you want."

I bite my tongue and count to ten. *Just tell them you can't entertain them,* a voice inside me urges. *Tell them your rent was increased by three thousand dollars. Tell them you're on the verge of failure, and you can't afford to take a weekend off. Tell them that Sebastian Ardalan, a two-star Michelin chef, didn't think your restaurant would survive another six months in business, and you're feeling bruised and damaged as a result.*

But I've never been able to effectively stand up to my mother. My moments of rebellion are few and far between. Most of the time, I just do as I'm told. It seems easier that way.

Kimmie's tapping her feet in annoyance. I need to get off the phone. "Fine," I sigh. "I'll see you in a few days. I have to go now."

I hang up and fight the urge to bang my head repeatedly against the ancient walk-in freezer. The damn thing is temperamental and will probably just stop working.

It's just after noon, and already, my day is a wreck.

Troubles always come in threes, Aunt Vera used to say.

I wonder what lies ahead.

CHAPTER TWO

The past is strapped to our backs. We do not have to see it;
we can always feel it.

— MIGNON McLAUGHLIN

Owen:

I meet Eduardo Mendez at a busy McDonald's, where a
constant stream of people enter and leave, and no one gives
two men seated in a corner a second glance.

"Lamb." The detective greets me, his voice a raspy growl,
as always, rendered hoarse by the two packs of cigarettes he
smokes each day.

I nod in reply, feeling the familiar excitement rush up
and grip me. Mendez has a job for me. He never makes
contact otherwise.

I take a sip of my steaming hot coffee and wait for him to
speak. In the seventeen years I've known him, I've learned
Mendez can't be rushed. Whatever he wants, he'll tell me
when he's ready.

"Hell's Kitchen," he says at last. "What do you know
about it?"

I know enough to avoid it. The Manhattan neighborhood of Hell's Kitchen has rapidly gentrified in the last
couple of decades, but before its revitalization, it was home
to poor and working class Irish Americans. Given my past,
it's not the safest neighborhood for me to spend time in.
The death sentence on me has never been lifted, and if
someone wanted to curry favor with those in charge back in

Dublin, they might think that killing me is the best way. "Not a lot."

He coughs. "Word on the street is that the Westies are moving back in."

"In Hell's Kitchen?" I raise an eyebrow. "The neighborhood's been clean for decades."

"I'm telling you what I know," he snaps. "The opium trade is flourishing, and these guys aren't dealing on street corners anymore. They're using local restaurants to distribute." He fixes me with a piercing look. "You know what that's like, don't you, Lamb?"

Just like that, the memories come rushing back. My mother's voice, raised in argument with my father. He wants to testify against the mob; my mom urges caution. *What if they come for us?* Even now, even after seventeen years, I hear the fear she's trying to conceal. *What about me? Aileen? Owen?*

And my dad replies, his voice always clear in my mind. *Someone needs to fight for what's right.*

They'd both been right and they'd both been wrong. Someone did need to fight for what was right, and the Gilligan's crime syndicate had come for my parents and baby sister. The only reason I'd survived was because I'd snuck out for a very illegal cigarette.

I shake my head to clear it. The past always threatens to overwhelm me. Mendez knows exactly what he's doing. My *da* died fighting the mob. I won't let them win.

"What do you need me to do?"

He pushes a list toward me. "I need intel," he says. "You're in the restaurant business. These are our list of suspects right now. Get close to them, see what you can find out about their finances."

I run my gaze down the names, and I recognize a few of

them. Two in particular jump out, *Emerson's* and *Aladdin's Lamp*.

Max Emerson came to us, looking for half a million dollars, but we turned him down last week. However, *Aladdin's Lamp* is still in play. My partner Wyatt and I have eaten there every day for the last two weeks, on the recommendation of our friend Sebastian Ardalan, but we haven't yet decided if we're interested in the place.

It's time to kick it up a notch. If Mendez needs to find out what's going on at *Aladdin's Lamp*, the easiest way is to invest in it.

"Let me see what I can do." I drain my coffee and rise to my feet. "I'll be in touch."

∾

CHAPTER THREE

All happy families are alike; each unhappy family is unhappy in its own way.

— LEO TOLSTOY

Wyatt:

When I walk into my office Thursday morning, my assistant Celia looks up. "Wyatt," she says, "I need to talk to you."

I gesture for her to follow me. "What's up?"

"Sandra from Reception called me this morning. She said there was a man in the lobby who insisted on seeing you." She pauses. "He told her he was your father."

I'm about to take a sip of my coffee, but hearing those words, I freeze. Twenty years ago, my father had ducked out to grab a drink at the local pub, and had never returned. He sent my mother a letter telling her he couldn't cope anymore, and he disappeared from my life. I was thirteen. I haven't seen him since that day.

"My father." My voice is even. Nothing betrays the sense of shock that explodes through me.

"That's what he said. I've never heard you mention your father, so I went downstairs to see what was going on, but he'd left by the time I got there." She gives me a worried look. "I didn't know what to do."

I clench my hands into fists. A vein pulses at my forehead. *Deep breaths, Wyatt. Calm down.* I force myself to bury all the emotion that rises to the surface. The feeling of abandonment when he left, the secret, shameful envy that my father was able to escape, leaving me stuck with my mother.

Celia shifts in her seat and I realize I've been silent for too long. I smile at her. "My father is dead," I lie easily. "I don't know who this man is, but he's an imposter. If he shows up again, have security deal with him, please."

She frowns in puzzlement, but doesn't contradict me. "Of course, Wyatt," she says. "Oh, and Owen called to say he'll meet you at the usual place for lunch."

Right. *Aladdin's Lamp.* "What time?"

Celia checks her notepad. "He'll meet you there at one."

"Perfect. Thanks, Celia."

My heart still pounds in my chest. Not even the prospect of finding a new restaurant to rescue is enough to distract me from my shock. *My father's back.*

I wonder what he wants.

My instincts warn me to stay away from *Aladdin's Lamp.* The place is a dump. Signs of benign neglect are everywhere. The red curtains have been faded pink by the sun. There's a large crack in the front window, with a strip of duct tape across it. At each table, a dusty vase with plastic flowers serve as decoration, along with a kitschy lamp. The table-cloth is stained, the menu is laminated and the waitress in her pink-frilled apron cannot stop chewing gum long enough to take our order.

I want nothing to do with it, but I will hand it to Sebastian Ardalan. He's right about the chef; the food shows flashes of brilliance.

"This is really good." Owen digs into his chili with gusto. "There's potential here."

"The place is called *Aladdin's Lamp*," I complain, not for the first time. "Why does it have chili on the menu, Owen? The tabbouleh is garlicky. The hummus doesn't have enough tahini in it. And this lentil soup has way too much salt."

"We've eaten here for two weeks," he points out. "The Middle Eastern food is terrible, and everything else is great. You should know that by now."

"Why are you so gung-ho about this disaster?"

"Come on, Wyatt." Owen gives me an amused look. "Since when did you get so boring? Think of this place as a challenge."

"I'm thinking of this place as one health-inspection away from being shut down."

Owen rolls his eyes. "Oh for fuck's sake," he says. "It isn't even close to failing and you know it. You just have an exaggerated need for cleanliness." He lifts his hand to catch the waitress' attention. "If the chef has a moment," he says, giving her a charming smile, "could you tell her we'd love to chat with her?"

She nods and departs. I look at him with exasperation when she's out of earshot. "We haven't investigated the place. Who knows what kind of deal we could be walking into?"

"Look around, Wyatt." Owen's eyes sweep the near-empty dining room. "This isn't a large restaurant. Worst case scenario, we put in two hundred and fifty grand in this place and it fails. So what?"

I don't like going investing in a restaurant before investigating it, but Owen seems committed. "You're doing this then?" I ask, already resigned to doing the deal.

"You don't have to," he replies. "But yes, I'm definitely investing in this place."

"Asshole." There's no rancor in my voice. "Fine, I'm in. But the chef had better toe the fucking line."

Owen leans back in his seat. "Your bark is worse than your bite," he says with a grin. Then his eyes widen and his smirk broadens. "There's the chef. Why don't you tell her what you told me?"

I look up to see a slender blonde woman thread her way toward us. She's got pale skin and red lips, and her hair is the color of the sun's rays at first light. Her hips sway slightly as she walks, and I find it suddenly difficult to breathe.

When she reaches our table, she glares at us, her hand on her hip. "You've eaten at my restaurant for two weeks," she says, her voice hard. "What are you playing at? Who sent you?"

Help me. When she speaks, her voice has a pretty Southern lilt that goes straight to my cock. Across me, Owen is struggling to hold back his laughter. He knows I can't resist a Southern accent. I've never been able to.

"My name," Owen says, "is Owen Lamb. My partner

here," he gestures toward me, "is Wyatt Lawless. Sebastian Ardalan suggested we stop by."

She goes still. That wasn't the answer she was expecting to hear. "Lawless and Lamb?" she whispers in shock. "Sebastian Ardalan sent you?"

Then our words register fully. Her back stiffens. "I'm not interested in anyone's pity," she snaps. "Not Sebastian Ardalan's, not yours."

My cock goes from being somewhat interested to rock hard in a second. Pretty, Southern, and feisty? *This woman is kryptonite.* "I don't invest in restaurants because I feel sorry for them," I reply calmly. "I invest in restaurants with potential." I look around the empty front room. "You clearly aren't setting the world on fire. The question is, do you want to?"

I sigh as I realize I've verbally offered this woman a deal. *Damn Owen.* The only thing I take comfort in is that someone in the kitchen can cook. The chili really *is* fantastic.

CHAPTER FOUR

The bargain that yields mutual satisfaction is the only one that is apt to be repeated.

— B. C. FORBES

Piper:

Trouble always comes in threes.

When Kimmie tells me that the two men who have eaten at my restaurant every day for the last two weeks are back again, my first instinct is to suspect my mother of sending them to spy on my restaurant. I wouldn't put it past her at all.

Then I come out and they introduce themselves, and my heart nearly stops. The names Owen Lamb and Wyatt Lawless are legendary in the New York restaurant scene. Five of their restaurants have Michelin stars. They own the top 10 list on Yelp. They run the best restaurants in the city. A Lawless and Lamb restaurant doesn't break even — it succeeds wildly.

Under different circumstances, I might also notice that they are very good looking men. When Wyatt Lawless' gaze bores into me, I wonder how his stubble will feel against my skin. Owen Lamb's blond hair glistens in the sunlight, and I want to lick the dimples on his cheeks.

But as soon as they open their mouths, I forget their good looks and their accomplishments go flying out of the window. Instead, I fight the urge to smack the silly smirk off Owen Lamb's face and punch Wyatt Lawless in the mouth. *You clearly aren't setting the world on fire.* I'm already reeling from Sebastian Ardalan's casual dismissal of my restaurant. Wyatt Lawless can take his callous words and shove them up his ass.

My mother's voice sounds in my ear. *Well-behaved Southern women don't punch strange men, dear.*

I grit my teeth and shove her out of my head. "What are you talking about, gentlemen?"

Wyatt Lawless surveys me with dark, expressionless eyes. "How long have you run this restaurant?"

People who answer a question with a question infuriate me. I pull up a chair next to them and sit down. "I inherited *Aladdin's Lamp* six months ago," I bite out.

Owen Lamb's blue eyes shine with curiosity. "And you want to run it?" he asks. "Why don't you sell it?"

Because cooking in a small cafe like this has been a dream of mine since I was a little girl. Because if I fail, I'm convinced my parents will make me move back to Louisiana. Because I'm running away from a lifetime of pleasing other people and all I want to do is live my own life.

I'm not going to tell these men that; I'm not going to tell them anything. Besides, I've been taught not to air my dirty laundry in public. *Well-behaved Southern women don't bitch about their family.* "I'm not ready to fail."

That seems to be enough. "Fair enough," Owen Lamb says. "Let me get to the point. Are you interested in a deal? If you are, we'll buy a stake in your business. We'll invest some money, but largely, what we bring to the table is our expertise. I've been in the restaurant business all my life. I'll help you in the back of the house. Wyatt," he gestures to his partner, "is the marketing genius. He'll get your name out there, bring the customers to your door."

God knows I could use help. I'm not stupid; I'm in over my head. *Aladdin's Lamp* has been losing money steadily ever since my family dragged Aunt Vera back to Louisiana. Aunt Vera was rich enough to afford to cover the losses, but I'm not. The restaurant needs a makeover desperately, but makeovers cost money and I have none. Even though I plow every dollar I make back into the business, progress has been glacially slow.

Yet I'm not delusional. This doesn't make any sense. A thousand chefs in the city would sell their firstborns for a chance to work with Lamb and Lawless. I'm not special. "Why are you here?" I ask bluntly. "Why me?"

"Like I said," Owen says, his gaze on the bowl of chili in

front of him, "Sebastian Ardalan suggested we check this place out."

Sebastian Ardalan dotes on my roommate Bailey. If she asked him to help me, he would move heaven and earth to fulfill her request. My heart sinks as I realize that this isn't about me, my abilities, my talents or my dreams.

But I can't afford to turn them down. My rent's been increased by three thousand dollars, and my bank account is close to empty. I've run out of options.

"Yes." It feels like I'm stepping on a new path, and there's no turning back. "I'm interested. Tell me more."

__Click to keep reading The Play.__

ABOUT TARA CRESCENT

Get a free story from Tara when you sign up to Tara's mailing list.

Tara Crescent writes steamy contemporary romances for readers who like hot, dominant heroes and strong, sassy heroines.

When she's not writing, she can be found curled up on a couch with a good book, often with a cat on her lap.

She lives in Toronto.

Tara also writes sci-fi romance as Lili Zander. Check her books out at http://www.lilizander.com

Find Tara on:
www.taracrescent.com
taracrescent@gmail.com

ALSO BY TARA CRESCENT

MÉNAGE ROMANCE

Club Ménage

Claiming Fifi

Taming Avery

Keeping Kiera - *coming soon*

Ménage in Manhattan

The Bet

The Heat

The Wager

The Hack

The Dirty Series

Dirty Therapy

Dirty Talk

Dirty Games

Dirty Words

The Cocky Series

Her Cocky Doctors

Her Cocky Firemen

Standalone Books

Dirty X6

CONTEMPORARY ROMANCE

The Drake Family Series

Temporary Wife (A Billionaire Fake Marriage Romance)

Fake Fiance (A Billionaire Second Chance Romance)

Standalone Books

Hard Wood

MAX: A Friends to Lovers Romance

A Touch of Blackmail

A Very Paisley Christmas

Boyfriend by the Hour

BDSM ROMANCE

Assassin's Revenge

Nights in Venice

Mr. Banks (A British Billionaire Romance)

Teaching Maya

The House of Pain

The Professor's Pet

The Audition

The Watcher

Doctor Dom

Dominant - *A Boxed Set containing The House of Pain, The Professor's Pet, The Audition and The Watcher*